PRAISE FOR STEVEN JAMES

"James writes smart, taut, high-octane th[riller]... books are not for the timid. The endings bl[ow]...
—MITCH GALIN, producer, Stephen King['s]...
and Frank Herbert's *Dune*

"A thought-provoking and thrilling mystery."
—NEW YORK JOURNAL OF BOOKS on *Placebo*

"The nail-biting suspense will rivet you."—RT BOOK REVIEWS

"[A] master storyteller at the peak of his game."—PUBLISHERS WEEKLY

"James delivers first-rate characters, dazzling plot twists, and powers it all with nonstop action."
—JOHN TINKER, Emmy Award–winning screenplay writer

"*Opening Moves* is a mesmerizing read. From the first chapter, it sets its hook deep and drags you through a darkly gripping story with relentless power. My conclusion: I need to read more of Steven James."
—MICHAEL CONNOLLEY, *New York Times* bestselling author of *The Drop*

"Pulse-pounding suspense."—FICTIONADDICT.COM

"Exhilarating."—MYSTERIOUS REVIEWS

"James clearly knows how to spin a yarn."—BOOKLIST

"His tightly woven, adrenaline-laced plots leave readers breathless."
—THE SUSPENSE ZONE

"James sets the new standard in suspense writing."
—SUSPENSE MAGAZINE

BLUR

STEVEN JAMES

SKYSCAPE

BLUR

SKYSCAPE

Text copyright © 2014 by Steven James
All rights reserved.

Published by Skyscape, New York

www.apub.com

Amazon, the Amazon logo, and Skyscape are trademarks of Amazon.com, Inc., or its affiliates.

ISBN 9781477847275 (paperback)
ISBN 9781477897270 (ebook)

Book design by Katrina Damkoehler and Susan Gerber

Printed in The United States of America
10 9 8 7 6 5 4 3 2 1

"Men are so necessarily mad, that not to be mad would amount to another form of madness."

—Blaise Pascal, seventeenth-century philosopher and mathematician

To Susanna and Meg

PROLOGUE

Daniel held up a blanket so that it hung vertically above his bed. Stacy stood beside his desk, her back to the wall. He noticed that she was tapping her fingers nervously against her leg.

"Alright," he said. "Imagine that everything on your side of the blanket is reality. Those are the things you can see, taste, feel, whatever. The things that are really there. Everything on my side of the blanket is . . ."

"Just imaginary." She finished his thought for him. "All in your head."

"Right. Now, from what I've found out in the last week, most people have a pretty thick blanket—barrier—that's in their minds that helps them know which side they're on."

She was watching him carefully; if he didn't know better, he'd say warily.

"So we can tell what's real and what's not," she said.

"Exactly. But now imagine that the blanket is a shower curtain or something and you can see through it, but everything on the other side is blurry. So you'd know the other side is there—"

"But you'd be able to tell which side was which." Stacy sounded slightly relieved. "You'd see the difference."

"Yes."

"And that's you?"

A pause. "No. Not quite." He dropped the blanket. "It's gone."

"The blanket is?"

"Yes."

"Completely?" She'd moved almost imperceptibly farther from Daniel.

He nodded. A moment passed.

Stretched thin.

"Does that scare you?" he asked her.

She didn't answer but said instead, "But can you tell this is real? That I'm really here, in front of you, right now?"

"Yes," he said.

But he wasn't sure. He wasn't sure about anything.

Not since realizing he was going insane.

CHAPTER ONE

The first blur occurred at Emily Jackson's funeral.

At 3:54 p.m., thirty minutes before it happened, Daniel Byers was staring out the car window, watching deep shadows pass across the pavement as his father drove along the pine- and birch-enshrouded northern Wisconsin county highway. A handful of autumn leaves skittered along the road ahead of them. The sky was steel blue.

Though it was still September, it'd already snowed twice. Most of the snow had melted, but a few stubborn patches remained in the corners of the forest where the sun never reached. More snow would be coming soon. Winter was not kind to this part of the state.

"Are we almost there?" Daniel spoke softly, without looking away from the window.

Silence from his father.

"Dad?"

"The church is just past Highway 14. Fifteen minutes maybe."

Outside, an intricate web of leaves passed overhead. Wisped into light. Merged into shadow again.

"How's your headache?" his father asked. "Gone?"

Daniel didn't want to worry him. "It's okay," he lied.

Get ready. You're about to see the body.

He suddenly felt cold and turned up the heater in the car.

It didn't seem to help.

13 MINUTES BEFORE THE BLUR

His father slowed down as they approached the Beldon Road Community Church parking lot.

"Don't worry," he told Daniel. "We won't stay long."

Daniel didn't know what to say. How do you deal with the fact that a girl who went to your high school, who you saw walking down the hall just a few days ago, is now dead?

They pulled into the lot. "Did you hear me, Dan?"

"Yeah."

"We won't stay long."

"Okay."

It felt a little weird coming to a church. He and his dad had only attended church twice since his mom left them six months ago—once for Easter and then the week after, as if they were about to start a new habit but never quite got enough momentum to carry things through.

The parking spaces closest to the building were filled, so his father eased into a spot near the back of the lot, then turned off the engine. After an awkward moment, he stated the obvious: "We're here."

Neither of them moved.

At last his dad rapped the steering wheel twice, then said, "Okay, then."

He eased his door open.

"I hardly even knew her, Dad."

His father hesitated.

"I know." He was still seated in the car but had one foot on the pavement. "But it's important to be here."

Daniel had never even officially met Emily Jackson, hadn't even known her name until the news story hit. After all, he was a junior and she was a freshman, so it didn't really make sense that he would know her very well. The thing was, he really *was* sad she'd drowned, he really *was*—and yet, in a way, he felt vaguely guilty that he wasn't sadder.

Emily Jackson.

A girl who was easy to miss.

He'd seen what happened whenever she entered the cafeteria and sat at a table. Suddenly, the other kids who were already there would remember something else they needed to do and would get up one at a time and leave. Or when a group of kids was talking in the hallway and she approached them, they would tighten up their circle so there wouldn't be any place for her.

And so she would walk past. Alone.

He didn't think they did it on purpose, treated her like that, it was just the way kids are sometimes.

Whenever he saw her, she was always alone.

And now she was dead.

A girl nobody seemed to want to be around when she was alive.

But now there was a parking lot full of cars.

Now everyone was coming to see Emily.

Now that she was dead.

11 MINUTES BEFORE THE BLUR

Daniel and his father crossed the parking lot and walked toward the church. He caught himself noticing what was in people's cars as they passed them—the fast-food wrappers and water bottles on the floors, the pet hair on the back seats, the baby toys and backpacks. For some reason everything seemed to be registering in his mind more than usual. More than ever.

An older man with bristly white hair who was leaving the building nodded to Daniel's father. "Sheriff."

"Tony."

Daniel recognized him: Mr. Kettner, the man who announced their home football games. Now he said, "I'm sorry about this, son. I know she went to school with you."

Daniel wasn't sure how to respond. "Thank you," he managed to say.

Mr. Kettner hesitated for a moment, as if he were wondering what he should say next. At last he told Daniel's dad, "Good of you to come."

"We thought it was important."

Mr. Kettner let out a small sigh. "Tragedy, though. What happened to her."

"Yes, it is."

Though brief, the conversation seemed like it had already gone on too long, and no one really knew where to take it from there. "Alright, then. We'll see you later, Sheriff."

"Alright."

"Daniel," Mr. Kettner said with a nod. It was his way of saying good-bye.

"Good-bye, Mr. Kettner."

As he ambled away, Daniel's dad said softly once again, "We don't have to stay long."

Thank you, Daniel thought.

"Yeah," he said.

And they walked up the steps of the church.

CHAPTER
TWO

A dozen men and women stood clustered in three groups just outside the front doors and as Daniel passed them, he heard them talking:

"She looks good."

"Yes, she does."

"And the flowers are nice."

"She would have been so glad to see you here."

It struck him how strange it was for people to be saying things like that.

Emily couldn't possibly look good, not after spending two days at the bottom of Lake Algonquin. And what difference did it make one way or the other what the flowers looked like? Didn't these people understand that the girl lying next to those flowers was absolutely and forever dead? And why would Emily have been glad to see a crowd of people she barely knew? Why, when they'd ignored her while she was alive?

So did you. You never talked to her. Not once.

A wash of guilt.

Daniel passed through the entryway and into the church.

All around the sanctuary, his friends and other kids he recognized from school were standing uneasily beside their parents.

Some of the guys looked anxious; others, like Brad Talbot, looked bored. All of them looked out of place, though—the guys wearing their fathers' ties, the girls dressed in dark, drab clothes that made them look much older than they were.

The air smelled of pinewood and old books.

Someone was playing a piano.

High overhead, dust floated through the air and passed across the streaks of sunlight slanting through the tall, narrow windows. It gave everything an unearthly, ethereal feel.

His friends, even the other guys from the football team, looked so fragile. So wounded. Some of the girls were crying, and so were some of the guys—but Daniel could tell they were trying their best to hide it. A lot of the kids were looking at him, like they did on the field when they were waiting for him to call the next play.

It made him uncomfortable.

Out there, he knew what to do, how to read the defense, how to respond. Here, he had no idea.

He avoided their gazes.

Daniel's headache seemed to be getting worse. He rubbed his thumb hard against his temple, but it didn't help.

Politely, his father excused himself and made his way to the back corner of the church to talk to Mr. McKinney, one of the teachers from Beldon High, leaving Daniel alone.

Everything around him was hushed. Even the piano music coming from the front of the church seemed to be hollower, fainter than it should have been.

He saw the casket positioned near the piano.

You ignored her.

No, you just didn't know her. There's a difference.

Trying to shake the thought, he glanced to the left, where it seemed like there weren't so many people. Near the last pew, Stacy Clern, a girl who'd just transferred to his school, stood beside a woman who Daniel assumed was her mother.

Stacy was pretty, but not beautiful. Dark brown hair. Gentle eyes. And unlike the giddy, airheady girls he seemed to attract like flies, Stacy seemed like the kind of real, down-to-earth girl he'd actually be able to connect with.

In fact, he'd wanted to ask her out ever since he'd first seen her around school, but he'd never quite gotten up the nerve to do it. On a football field or a basketball court he was fine—no problem figuring out what to do there. But stick him next to a girl like Stacy and he would fumble around all day for the right things to say.

From where he stood he couldn't tell if she'd been crying, but she looked really sad and he wanted to go and talk to her, tell her that things were going to be alright, but he couldn't figure out exactly what he might say. And he doubted he'd have the nerve to say anything at all once he got there.

Finally, he nodded to her and she offered him a small nod back.

A line had formed, leading to Emily's corpse.

Everyone was moving in slow motion, like animated shadows, circling and hovering around each other in tight bunches. Everything people said was lowered to a whisper.

You should have talked to her.

Somehow it seemed both unnatural and natural to feel guilty for not having talked to Emily. But he felt like he needed to do this thing now, to see her one last time. Maybe to redeem himself in some way for not knowing her better. Maybe paying his last respects—whatever that actually meant—would help to quiet the murky shame he felt crawling through him.

Daniel got in line.

CHAPTER THREE

There were sixteen people in front of Daniel Byers, and he was standing right behind the guy who took their team photos. One of the other girls from his class, Nicole Marten, handed him a church bulletin. The makeup all around her eyes was smeared.

"Thanks," he said.

"It's so sad, isn't it?" Daniel had known Nicole for six years, in a friendship that had been pretty close but had never moved into anything beyond the just-being-friends stage. "I mean, how could this *happen*?"

"Yeah," he replied. "I don't know."

She brushed away a stray tear, and then, without warning, she leaned against Daniel's shoulder and gave him a small hug. It made him feel a little conspicuous but he didn't pull away. He put his arm around her for a moment, then she backed up, rubbed at her eyes again, gave him a faint smile, and left to deliver more bulletins.

He noticed Stacy staring in his direction.

Not the best timing in the world, watching another girl hug him. Especially a girl as popular as Nicole.

He hid by looking at the bulletin Nicole had given him.

Printed on the front was Emily's name and date of birth.

And date of death.

She'd lived fourteen years, four months, and twenty days.

Immediately, and without even realizing it, Daniel calculated that he had already lived 845 days longer than she ever would.

He didn't open the bulletin. He didn't want to see all fourteen years, four months, and twenty days of her life summarized in one tidy little paragraph. It didn't seem fair.

The line edged forward as the first few people finished looking at Emily's corpse and then made their way to a semicircle of mourners, presumably Emily's family, standing near the piano.

845 days.

The idea that death is the end, the end of every dream and memory that a person will ever have, every hope and smile and tear . . . it was unsettling.

Teenagers weren't supposed to have to think about things like that.

845 days.

The casket was adorned with flowers. Only the left half was propped open.

The line of people shuffled slowly toward it.

Someone had placed fifteen framed photos of Emily on a table nearby.

A couple of them were pictures of her at birthday parties

when she was a kid; one showed her at the beach walking by herself. In another, she was inside a cabin with an older man who might've been her grandpa. In the biggest photo—a studio picture—she was kneeling beside a golden retriever. In the most recent photos she had on a silver necklace with a heart-shaped locket.

In all the pictures Emily was smiling, but it struck Daniel that he had never seen her smile at school.

Two people finished their viewing and stepped aside. As Daniel moved forward, a man who was walking past patted him on the shoulder. The man's face was drawn and sad. Daniel didn't recognize him.

"Were you a friend of Emily's?" the man asked.

Actually, no. I barely knew her.

"Um. Sort of."

The man nodded and patted his shoulder again and told him, "Thanks for coming. It really means a lot to us." Then he left to go stand by the piano, and Daniel realized he was probably a relative of Emily's, maybe even her dad, and he felt worse that he hadn't known her better, as if somehow it would have meant more to this man if he'd been Emily's good friend.

Daniel wanted to go and tell him, "Really, you know what? She was one of the nicest girls I've ever met."

But instead, he stepped forward with the line.

It was moving faster now. Just eight people ahead of him.

He wished his headache would go away.

As he took another step, it struck him that if Emily had gone to another high school or lived in a town fifty or a hundred miles away, he might not have even heard about her death, and he would be at football practice right now—the one that had been canceled in light of the funeral—and that would be that. Anonymous people die in distant places every minute of the day, but death doesn't seem to mean anything to us until it somehow touches our life.

Four people.

Finally, he caught a glimpse of Emily Jackson's face.

CHAPTER
FOUR

Actually, he could see only the top half of her face—her eyes, her forehead, a blond fringe of hair. Somehow they'd made it look like she hadn't really been underwater all that time, but still her face didn't look natural.

Her eyes were closed. The acne on her forehead had been covered up with the makeup they use on the dead. He'd never really thought about it before, but someone at the funeral home's job was to put makeup on corpses for a living.

That's how the guy paid the bills.

Daniel forced himself not to think about that.

Only three people stood between him and the body.

He felt his heart beating faster now, nervous with a quivering, expectant kind of fear.

Then he saw the rest of her face.

Some people say that dead people look like they're sleeping, but Emily didn't. She looked dead and that was all.

Two people.

Then one.

And then Daniel was standing in front of the casket, staring down at the pale dead face of Emily Jackson.

THE BLUR

Her lips were closed just like her eyes. Hands folded neatly across her chest.

She looked smaller, more frail than he remembered her.

For a brief, macabre moment, he had the desire to touch her hand, to somehow comfort this girl who would never go to a homecoming dance, never stay out too late on prom night, never graduate, go to college, get married, raise a family.

What does the skin of a dead person feel like?

The idea evaporated in a swirl of fear and repulsion.

You ignored her.

She looked both familiar and like a stranger.

Lying still, so still.

And then Emily Jackson opened her eyes.

CHAPTER FIVE

Daniel gasped and stumbled backward, bumping into the person behind him. He turned to see an elderly woman looking at him concernedly. "I'm sorry," he muttered. "Did you see that?" His voice sounded like dust.

"What?"

"Her."

He pointed at Emily. He couldn't bring himself to say any more.

The woman leaned to the side and tipped her gaze toward the casket, but acted like nothing was out of the ordinary and looked at him with mild suspicion.

Slowly, his heart hammering, Daniel peered into the casket again.

A deep chill.

Emily was still lying there but had tilted her head and was staring at him, her eyes ghostly white, drained of color. She opened her mouth slightly and a trickle of stale water oozed out.

She's dead, she's dead, she's dead. This isn't happening. This can't be happening!

He pinched his arm, hard, but the image of Emily staring at him did not go away.

Then her lips moved and he heard his name in a voice wet and soft: "Daniel."

This isn't real!

Right before his eyes, weeds from the soft-bottomed lake appeared in her hair. Her clothes became soaked. The color of her skin changed from imitation-Caucasian-white to the bluish gray shade of death that it must have been when the two fishermen found her. Then she spoke to him again, her voice moist and gurgly, more water seeping from her mouth with every word: "Trevor was in the car."

Pain buzzed through his head.

The moment overtook him. He was too petrified to move.

"Trevor shouldn't have been in the car," she said. Then, with one swift and abrupt motion, she sat up. "Find my glasses." She slung her arm toward him and clenched her dead fingers around his forearm. "Please, Daniel." A gush of filthy water spilled from her drooping mouth.

He yanked his arm away and stumbled backward again, his head throbbing, pounding, the world growing dizzy, dizzy black. Emily slumped back into her casket, and then everything was turning in a slow, wide circle, and he realized he was on the floor of the church and people were leaning over him, asking what was wrong, if he was okay.

The darkness curling through his mind turned into a sharp blade of light that sliced through everything.

"She's alive," he said as loudly as he could, but it didn't sound loud to him at all. "Emily's still alive."

And that was the last thing Daniel remembered before he blacked out.

CHAPTER SIX

He woke up disoriented, his thoughts in a fog. As far as he could tell he was lying on one of the stiff couches in the lobby. His dad, along with some adults he didn't recognize, were staring down at him.

The ceiling lights glared above him. He had to blink and look away.

"Dan?" There was both concern and relief in his father's voice. "Are you okay?"

Daniel blinked again. It was all coming back to him now—entering the church, approaching the casket, seeing Emily. . . .

She spoke to you. She called you by name.

"Are you okay?" his father repeated.

"Yeah." He nodded. "Um, is she . . . ?"

"Who?"

"Emily. Is she . . ." Man, this was going to sound weird. "Is she really dead?"

His dad nodded somberly. "We can talk about this more at home, alright?"

"So she . . . ?"

"Yes."

The vision of Emily in the casket, the sight of the water pouring from her mouth, the gurgling sound of her voice, the firm grip of her hand on his arm, all of it had seemed so *real*.

How could any of that have happened if she were dead?

But it couldn't have been real either. Emily had drowned and she was dead, and dead people don't open their eyes, don't sit up in their coffins, don't talk to you, and they certainly don't reach over and grab your arm.

You're just seeing things. That's all it is. Your mind is playing tricks on you.

But it'd seemed just as real as this conversation he was having with his dad.

He was still dizzy and it took a little effort to sit up. A couple of people who were standing beside his dad eased away. Then the others did as well, until it was only Daniel and his father.

"You fainted," his dad told him, as if he were anticipating a question that, in truth, Daniel hadn't even been intending to ask.

"I've never fainted before."

"Was it the headache?"

"I don't know."

Daniel's dad helped him to his feet, and amid the stares and anxious glances of some of his classmates, they left the church.

"I guess it was the shock," his dad said, "you know, of seeing her like that."

"I guess it was."

On the drive home, Daniel tried to shake what'd happened

from his mind, tried to convince himself that he had not seen what he had, that he had not heard Emily tell him that Trevor was in the car, that a dead girl had not asked him to find her glasses.

Now that he thought about it, in the photos at the front of the church she'd been wearing a pair of glasses, and in school when he'd seen her, she'd had them on then as well.

He didn't know if it was typical to put people's glasses on them when they were lying in their caskets. It seemed like an odd thing to do, but it was possible that it happened, if maybe someone wore glasses all the time and the funeral home staff was trying to make them look as normal as possible.

But in this case, no one would have found Emily's glasses anyway. After all, she drowned, and it seemed pretty unlikely that she would have somehow been able to keep her glasses on while the currents in the lake dragged her down and carried her into that inlet where her body was found.

They arrived home and Daniel headed to his room.

He'd never known what to believe about ghosts. On the one hand, the supernatural or the paranormal, whatever term you wanted to use, wasn't something he could easily accept. He believed science would eventually wrap its arms around those things and come up with an explanation that made sense.

On the other hand, lots of people really did see unexplainable things, and there was no discounting what they experienced—visions, hauntings, strange noises in the night, doors or windows slamming on their own. Patches of freezing air where nothing cold should be.

Before today, he could barely imagine what that was like.

But was it Emily's ghost he had seen?

He really couldn't come up with any other explanation.

Daniel removed his tie, the only one he owned, and hung it in his closet.

But even if it had been Emily's ghost, why would it ask him to find her glasses? Daniel had seen his share of scary movies and heard his share of ghost stories around campfires—especially from his friend Kyle.

According to what people said, ghosts, if they were real at all, were sometimes harmless—benevolent even—bringing help to the living. Sometimes they were seeking justice or a place to find their final rest, or the opportunity to finally slip out of limbo and into eternity. But sometimes they were vengeful or just plain evil.

The stories Kyle liked to tell were usually about the vengeful ghosts or poltergeists who wanted nothing more than to terrify or harm people who were still alive.

Or kill them.

Sometimes they wanted that.

Daniel reassured himself that all those things were just made up, that in real life ghosts didn't exist.

But as he took his shirt off, a thin cold shiver slithered down his spine.

He stared at his arm.

Clawlike marks, swollen and red and shaped in the form of a hand, encircled his forearm in the place where the dead girl had grabbed his arm during her funeral.

CHAPTER SEVEN

Daniel did not sleep well.

It wasn't just the disquieting feeling of being at the funeral, or the fact that his arm hurt; it was mainly that image of Emily staring at him, moving, sitting up. It wouldn't leave him alone, even in his dreams. She kept rising in her casket and speaking to him.

Trevor was in the car. Trevor shouldn't have been in the car.
Find my glasses.
Please, Daniel.

In his dream she called him by name, over and over.

Please, Daniel.
Daniel . . .

The photos from the front of the church came to life, and he saw her as if she were moving from one to another, morphing and changing and merging, picture by picture—the cabin to the beach to the studio photo with her dog—with glimpses of her walking through the halls of school in between.

Finally, when he did roll out of bed, he felt like he needed a few more hours of sleep.

The marks were still on his arm.

Still sore.

He chose a long-sleeved sweatshirt so no one would see them.

He wasn't sure how he'd cover them up during football practice, but maybe using his arm warmers would take care of it—as long as no one noticed anything in the locker room while he was changing.

Just like usual, his dad was in the kitchen scrolling through the news feeds on his iPad as he finished his coffee, with a copy of the local paper that he'd already read folded up next to his empty cereal bowl. He wore his sheriff's uniform. Radio. Flashlight. Handcuffs. Gun. Ready for the day.

"Feeling better this morning, Dan?"

"Yeah. Thanks." He didn't realize he'd turned his wounded arm away from his dad until after he'd done it.

Man, he hoped he wasn't going to be self-conscious about that at school too, or it was going to be a really long day.

"What time will you be home from football practice tonight?"

"We're reviewing game films of the Pioneers afterward, so it might not be until six thirty or so. Kyle's coming over at eight to study for our history test tomorrow."

His father finished his coffee. "You want me to pick up something for supper on the way home?"

"I'll throw some fajitas together." When his mom moved out, Daniel and his dad had split up the cooking responsibilities, and his specialty was homemade tortillas, so his father didn't argue at all about the idea of fajitas.

"That'll work." He rose and gently patted Daniel's shoulder. "Hey, bud, I know there's been a lot going on this week, a lot of really intense stuff. Hang in there."

"I will."

Things had been pretty good between the two of them since the day last spring when Daniel's mom had said things no woman should ever say to her husband, and then walked out the door.

The separation had really affected his dad. He didn't smile so much these days. He worked hard, he was a good dad, he was there when Daniel needed him. But his heavyheartedness had weighed on them both, and Daniel wasn't sure how to help lift him out of it.

The divorce still wasn't final. Daniel's mom talked to him occasionally on the phone and told him how much she still wanted to be part of his life, but since she still hadn't come back to Beldon from the Twin Cities, where she was living with her sister, not even come back once, her words didn't mean much to him. It was clear to everyone that she wasn't returning, at least not for good.

Outside, a thin layer of frost covered everything, and Daniel had to scrape his car before backing down the driveway.

On the way to school, he tried to put Emily's death and the funeral out of his mind, but had a hard time dismissing what'd happened there at the front of the church. It had to have been more than a hallucination. He'd seen her ghost, he'd heard it speak, and he bore the proof of the encounter on his arm.

But what was he going to do about any of that, apart from

hiding the hand-shaped, swollen mark and trying to forget what'd happened?

That really was the question.

And he didn't have any clue as to the answer.

But one thing he was pretty sure about: it wasn't something he was ever going to be able to forget.

Daniel found his typical parking spot on the edge of the lot near a quiet grove of pines where he sometimes saw deer in the mornings, especially in the winter, when it was just barely getting light when he drove up. The football stadium lay to the left, near a farmer's cornfield bordering the school.

After grabbing his backpack and slinging it over his shoulder, he headed toward the building.

Beldon High School was relatively large, considering how many people lived in town. About a decade ago someone had decided that busing students in from the region would be cheaper than building or remodeling smaller high schools throughout the area, and they'd been doing it ever since. Daniel's class was the smallest, but even it had a couple hundred kids. There were more than enough students at the school for some of them to slip through the cracks.

Just like Emily did.

He found his friend Kyle Goessel pulling to a stop in his twenty-year-old midnight black Mustang.

Kyle climbed out and tossed the door shut. "What's going on, Dan?"

"Hey."

"You okay? I heard about what happened at the funeral."

"I'm good." They started toward the school and Daniel said, "So you weren't there?"

"I got there after you left."

Ever since Kyle and his family had moved to town five years ago, he and Daniel had been friends, even though they were pretty much total opposites in a lot of areas.

Daniel was into sports. Kyle was all about his electric guitar, comic books, and working at Rizzo's, their favorite local pizza place.

Kyle, English. Daniel, math.

Daniel, classic rock. Kyle, indie bands.

This morning, Kyle's shoulder-length, dirty blond hair was still a little tangly damp from his shower, and he spread his hand across it to tame it.

Kyle was taller than Daniel, but lanky and a little uncoordinated—unless he was running. It was sort of strange. His limbs all seemed to move at different speeds as he loped through the school halls, but when he took off sprinting, he was fluid. Smooth. The kid could run, but even though the cross-country and track coaches were after him to join their teams, he refused, for reasons he'd never fully explained to Daniel.

In a way, it was like this other guy in their class, Jacob Lawhead, who stuttered when he talked, but when he sang, his stuttering completely disappeared.

Some people said it was all just in his head, but ultimately, what did that really matter? It didn't make it any less real. Whenever someone says something is just in your head, they should leave out the word *just*, because whatever happens in your head also happens in your body. There's no other way around it.

Some kid must have pressed the wrong button on his key fob, because as they approached the school, a car alarm started blaring. Kyle mumbled, "I'm really glad someone invented those things. What a brilliant idea that turned out to be—I mean, how many crimes have car alarms helped deter? Tons, I'm sure."

They passed through the front doors and into the hallway that paralleled the office and led toward the science wing.

Kyle had his phone out, with the calculator app open.

"Not this morning, Kyle."

"Just do one."

"I'm not really in the—"

Kyle was already tapping at the keys. "1489 times 783 divided by 4.4."

"264,974.318," Daniel replied without missing a beat.

Kyle shook his head. "Man, I have no idea how you do that."

"It's the same as when you play guitar."

"How's it the same?"

"You read the music, you translate it without even thinking about it, and you know exactly what to do—which strings to press down, when to do it, all that. When I look at a sheet of music, I'm completely lost. I guess I could eventually translate which note is which, just like you could do the longhand in math, but only if I worked at it for a while. For you, music comes naturally."

"And for you, math does."

"Pretty much."

Kyle slipped his phone into his pocket. "Hey, I need to grab something from my locker. Come on."

They cut through the hall, navigating through the crowd of students heading to their lockers or their first-hour classes.

Five minutes until the bell.

Nicole Marten walked past on the way to their English classroom. "Hi, Kyle. Hey, Daniel."

"Hey," they replied.

When she was gone, Kyle gave Daniel a look.

"What?"

"Dude, she's *so* into you. You should ask her to homecoming."

Daniel stared at him blankly. It'd never occurred to him that Nicole might like him in that way. "She likes me?"

Kyle shook his head. "For being the class jock, you are staggeringly clueless when it comes to girls. No offense."

"None taken." They arrived at the locker. Daniel leaned a hand against the wall. "I was kinda thinking about asking that new girl, Stacy."

"Yeah." Kyle was digging through his things. "You keep telling me about her. When am I gonna meet her?"

Normally, when a new kid comes to school everyone talks about her, but no one seemed to be mentioning Stacy. Daniel wasn't sure why—probably because they were preoccupied with everything that was going on with Emily's death.

"I'll introduce you."

"The dance is—" Kyle began.

"Saturday. Yeah, I know."

"You're cutting it close, amigo. I mean, if you're gonna ask anyone."

"You taking Mia?"

Kyle nodded. He'd been going out with Mia Young since the beginning of summer—the longest he'd ever dated anyone. "You know it."

He finished rooting through his locker, closed it, and said to Daniel, "Well, just don't discount Nicole. She's cool. And from what Mia tells me, she doesn't have a date yet." As they left for English, Kyle indicated toward a locker near the end of the hall. "That was Emily's."

"How do you know?"

"I saw her sometimes, here in the hall, getting her things. I heard they cleared it all out." He paused. "I wonder what they found."

Thinking about what might have been in Emily's locker brought back memories of the funeral, and that was something Daniel did not want at all right now.

The place on his arm where she'd grabbed him began to itch terribly, but he resisted the urge to scratch it, and, merging with a group of other students, he and Kyle filed into their English classroom.

Everyone was quieter than usual today, almost certainly because they were still trying to sort through their feelings about what had happened to Emily.

A few people asked Daniel if he was okay, but thankfully most of his friends didn't bring up anything about what'd happened at the funeral.

Emily's body had been found on Sunday afternoon and on

Monday morning the school administrators had brought in counselors to meet with the students.

Everything had happened so fast. Daniel's dad had told him that typically the family wouldn't have the funeral so soon after a family member's body was found, but apparently in this case they wanted to have it as quickly as possible.

There weren't enough therapists in Beldon for the school, so they called in some from Superior and Ashland. Most of the kids Daniel knew didn't really feel comfortable talking to the counselors, and he wondered if maybe it was mostly under-classmen who ended up being helped by them. Hard to know.

The counselors all gave out their phone numbers and e-mail addresses and promised to be available if the students needed to contact them, and that was that. They'd seemed like they cared, seemed genuine enough, but, honestly, Daniel didn't know how much good any of it was going to do.

Time might heal some wounds, but from dealing with his mom moving out, he knew that sometimes it just makes the pain fester even more, like an infected wound in your heart that refuses to heal.

Their English teacher, Miss Flynn, glanced at the wall clock and then shuffled through the myriad of papers spread across her desk. She was single, mid-twenties, and wore skirts that none of the other teachers at the school would have ever been able to get away with.

She wasn't into the classics, but had an unsettling inter-est in stories about death, gothic horror, and the macabre. Although the students thought it was a little weird, admittedly, it did keep class interesting.

On the first day of the school year she'd told them that if they called their coaches "Coach," they should call her "Teach," which they'd done ever since.

Kyle leaned across the aisle and said to Daniel, "How much you wanna bet she assigns us a story about overcoming grief? Something like that?"

"I'm with you there."

For a moment he glanced at Nicole as she got out her books, then he averted his gaze before she could notice he'd been watching her.

The rest of the kids took their seats, the bell rang, and Miss Flynn stood up to begin class.

CHAPTER EIGHT

"Today we're going to take a look at a story from Richard Brautigan, a beatnik poet and essayist from the 1960s."

Okay, that was out of nowhere. A hippie poet from fifty years ago—not exactly Teach's typical fare.

She took a seat on her desk, crossing her legs in a manner that might well have been calculated to keep the attention of the guys in the class focused intently on the front of the room.

"The story is called 'Greyhound Tragedy.' It's found in his book *Revenge of the Lawn*. Here's how it begins: 'She wanted her life to be a movie magazine tragedy like the death of a young star with long lines of people weeping and a corpse more beautiful than a great painting, but she was never able to leave the small Oregon town that she was born and raised in and go to Hollywood and die.'"

Long lines of people weeping at a funeral.

A corpse of a young woman.

That sounded uncomfortably familiar.

Suddenly, it didn't seem so strange that Miss Flynn had chosen this story for today's class.

She paused as if to let the image of the funeral sink in, then continued reading about the young woman who wanted to become a Hollywood starlet. In her hometown she was on a path toward a safe, generic marriage she didn't want to a car salesman. At the climax, there was this really sad scene where she was at a bus station trying to get up the nerve to follow her dream, but couldn't do it and ended up leaving without the ticket.

Miss Flynn read: "'She cried all the way home through the warm, gentle Oregon night, wanting to die every time her feet touched the ground.'" In the end, the woman married that Ford salesman and tried to forget about her dream, "'but now,'" Miss Flynn finished, "'thirty-one years later, she still blushes when she passes the bus station.'"

No one spoke. Hardly anyone moved.

She still blushes when she passes the bus station.

Thirty-one years later.

"Dreams and death come to us all," Miss Flynn told them quietly. "What we do with the first before we experience the second makes all the difference. For Friday's class you're all going to write two blog entries—you don't need to post them online or anything like that—but I want you to write about what you'd like to accomplish before you die so that you won't have to blush when you pass the unopened portal to your dreams three decades from now."

Death and dreams.

And final regrets.

For a moment, Daniel wondered what Emily had dreamt of. *Maybe being accepted for who she was.*

Maybe—

One of the girls in the front row flagged her hand in the air. "Teach, are we seriously gonna be graded on our dreams?"

"I'm not going to grade this assignment."

A few sighs of relief throughout the room. Someone behind Daniel whispered, "Then why do we even have to do it?"

"What was that, Mr. Talbot?"

He cleared his throat. "I was just wondering why we need to do it if we're not gonna get graded on it."

"I'll give you a completion grade if I feel you've put forth an adequate effort. And as far as length, I'll leave that up to you. I'd rather you express yourself succinctly than write something meandering and unfocused just to meet a certain word count. This unit is on creative writing, so keep that in mind. Oh, and I will be asking you to share one of your blog entries with the class on Friday."

Oh, perfect.

Daniel didn't mind a thousand people watching him when he was on a football field or basketball court, but for some reason reading his work in front of his class always made him feel like he wanted to climb into a hole.

Nicole glanced at him knowingly, as if she could read his mind and knew how apprehensive the assignment made him.

Miss Flynn handed out a photocopy of another story.

"Now, let's take a look at 'The World War I Los Angeles Airplane,' the last story in Mr. Brautigan's book."

As it turned out, that one was about death too, or about life, depending on how you looked at the ending.

The rest of the morning went pretty much like normal. For the most part everyone left the topic of Emily alone, but there were occasional hushed conversations about it, a few tears here and there. Rumors swirled around about how at Windy Point there'd been other deaths in the past, that it might be haunted or something, that if you got too close to the edge, someone—or something—would pull you over to your death.

Windy Point was the highest bluff in the area. Not a mountain by any means, but it did rise nearly a hundred feet above Lake Algonquin.

Daniel reassured himself that those were only the kinds of stories kids tell to try to make sense of something as senseless as all this.

It was just an accident that happened to Emily.

That's all it was.

Maybe. But it was no accident what happened to your arm.

After lunch, he and Kyle were on their way to class when they saw a cluster of students forming near the doors to the gym. From the looks of it, a tall husky boy stood in the center of the group.

Daniel recognized him.

Ty Bell didn't laugh much, and when he did, he didn't laugh at the things other people thought were funny. It was more this distant, detached kind of laughter that seemed to drain humor out of the moment rather than add anything positive to it— almost like he was laughing simply because life had run out of humor and nothing was really funny anymore.

He was a senior, but had started late and been held back one year, so now he was a hardened, tough nineteen-year-old. He'd had a few run-ins with Daniel before, and also with Daniel's dad.

According to what people said, Ty carried a switchblade to school, and everyone pretty much steered clear of him and his three friends—if you could call them "friends." They were the three guys he made carry his books for him, open the doors for him, buy his cigarettes for him.

Daniel had always gotten the sense that they hung out with him because it made them feel more dangerous than they would've ever felt on their own—or maybe they somehow felt safer. He didn't know them well enough to be sure.

They weren't a threat by themselves, but Ty was a time bomb. Even the teachers seemed uneasy around him, as if they knew he was the kind of kid who might lose it at any time and show up the next day with a shotgun, ready to start picking people off, laughing that wild laugh.

A circle of students had gathered around him, and in mob mentality, some of them were egging him on. A couple of girls were telling him and his friends to "let the kid go," but no one was taking any steps to stop them. Four against one were bad odds, especially when one of them was Ty Bell, and if he was in the middle of this pack, it could only mean trouble.

Daniel shouldered his way through the crowd.

By the time he made it to the center, he could see that Ty and his buddies had just shoved someone into a hall locker. One of the boys was sticking a pencil through the padlock hole to keep him inside.

Daniel could hear the trapped boy trying to jimmy the lock open, but with the pencil in there, that wasn't going to happen.

Ty grinned and shook a can of soda to spray through the ventilation holes at the top of the locker.

"Put it down, Ty."

He gazed at Daniel flatly with his slate gray eyes. "Oh, look, it's Johnny Football Hero, here to save the day." His buddies seemed to think that was funny.

"You're not going to spray that into the locker."

He gave it another shake and held it closer to the vents. "What? Are you gonna stop me?"

"Yes."

A pause as Ty considered that. His friends closed in around him but Daniel just eyed Ty coolly. He felt Kyle slide in beside him.

Ty sneered. "And here comes our local rock star. I heard all about you and Emily."

"Nice," Kyle said. "Two complete sentences in a row. I'm proud of you. The remedial classes must be paying off."

Ty set his jaw.

Daniel said to him, "Back away from the locker."

Okay, what was with the comment about Kyle and Emily? What on earth did Ty mean, he'd heard about them?

Ty shook the can again, then suddenly aimed it at Daniel

and flicked back the pull tab. The soda exploded out and sprayed across Daniel's shirt, face, and neck.

Smiling, Ty turned toward the crowd of students as if he were looking for affirmation, but the only people snickering were his three buddies. The crowd might've laughed, at least a little, if he had done it to someone else, but they didn't laugh at all when he messed with their all-conference quarterback.

Daniel brushed gently at his shirt to rub the drops of soda off. "I told you that you weren't going to spray that into the locker."

Ty's gaze hardened once again. "You get into a fight, you can't play on Friday night, am I right? Miss the big homecoming game? How'd you like that, Danny boy?"

Daniel hadn't been in a fight since middle school. That summer he and his family had gone to the East Coast, and he'd been down by the ocean one night when three boys cornered him.

He'd warned them to leave him alone, but they'd rushed him. He came away from that fight with a black eye and two bruised and bloodied knuckles. The other boys hadn't fared quite so well.

But today Ty was right about him missing Friday night's game if he got into a fight, and that was not something he was about to do unless he absolutely had to.

However, Ty had made up his mind and took a swing at Daniel, who ducked and evaded the punch. Ty lurched forward, off balance, and Daniel had a clear shot at an uppercut to his abdomen, but he held back. Instead, he grabbed Ty's arm and twisted it around behind him to hold him secure. When

Ty tried to pull away, he put more pressure on his wrist to stop him.

Daniel didn't know martial arts or anything like that, but his dad had shown him how to immobilize someone if necessary. It was one of the advantages of being the son of a guy who'd been in law enforcement for nearly twenty years.

"Open the locker," Daniel said, "and let him out."

"No, I— Ow!"

"Teacher!" someone shouted. Immediately, the crowd began to melt away.

Daniel released Ty, shoving him firmly away from the lockers.

He shook out his arm angrily as he and his three friends backed down the hall. "You're dead, Byers. You're all mine."

Daniel quickly removed the pencil and unlatched the locker as Ty and his buddies vanished into the dispersing pack of students.

One of the freshman math teachers, Mr. McKinney, was striding toward them, but he was still only halfway down the hall.

When Daniel opened the locker he could tell right away why Ty and his friends were picking on this boy. He wore clothes that were way out of style, had a bad case of acne, and he was short and didn't look very athletic. Bullies are cowards. They always prefer to pick on people smaller or more helpless than they are. Daniel had seen this boy around school, but only this year. He guessed he was a freshman.

And he'd seen him one other place.

At the funeral yesterday, standing near the front of the church.

Even though the boy was trying his best to hide it, Daniel could tell he'd been crying. "What's your name?"

"Ronnie."

"You okay, Ronnie?"

"Yeah." He was trying to smile, trying to pretend everything was alright, but he couldn't hide the fact that he was trembling. Despite himself, he sniffed back a tear.

Mr. McKinney called, "What's going on here?"

"They mess with you again," Kyle said quietly to Ronnie, "you tell me. Alright?"

Ronnie nodded to Kyle as Mr. McKinney arrived. "I said, what's going on down here?"

"Nothing," Kyle replied. "We were just helping show Ronnie around the school."

"That true, Mr. Jackson?"

"Yes, sir," Ronnie said.

His last name is Jackson? Is he related to Emily?

Mr. McKinney let his gaze move from one boy to the next. Daniel and Kyle had both had him for freshman algebra. One time he'd told Daniel that he was one of the brightest students he'd ever had in a decade of teaching and had encouraged him to join his math club. Daniel hadn't, but they'd always gotten along pretty well. In addition, although Kyle and Daniel had been in trouble a few times over the years, it was never for anything serious, and never for bullying.

Now Mr. McKinney glanced sternly at his watch. "I think you three had better be getting to class."

After they were out of earshot, Daniel asked Ronnie, "Are you related to Emily Jackson?"

"She's my sister." He wiped a tear from his cheek. "My twin sister—or she was. Until she was killed."

"Killed?" Kyle sounded as surprised as Daniel was by what Ronnie had said.

"She knew how to swim. There's no way she just happened to fall in and drown. Not without someone holding her under."

CHAPTER NINE

"But she might have fallen off Windy Point," Daniel suggested.

"Or been pushed," Ronnie said.

"You really think she was killed?"

This time he hesitated a little. "How else could it have happened?"

The explanation seemed simple enough—she fell into the lake, it was too cold to swim to shore, and the current pulled her under.

But Daniel thought that pointing that out might upset Ronnie or hurt his feelings, so he held back. However, he did bring up something else. He had no idea why this boy would be in school the day after his sister's funeral. "Shouldn't you be at home?"

"I wanted to come." His voice was soft, distant. "To be with my friends."

Daniel couldn't help but wonder how many friends Ronnie really had. "Yeah, that makes sense," he said, trying to help him feel better.

He did his best to figure out what was going on. It seemed like an awfully big coincidence that Emily died and then Ty and his friends just happened to start bullying her twin brother the day after her funeral.

Probably just taking advantage of the situation—knowing that messing with him today when he's upset about his sister will bother him even more.

Daniel felt his hands tighten into fists and he wondered if he should have taken a swing at Ty after all.

Ronnie left and Kyle mentioned that he needed to get going too, but before he took off for his chemistry class, Daniel asked him, "What did Ty mean when he said that about you and Emily? About how he'd heard about you two?"

"I have no idea."

"So you didn't know her or anything?"

He shook his head. "No."

"But why would he—"

"I said I have no idea."

A pause. "Okay."

"I'll see you tonight. Eight o'clock. Your house."

"Sure."

Kyle headed to class, and Daniel stopped by the restroom to wash the soda off his face.

As he did, he wondered why Kyle had seemed defensive when he asked him about Emily. It wasn't like him at all. Based on Kyle's reaction, Daniel couldn't help but wonder if there was something his friend wasn't telling him.

With that bothering him, he finished cleaning up. He tried

not to disturb anyone when he walked into the physics lab late, but ended up getting a tardy slip anyway.

After that, the day went by quickly, but a swarm of questions pursued him everywhere he went.

Could Emily really have been killed?

Why had she appeared to him?

Was Ty just trying to get on Kyle's nerves, or, if not, what'd he been referring to?

After school, when Daniel was in the locker room changing for football practice, he was surprised to discover that there were no marks on his arm. None at all. Somehow the wound, which had been burned so deeply into his skin that morning, had healed during the day.

Or maybe it was never there at all. Maybe you imagined the whole thing.

He rubbed his head.

No matter what was going on, it was like normal life was being warped out of shape little by little and he was getting drawn into something dark and confusing, something that was way beyond his control.

Practice did not go well.

The team was distracted, their timing was off, and their concentration was at zero, but the coaches must have understood that it had to do with the recent tragedy at their school and didn't get on anyone's case.

Afterward, Daniel and his wide receivers met with the offensive coordinator and the head coach to review the film of the Coulee Pioneers dismantling the Spring Hill Panthers last weekend. He had a lot on his mind, but he tried to ignore everything except the game film and did his best to concentrate on analyzing the plays.

The Pioneers' defensive ends were crashing a lot. "We should go with read options on Friday," Daniel suggested, anticipating what the coaches would be thinking.

"Right," Mr. Jostens, the offensive coordinator, agreed. He was a trim, fit guy in his late twenties who'd been a wide receiver for UW–La Crosse and had been an assistant coach at Beldon for the last four years. He didn't teach any classes and Daniel wasn't sure what other job he might work at to help pay the bills.

Coach Jostens paused the video and pointed to the Pioneers' all-state tackle, a kid who weighed more than 260 pounds. "They have an enormous line. This guy's trouble, but you're good out of the gun. Read the defense, fire it fast, and we'll roll over these guys."

When they were done, the head coach, Mr. Warner, called Daniel to his office and looked at him sternly. "Have a seat, son."

Daniel did.

With his round, stylish glasses, perceptive gaze, and meticulous mannerisms, Coach Warner looked more like a statistician than a phys ed teacher and hard-nosed football coach.

But looks can be deceiving.

"I heard about an incident earlier today between you and Ty Bell. Care to tell me what happened?"

"I was just trying to help this other kid out of a locker. He was a freshman."

"Did you fight with Ty?"

"No."

"That's not what I heard."

"He swung at me, I stopped things from escalating. That's all that happened."

Daniel wasn't sure that would be enough to reassure his coach.

"You need to be careful, Daniel. Bell is trouble and he'll drag you down with him if he's given half a chance. You understand that?"

"Yes, Coach."

"Alright." With that, he dropped the subject of the almost-fight. "Hey, listen, I've got some good news. There are two scouts coming this weekend. One from the University of Minnesota, the other from Ohio State. Have either of the schools talked to you yet?"

"Just letters so far."

Daniel's grades were good, especially in math and science, but all he could really count on would be a small academic scholarship. His dad's salary wasn't that much—a small-town sheriff wasn't exactly the best career choice if you were hoping to make a ton of money.

So even though his dad didn't tell him in so many words, Daniel knew the only way he was going to make it through college without working or taking out some major loans was with a football or maybe a basketball scholarship.

So, yes, a lot was riding on this year.

On this game.

Especially if scouts from two Big Ten schools were going to be there.

"They want to meet you after the game," Coach Warner said. "No guarantees, but just the fact that they're coming is a good sign." He rapped a finger against the side of his own head. "Don't let this mess with you. Just go out there and play. Hit your receivers. Do what you do best. Got it?"

"I will."

"And stay clear of Bell."

"I will, Coach. Thanks."

As Daniel was grabbing his things, Randall Cox, one of their wide receivers, caught up with him in the hallway. "What's up, Dan?"

"Hey."

"Listen, did you hear about this thing Coulee has going on? The pizza thing?"

"No. What's that?"

"Their defensive unit has this deal that they'll buy a pizza for anyone who makes a hit that ends up with one of our guys being carried off on a stretcher."

"You're kidding."

"My cousin goes to school over there. That's what she said."

"Fabulous."

It didn't take a lot of insight to translate that "one of our guys" meant the quarterback and wide receivers would be some of the primary targets.

Randall glanced at the wall clock. "Well, see you tomorrow."

"You too."

At home, after making fajitas for himself and his dad, Daniel ate supper, then waited in the living room for Kyle to come over and for his father to get off work. While he did, he spent some time surfing on his laptop, pulling up whatever articles he could about Emily Jackson.

He found her Facebook page and was surprised to see that the privacy settings were turned off, so that even though they'd never friended each other, he could see all her posts and pics.

Maybe she'd done it herself before she died, or maybe her parents had changed the settings so people could find out more about her life now that she was gone.

A couple of boys and a bunch of girls had left comments since her death telling her how much they'd miss her, how nice she was, how sad they were about what'd happened, and it was a little creepy to see the posts like that on a dead girl's page, but it struck Daniel that it was sort of like the twenty-first-century version of leaving flowers on someone's grave.

Still, he didn't like reading the comments. It made him think of the funeral again and how all those kids who'd ignored Emily had shown up after it was too late for her to ever feel wanted or a part of their group.

She had Ronnie listed as her brother.

Daniel studied who her friends were and read her status updates, which didn't take long, because there weren't too many of either of them.

And she didn't have that many comments or likes on the posts that she had put up there.

She tended to post photos, which actually helped Daniel get a feel for her life.

One of the pictures of her and her bushy golden retriever caught his attention.

She'd taken it herself, hugging her dog close and holding her camera out to snap the photo. Behind her, a lake stretched back until it met a forest folding into the horizon. The caption read, "Me and Trevor at Windy Point!"

Daniel stared at the words, a knot forming in his stomach. Trevor.

That was the name of her dog.

At the funeral, she'd told him—or at least he'd imagined she'd told him—that Trevor was in the car: "Trevor shouldn't have been in the car."

Daniel couldn't think of any way he might have known before now that her dog was named Trevor. He hardly even knew who Emily was—how could he have known the name of her golden retriever? So, if it wasn't her ghost, what explanation made sense? There was no way all this could be a coincidence.

And apparently she'd been up to Windy Point at least once by herself.

Did she fall? Did she jump? Was she dragged over the edge? Or maybe, was she pushed?

Ronnie had told him he thought his sister was killed.

Maybe he was right.

CHAPTER
TEN

As it turned out, a domestic disturbance call kept Daniel's dad out a little later and he didn't make it home until after seven. He warmed up a fajita for supper, but didn't say much to his son.

He usually took some time to himself when he got home from work and they didn't always talk much with each other—but it wasn't a strained silence. It was more the comfortable kind a father and son can develop over time when they've been through a lot together and come out on the other side respecting each other more than ever before.

Kyle showed up just before eight. Even though he'd eaten at home, he microwaved a fajita for himself and they headed to Daniel's bedroom.

Basketball and football trophies cluttered the shelves and the top of Daniel's dresser. Since his dad wasn't too excited about the idea of his having *Sports Illustrated* swimsuit-issue pics all over his walls, Daniel stuck with posters of his favorite Mavericks and Packers players instead. It was clearly the room of a kid who was into sports.

Kyle dropped his backpack on the desk, quickly finished off his fajita, and then flumped onto the bed and started throwing Daniel's Nerf football into the air. "So, did you call her yet?"

"Who?"

"Stacy, dude. The new girl. Did you ask her to the dance on Saturday?"

"I don't have her number."

"Oh, that's lame."

"How's that lame?"

"Google her. Whatever. Facebook. See if it's listed. Some people do that. You can at least message her through there, anyway."

"No . . . I don't know. Asking someone out that way, it's just . . . I don't really want to do it through a text message. Seems sort of cowardly."

Kyle looked at him disbelievingly. "Has no one informed you that you are now living in the twenty-first century?"

"I need to talk to her in person, or at least on the phone. I don't know. It wouldn't feel right."

"Well, I could call Mia, see if she has her number?"

"I don't know. I guess not. Not right now."

Kyle shrugged. "Your call." He tossed the football into the air a few more times. "So, do you have either of your blogs written for Teach's class yet?"

"Still working on 'em. You?"

"I've been kicking around a few ideas. What do you have so far?"

Daniel turned his laptop so Kyle could see the blank page on his word processor.

"Ah."

"Yeah."

"So just jot down your thoughts."

"This kind of thing comes naturally to you. I'm not a writer."

Kyle stopped with the football. "Do you have a journal? What about that one your mom gave you last year?"

"A journal? You mean write it out instead of typing it?"

"Exactly."

"Now who's stuck in the twentieth century?"

"Humor me."

How the process of writing his blog by hand rather than typing it was going to help him do better with the assignment was beyond him, but if Kyle thought it was a good idea, Daniel figured it was at least worth a shot.

He dug the journal out of his desk. He'd dabbled with writing some thoughts in it after his mom left, but he didn't really want to see those entries, so he quickly flipped past them to a blank page.

"So," Kyle said, "tell me about a dream you have."

When he put it that way, Daniel immediately thought of the distressing dreams he'd had last night. He knew what Kyle meant, though, so he tried to think of his dreams for the future.

Honestly, however, it wasn't those kinds of dreams that were on his mind as much as the hope that he would be able to move past Emily's death without anything else mysterious or unexplainable happening to him. "Lately, I've been having a hard time . . . well, focusing. You know, like my thoughts are getting away from me."

"Getting away from you?"

"Wandering out of formation. But that's not a dream, so much, it's more of—"

Kyle tapped a finger against the air. "Keep that. It's a good image. Thoughts wandering out of formation. I like that. Write it down."

Daniel made a note of it.

"So, you've got this deal going on with your thoughts wandering out of formation—maybe flying out of formation, something along those lines. Who knows. Any other impressions about what's happening—something to do with flight?"

"Vultures."

"Vultures?"

"Yeah, picking them clean."

"Picking your thoughts clean?"

"Picking clean the carcass of my dreams." The words just came out.

Kyle stared at him oddly. "You just come up with that?"

"I guess so."

Where did that even come from? What's going on with you?

"Write that down, bro. You're on your way."

It went like that for the next fifteen minutes—Daniel throwing ideas out, Kyle helping him sort through them. It reminded him a little of how he helped Kyle sometimes with calculus—not giving him the answers, but reviewing the equations so he could find the answers himself.

At last, Kyle said, "Read me what you have so far. I want to see where this thing's at."

"Give me a sec." Daniel drew lines across the page from one idea to another, marked off the phrases he definitely did not want to use, wrote a few transitions, then read,

> *The boy remembered a time not long ago, when he was in control of his thoughts, when they lined up where he asked them to, with only the usual flutter of spontaneity, with the stray ideas wandering into and out of formation like they're apt to do.*
>
> *Back then, like most people, he was able to pull them together, keep them in order, and there was a comfort to that, a sense of saneness and rightness.*

"Why's it in third person?" Kyle asked.

"I don't know, exactly. It just came out that way."

"Works for me. Go on."

> *But now he sees them, like birds in flight, and they wing into the spaces beyond his understanding. And sometimes vultures land in their place.*
>
> *Vultures.*
>
> *Dark birds that feed on the flesh of his dead dreams. Picking them clean until only the bones remain.*
>
> *White bones, clean in the sun. Bones where his carefully ordered thoughts used to live.*

Kyle stared at him. "I've never seen you write anything like that before."

I never have.

"Well, I'm definitely not reading this one in front of everyone. People would think I'm going nuts. I mean, dead dreams being eaten by vultures? That's pretty depressing. And besides, it's not really about what I hope to accomplish before I die."

"I don't think Teach will have any problem accepting that. It's implied that you want the vultures to go away. She'll dig it." He tossed Daniel the football. "And besides, I know one of your dreams, even if it's one you don't want to write about."

"What's that?" He tossed the football back.

Kyle went over to the desk, picked up Daniel's cell phone, and handed it to him.

"What's this for?"

"Calling Stacy."

"No, listen, even if I wanted to call her, I—"

"Which you do."

"Okay, yes, which I do—but I told you, I don't have her number."

Kyle pulled out his own phone and before Daniel could stop him, he'd speed-dialed Mia.

Daniel just shook his head and listened to one side of the conversation. "Yeah, no . . ." Kyle said. "I know. . . . Hang on." He asked Daniel for Stacy's last name.

"Clern."

"Clern," he told Mia. "I don't know. . . . Seriously? Cool. Okay."

End call.

"What did she say?" Daniel asked.

"She doesn't know her, but she's gonna ask around." Kyle

put his phone away. "So, dead end number one, but that just makes it all the more interesting. I'll go to Facebook. You Google her, like we were talking about before. Let's see if we can pull up some way to contact her."

"I don't really want to—"

"Of course you do." Kyle already had his laptop open. "You're just scared."

"I'm not scared."

"Uh-huh."

"I'm just . . . slightly apprehensive."

"Which qualifies as scared." He typed. It took him only a few seconds to do the search. "Huh. Nothing's really coming up. Tons of Stacys, but nothing for her specifically. You?"

Daniel finished tapping at his keyboard. "No."

"Do you know where she moved from? Her name could still be under some previous town or school or something, you know, in their class rosters."

Daniel shook his head. "I'm not sure where she's from. I've . . . well, I've never actually talked to her."

Kyle blinked. "You've never actually talked to her."

"Not exactly, but I've come close a few times."

"Oh, you are seriously snargled over this girl."

"Snargled?"

"Needed a word, couldn't think of one, made one up." Kyle gave his attention to his computer. "Well, still, I'd have to say this is weird. I just can't believe she doesn't have a Facebook page."

"It's not that unusual. A lot of kids are moving off it, you know, because their parents and grandparents are on it."

"Sure, I get that."

"Maybe something happened to her at another school—something she doesn't want the kids at her new school to know about—and she closed it down. It happens."

"You mean maybe she was embarrassed about something or hurt somehow?"

"Yeah."

"Or maybe she had something to hide."

Daniel eyed him. "What would she have to hide?"

"I don't know. Just throwing it out there."

Neither of them seemed to know where to take things from there.

Finally, Kyle dug out his U.S. History book. "Man, to do well on this test, I'm gonna have to dust off a part of my brain I haven't used in a while."

"Well, let's start dusting."

They spent the next hour poring over the chapter summaries and review questions.

Sometimes when Daniel studied with people, it was more just hangout time than anything else, but, despite the fact that Kyle acted like school wasn't a big deal to him, he took studying seriously, and Daniel could always be sure to get more done with him than with any of his other friends.

The whole time they were reviewing the material, Daniel was wondering if he should bring up anything about what he'd seen at the funeral, or about the weird mark that'd appeared on his arm.

He'd already told Kyle that vultures were picking away at his dead dreams, but the stuff concerning Emily was on a whole different level.

In the end, he decided he didn't want his best friend to think he was losing it, and kept everything to himself.

Maybe, when the time was right, he'd tell him what was going on, but right now the time did not feel right.

When they'd finished studying, they got some chips and salsa, so Kyle's mouth was full when he said, "So that was pretty wild, huh, that Ty was picking on Emily's brother today?"

"Knowing Ty, it doesn't surprise me." Daniel was still curious about what Ty had been referring to when he said he'd heard about Kyle and Emily, but after seeing Kyle's reaction to his questions earlier about it, he knew better than to bring that up.

Kyle swallowed, then used a mutantly large chip to snag a heaping dollop of salsa.

"That's a lot of salsa."

"I'm occasionally prone to excess."

"Really."

"I've had my moments. Hey, I heard they did go through her locker, you know, like we were talking about at school."

"Who went through her locker?"

"I don't know, the school administrators maybe. Or her parents. Or the cops. But supposedly they found a notebook in there that she'd been writing in on the day she died. Could have been the last words she ever wrote. You never know." He devoured the salsa-laden chip. "Makes you think."

Given what'd happened the last couple days, Daniel was more than a little curious about what was in that notebook.

Kyle checked the time. "Listen, I gotta fly or my mom'll kill me." He gathered his things. "I'll catch up with you tomorrow."

"Sure. Yeah."

After Kyle left, Daniel stood at the window and watched him drive away.

Partly he wished that he'd told him about Emily rising in her casket and grabbing his arm and leaving her handprint behind, but partly he thought that was something he should keep to himself.

For now.

Probably forever.

As long as nothing else like that happened again, he would be alright. Life would go on and eventually he would be able to make sense of it all.

And that's what he tried to do as he lay down to sleep.

But even if it wasn't her ghost that had grabbed his arm, he still couldn't understand how he'd known Emily's dog was named Trevor.

CHAPTER ELEVEN

Thursday.

Time whipped by.

The history test seemed to go alright.

Then government. Spanish. Study hall. AP Calculus.

He saw Nicole around, talked to her a little, just in a passing-someone-in-the-halls, how-are-you-doing? sort of way. But he couldn't help but think of what Kyle had told him about her, that she didn't have a date for Saturday's dance. That she liked him.

Since there was a game tomorrow, football practice was pretty light. At least it went better tonight—the guys were more in sync than they'd been the night before, and things were clicking.

Daniel was a little slow getting out of the locker room afterward and was one of the last guys to head to the parking lot.

He was nearly to his car when he saw Stacy emerge from the edge of the woods.

"Hey," she said.

"Hey."

She hugged her books to her chest. "I don't know if we ever officially met. I'm Stacy."

She was waiting for you. She wanted to talk to you!

"I'm Baniel Dyers—Daniel. I'm Daniel Byers."

Oh, you are such an idiot!

A glimmer of a smile. "I know who you are."

"I know you too."

"Really?"

"Uh-huh."

"How?"

"I've seen you around."

"Oh."

A long pause.

"So."

"So," he replied lamely. "Well, it's good to meet you. Officially."

"Good to meet you too." He had the sense that she would reach out to shake his hand, but instead she stared down at the ground between them for a moment, then back at him. "You played good against Spring Hill."

"You were there?"

A slight eye roll. "Of course I was there."

"Not everyone comes to the games."

"I do."

"Me too."

Dude, that was the stupidest thing ever to say!

"Of course you do," she said lightly.

He felt like he wanted to hide somewhere—anywhere—but when she spoke again she just did so matter-of-factly and not the least bit in a way to make him feel more put on the spot. "Um, I just wanted to wish you luck on the game. I mean, the one tomorrow night."

"Thanks."

She waited.

Ask her to the dance on Saturday—at least get her number.

"Um . . ." He repositioned his feet. "Say, I was wondering . . ."

"Yes?"

"About the game."

No, not the game, the dance—

"Yes?"

He took a deep breath. "So, I was . . ."

Go on!

"Um . . . So maybe I'll see you there. At the game."

"Oh. Sure. So, good luck," she repeated.

"Right."

Ask her for her number.

But he didn't.

And then she was saying good-bye and he was fumbling out a reply. "See you around, Stacy."

"See you around, Baniel," she replied good-naturedly.

As she stepped away he opened his mouth to call her back, but nothing came out.

And then she was gone.

But at least he'd talked to her.

You can't be expected to ask a girl out or get her number the first time you officially meet her, can you?

Um, yeah.

He climbed into his car and leaned his forehead against the steering wheel.

Man, you sounded like a moron!

Well, talk to her tomorrow. You can still ask her.

The dance was Saturday night, but at least that gave him one more day.

Before starting the car, he saw a text from Kyle asking what he was up to tonight, and he texted back that he was going to be at home finishing up his homework and then head to bed early to get a good night's sleep before game day.

He didn't bring up anything about the conversation with Stacy. It would have only made him more embarrassed if Kyle knew how he'd failed to sound like even a halfway intelligent human being talking with her.

Imagine that. Daniel Byers not knowing how to talk to a girl.

What else is new?

That night back in his bedroom, it took him a while to write his second blog entry, the one he was going to have to read in front of Teach's class tomorrow.

Without Kyle there to help him, he felt like a guy stuck on a boat in the middle of the ocean with no idea which direction to row toward land.

Eventually he got something out, this time about hoping to send the vultures away, but it wasn't nearly as good as if he'd had Kyle brainstorming with him.

Then he went to bed, but his thoughts of Stacy kept him awake.

Talk to her tomorrow at school, or at least before the game.

But he also found that, just before falling asleep, his thoughts were drifting toward Nicole as well.

CHAPTER
TWELVE

The next day before class, he kept an eye out for Stacy but glimpsed her for only a moment in a crowd at the end of the hall. In English, when he saw Nicole taking a seat, he felt conflicted. Truthfully, he was interested in them both, but in different ways.

He'd known Nicole since fifth grade, so there was this history they had together, but Stacy was new, so there was a mysterious, alluring air about her that he found intriguing.

A few days ago if you would have asked him, he would've said he was sure he wanted to go with Stacy—that is until Kyle told him that Nicole liked him. That, along with the fact that Stacy had waited around after school to meet him, just made everything more confusing.

Miss Flynn got things rolling and began calling on students to get up and read their blog assignments about dreams and death.

When it was Nicole's turn, she said to Miss Flynn, "I wrote mine as a prayer."

"A prayer?"

"Yes."

Of course, they were at a public school, a place where it was okay to utter God's name as a swear word but not in a prayer—something that even Daniel, who wasn't overly religious, found ridiculous.

"Well." Miss Flynn sounded vaguely uncomfortable. "Go ahead. Let's hear it."

Nicole read:

> God, I thought I should probably let you know that a demon showed up at my doorstep yesterday. He was returning my shadow-clothes. I must have left them at his place when I stopped by for a visit last week, and he was just being kind enough to return them.
>
> So, to make sure they hadn't shrunk, I tried them on and found that they fit just as snugly as ever.
>
> I'm telling you this because I noticed the outfit you set out for me on my bed. And I'm curious, are you trying to get me to revamp my wardrobe?
>
> Truth is, I'm pretty comfortable with the clothes I already have.
>
> Just let me know what you're up to and then I can decide whether or not to try on those glowing clothes waiting for me in my room.

When she finished, there was a long stretch of silence before Miss Flynn finally asked, "And how is that your dream, Nicole?"

"My dream is to be wearing the right outfit when it matters most."

"When you die."

"Yes."

Everyone stared at Miss Flynn to gauge her reaction. "I think that's the most admirable dream of all," she said at last. Then she went on to the next person.

And the next.

Right around the room.

Daniel wasn't excited about the second blog entry of his, but he didn't want to read the first one either, so the closer it came to his turn, the more unsure he became about which one would be the best to read.

Brad Talbot read his, the briefest one so far: "I dream of being rich and famous."

Miss Flynn waited. "And?"

"That's it."

"Well, thank you for not wasting our time with unnecessary verbiage."

"No prob, Teach."

"You might have dialed up the creativity factor a little, but I appreciate your honesty."

Then Kyle went. He called his entry "Wind and Rain," and somehow his words were both hope-filled and remorseful at the same time:

> Grain by grain the sand erodes
> through my moments, slipping down
> the fragile slopes of my days.

And I wonder, as I tumble down the side,
  who will change the weather
and give my life another shot
at glory?

Miss Flynn nodded. "The sand tumbles down quickly," she told the class. "For us all."

It sure did for Emily. No question about that.

Daniel wondered how long it'd taken Kyle to come up with that. Knowing him, he might very well have thought of it in the hallway on the way to class.

Two more students went, then it was Daniel's turn.

Still debating which entry to read, he decided at the last minute that he'd be more embarrassed about the second than the first, so he went with the one he'd written when he was with Kyle.

He was seriously nervous and felt like he stumbled all the way through it, but at least he managed to finish without any major flubs. When he was done, Miss Flynn quietly jotted something in her grade book and then, without any comment, asked the next person to go.

There was something about her lack of response that made Daniel uncomfortable—especially since she seemed to be commenting on everyone else's, no matter how weak they were.

After the last person had gone, she collected all the blog entries, then announced that since it was homecoming weekend she wasn't giving them any assignment for Monday. "Enjoy your break."

Nods and a few thank-yous around the room.

"And, as you know, next Wednesday is a parent-teacher conference day, so there won't be any classes. We'll only be meeting Monday and Friday. Have a good weekend."

The bell rang, and everyone grabbed their things and headed for the hall.

Nicole happened to be heading in the same direction as Daniel.

"Hi," she said.

"Hey. I thought it was cool that you wrote a prayer and felt okay sharing it with everyone," he told her candidly.

"Well"—she avoided discussing her blog entry—"I thought yours was awesome—but sad too. Where did you learn to write like that?"

"Busted. Kyle helped me piece it together."

"Well, I'm just glad that's over with, huh?"

"I'm with you there."

They walked in silence for a few steps, and then, out of nowhere, Nicole said, "So, are you going to homecoming dance with anyone?"

"Am I . . . ?"

No—but you might be.

If you can get up enough guts to ask . . .

He was still trying to figure out how to finish his sentence when Nicole did it for him: "Going to homecoming dance with anyone? Call me curious."

Tell her you're going with Stacy, that you're—

But you're not. You never asked her. You don't even know if she would go with you.

"No, not yet," he admitted. It was the truth. He didn't

want to lead Nicole on, but he did want to be honest. Then it came out: "But there's someone I was gonna ask." It was one of those things you say and then immediately wonder what in the world led you to say it in the first place.

"Oh?" she said in a tone that was impossible to read.

"Yeah, but I guess I haven't gotten up the nerve yet."

"It's not that big of a deal. Just ask her."

Yeah, I wish it was that easy.

"The worst she can say is no," Nicole reassured him.

Exactly.

"I guess."

She stopped walking. "Practice on me."

"What?"

"Practice. Ask me to go to homecoming with you."

"Ask you . . ."

"Go on, pretend you wanna go with me."

"Nicole, I was . . . Well, actually . . . It's just that . . ."

She read volumes in his hesitation and her eyes grew large. "Oh, you're . . . I heard that you weren't . . . I thought . . ." She blushed and shook her head. "Seriously, I didn't know—" She closed her eyes as if she were trying to disappear. "Please, please, please pretend this never happened."

"I mean, it's not that I—"

She held up her hand to cut him off. "It's okay. Seriously." Before he could reply, she turned abruptly. "I gotta go. I'm sorry."

"You don't need to apologize for anything, Nicole."

But she was already hurrying down the hall. He watched to see if she would turn around and glance back at him.

She did not.

And she was staring down at the floor as she went.

Which made Daniel feel even worse.

He didn't want to assume too much, but he wasn't a complete idiot and he could read between the lines of what had just happened.

For the rest of the day he didn't see Stacy or Nicole, and he found himself going back over the awkward conversation with Nicole again and again, replaying it in his mind, thinking of things he might have said differently, things that would've led their exchange in a different, more positive direction.

But ultimately, it didn't matter. He might think of a thousand other things he could have said, but he hadn't said them. His friend had left feeling bad, and it was all his fault.

After school he tried to ignore the headache that was coming on. The last thing he needed tonight was to be distracted during the homecoming game against the Coulee Pioneers.

Daniel told himself it would pass, that it was no big deal.

That's what he tried to convince himself of as he hung out with some of the guys from the team at Rizzo's pizzeria before leaving for school to get suited up for the seven-thirty game.

CHAPTER THIRTEEN

It was autumn.

Football season.

Daniel's time.

He loved all that it was: the rub of the shoulder pads, the dirt beneath your fingernails, the taste of blood in your mouth after you took a hard hit, the shot of adrenaline when the ball was snapped, running through the banner the cheerleaders made for the players, the invigorating evening air, the crowd going crazy. Everything.

Tonight, the smell of moist soil, someone's wood-burning stove, and the faint odor of manure from a dairy farm not too far from the football stadium mixed in the gentle evening breeze.

The headache didn't go away.

This year, homecoming was senior night, so all the seniors from the football team, as well as from the cheerleading squad, the cross-country team, the marching band, and the color guard, all got honored.

Before the game, one by one they met their parents at the fifty-yard line, where Mr. Ackerman, a newspaper photographer who did this at high schools throughout the area, stood and snapped their pictures. The parents smiled; the football players all tried to look tough.

The school also took time to recognize the homecoming king and queen. At Beldon High, either juniors or seniors could be chosen, and there'd been talk of nominating Daniel. However, he was only a junior and he didn't like the idea of taking that honor away from a senior, so he'd pulled his name.

Besides, even though he was captain of the football team, that kind of attention off the field made him feel a little awkward.

Beldon's concession stand was stocked with popcorn, hot chocolate, candy bars, pizza, and nachos with cheese. Some parents had been pushing for "healthy alternatives," some sort of vegan health bars, but as far as Daniel knew, they'd never sold any of them yet except to themselves.

Parked beyond the southern end zone were two emergency vehicles: Daniel's dad's squad car and an ambulance for any trouble, on the field or off it, that might sprout up at a game between these two rivals.

After the players had warmed up, the school district superintendent went to the announcer's booth at the top of the Eagles' stands, took the microphone and offered a moment of silence in honor of Emily and her family.

Then the marching band played the national anthem, the two teams took the field, and the game began.

During the first half, the headache was still bothering Daniel, but he managed to throw for two touchdowns, one in the first quarter, one in the second.

Coulee ran back the second kickoff and then, after the change of possession, hit a thirty-three-yard field goal with twenty seconds left in the half to bring the score to within four.

Home 14.

Visitors 10.

At halftime in the locker room, Coach Warner offered a few words of encouragement to the team as a whole, then the assistant coaches met with their offensive and defensive units.

"Byers," said Coach Jostens, "you need to keep an eye on that defensive end and stay focused on reading your keys. Recognize the coverages on those pass plays. We're gonna be throwing the ball a lot in the second half."

"Yes, Coach."

He spent a few minutes reviewing blocking schemes for pass protection with the offensive linemen, then turned to the receivers. "We can break this open in the second half. We need you to run disciplined routes. Crisp. Clean. Got it?"

Nods of agreement from the players.

However, as Daniel ran onto the field to throw a few balls to loosen up his arm, the headache that'd been lurking somewhere in the back of his mind crawled forward and tried to swallow up all of his focus and attention.

CHAPTER
FOURTEEN

The third quarter began with the teams exchanging touch-downs and converting the extra points, bringing the score to Eagles 21, Pioneers 17.

Run.

Evade.

Pass and play.

The fans were loud and wild and it was hard to hear, so when Coach wasn't sending in plays with the running back, he was holding up signs with the names of college teams on them to signal Daniel which plays to call.

First and ten, their own thirty-five yard line.

This time the sign read, "Alabama," which was a gun slot left slant trail pass. On this play, Daniel would have four possible receivers to throw to.

In the huddle he told them, "You get open, I'll get you the ball."

They broke huddle and the guys took their positions. Daniel started in a gun set, gave the count, and the center snapped the ball.

The Pioneers had gone to a 4-2-5 defense and Daniel found his wide receiver, Randall Cox, in the middle of the field for a twelve-yard gain just before the end of the third quarter.

At the start of the fourth, after a botched running attempt, Daniel found himself at second and ten, at his own forty-nine yard line.

Beldon High's band started in with some type of chant song and, because of the noise, Coach Warner held up a sign with "Nebraska" written on it, code for a read option right out of the gun.

On a read option, Daniel's line wouldn't block the defensive end. If he crashed at the running back, Daniel would keep the ball. If he didn't crash, he would hand it off to his running back. So at the snap, when the left defensive end came at him fast and hard, Daniel made his read and gave to the running back for a gain of three.

Third and seven.

And that's when it happened.

Daniel went with gun bunch right, a play with three receivers on the right side. He liked to hit Cox on a flag route as he angled toward the corner of the field. If he could connect with him it would typically be good for a nine- to thirteen-yard gain.

They lined up.

Daniel gave the count, received the ball from the center, and was scanning for an open receiver when he saw her.

A girl had climbed over the fence and stepped onto the field.

She walked in a stiff, jerky, unnatural way, keeping her head down. All Daniel could think was why the refs didn't throw a flag or try to stop the play, to protect her.

But they didn't, and Daniel couldn't stop the play himself. The defense blitzed.

And as they did, time seemed to grind to a halt and then tick forward slowly again, frame by frame, all within the breadth of a moment.

Everyone around him was moving at an impossibly slow speed. He could see what he should never have been able to see—the fierce expression on the face of one of the advancing defensive linemen, the flicks of grass left in his wake as he came toward him.

He heard the wash of sound from the crowd sharpen and suddenly become clear, almost as if he could distinguish between the separate people, each shouting.

An air horn went off.

He became aware of the lights shining brilliantly down at him, the moon high above the cornfield south of them, the world quickly dropping off into darkness beyond the bleachers.

And the slow, distinct movement of players surrounding him.

The only thing that didn't change speed was the girl, who lurched forward, with her head still bent forward, staring at the ground.

When she was maybe ten yards away, she lifted her head and looked directly at him and he saw the blank eyes, the gaping mouth, the pale and bloated skin.

Emily Jackson.

The dead girl.

And she was coming straight toward him.

She reached up and grabbed a silver chain necklace she was wearing, yanked it, and it floated right through her neck, leaving a thin streak of fresh blood behind it, as if something really had passed through her muscle, her bone, her skin.

Then she held up the necklace, a locket dangling from its center, and opened her mouth trying to say something, but no words came out, just a slurp of ugly water.

Blood oozed from the thin red line encircling her neck.

In a fraction of a second, all Daniel's senses seemed to become one: the sound of the crowd somehow merged with the damp autumn scent of the field, the sight of the sharp lights, the feel of the smooth-rough leather of the ball in his hand—everything flowed together, leaving him dizzy and off balance.

And then time caught up with itself.

Out of the corner of his eye, he saw Cox open downfield, but he didn't have time to throw—two defensive linemen had gotten past their blockers and were closing in.

Fast.

He only had time to protect the ball as he felt the crushing blow of the two guys sacking him together, one of them grabbing his face mask, snapping his head around, and when he landed on the ground, he hit hard on his left side, and his head smacked into something—another helmet, the ground, someone's knee, he couldn't tell and it didn't matter.

The huge tackle, the guy who weighed over 260 pounds, landed right on Daniel's stomach.

And the world went black. Just like it had at Emily Jackson's funeral.

CHAPTER
FIFTEEN

Lost in a waking dream.

The girl.

The game.

He heard words as if they were coming from the inside of his head rather than from the outside world: *Stay on this. Seek the truth. Learn what happened.*

The team doctor was leaning over him when Daniel opened his eyes: the second time in less than a week that he'd blacked out and awakened to see someone's anxious face bent over him.

"Hey, buddy? You alright?" the doc asked. "Can you see me?"

Daniel felt himself nod. "Yeah." It was different from when he woke up in the church on Tuesday. This time he'd had the air knocked out of him when he was sacked, so he was also short of breath.

"What's your name?"

"My name?" he mumbled.

"Yes."

"Daniel."

"And your last name?"

"Byers. Daniel Byers."

"Do you know where you are, Daniel?"

He turned his head, looked for Emily coming toward him across the field, but didn't see her. "Yeah. In the stadium. It's homecoming."

The doctor held up four fingers. "Daniel, can you see how many fingers I'm holding up?"

"Four."

Daniel found his attention shifting to the sidelines, but there was no sign of Emily.

Where is she?

Where—

"And what day is it?"

Person, place, and time. Daniel had been playing sports long enough to know that those were the three things they ask a player after he wakes up from blacking out. That, and checking his visual acuity, which the doctor was testing when he asked about the number of fingers he was holding up.

"Friday. September twenty-ninth," Daniel said.

The worry on the man's face eased. He glanced to the side, making eye contact with Coach Warner, who stood nearby. "Good." Then he stepped back and a couple of people helped Daniel to his feet.

He was slow getting up, and a little wobbly. Relieved applause from the crowd greeted him as he headed off the field with the coaches beside him.

At least he wasn't on a stretcher. Randall had told him the Coulee defense was trying to earn a pizza by tackling a player so hard he couldn't walk off the field. So, no pizzas on that play.

On the way to the sidelines, Daniel scanned the field, the track encircling it, and the stands, but he didn't see her. Thank goodness he didn't see her.

Please don't let me see her again.

Don't let me see her ever again.

He knew better than to tell the doctor and his coaches about Emily's appearance. They would only think he was hallucinating, that the knock on his head was worse than they'd imagined. And they would undoubtedly do a bunch of tests on him, since they'd be convinced he was seeing things that weren't there.

And they'd be right.

You are.

He pushed that thought aside.

When he reached the side of the field, he realized they'd already taken his helmet and hidden it. That was typical if the coach or the doctor wanted to make sure a player couldn't go back on the field.

Daniel was forced to confront the fact that he was not going to be playing any more in the game tonight.

With the recent national attention on head injuries in football, Beldon High's coaches had gone over all of this with the team at the beginning of the year: whenever a player blacks out, it's classified as a grade-three concussion, and after any concussion, at least in high school, you're sidelined for the rest of the game.

There was just too much public concern over repetitive traumatic brain injuries these days—especially with teenagers—to chance it.

But still, when he first woke up, Daniel had been hoping that maybe things would work out for him this time. That he would be the exception.

Usually, they would even take the guy to the hospital to look him over, but since Daniel had answered all the doctor's questions correctly, he hoped he wouldn't have to mess with any of that after the game.

He'd lost consciousness.

Yes.

But he didn't know if he'd blacked out from the headache or from the shock of seeing Emily again, or maybe from being hit in the head when he was tackled.

In the end, it really didn't matter. He'd seen what he had seen. There was no getting around that.

Twice now.

First speaking to him.

Now holding up her necklace—after pulling it through her neck.

Emily Jackson, the dead girl, had appeared to him.

And since no one else was acting strangely—just like at the funeral, when they didn't respond to what he'd seen in the casket—evidently she had appeared only to him.

The guys on his team fist-bumped him or smacked his shoulder pads and told him they were glad he was okay, and how well he'd played, and how tough he was to walk off the field after a hit like that.

His dad was making his way across the track, hurrying toward Daniel.

"You banged your head pretty hard out there, Dan. You alright?"

"I'm good."

"You sure?"

"I'm fine, I—"

But he never finished his sentence. There'd been a face-mask penalty when Daniel was sacked, but play had resumed on the field and the second-string quarterback had fumbled the ball on the first snap.

Half a dozen players piled on each other trying to recover the ball and it wasn't clear which team had gotten it, but the Pioneers guys were all pointing to their side of the field.

The refs dug through the pile of players and when they got to the bottom, they made the call.

Pioneers' ball.

Some of the guys around Daniel swore in frustration. He felt like doing the same.

Since he'd lost consciousness, even though it was only for a short time, his dad could have stayed there at the sidelines with him without any issues—but after he'd confirmed that Daniel was alright, he got a call on his radio and left to take care of some sort of altercation near the concession stand.

After his dad left, Daniel watched the dismal ending to the game.

The Pioneers scored.

Hit the extra point.

Took the lead 24 to 21.

Man, he wanted so badly to be out there. He assured his

coaches that he was fine, but school policy was clear: after what'd happened, he would be out for the remainder of the game.

After stopping the Eagles in three plays, Coulee High controlled the ball the rest of the game until the last few seconds, when they hit a field goal to make the score 27 to 21.

The only hope Beldon had was running back the kickoff, but that didn't happen.

They failed to score at all.

Lost homecoming.

To the Pioneers, their archrivals.

Because you were too distracted by a ghost to be focused on the game!

Although there was no way to be certain, Daniel knew—*he knew*—he wouldn't have fumbled that ball. He would have hit Cox for the first down. And they would have moved downfield and scored. If only he hadn't seen Emily Jackson walking toward him, then everything would've turned out alright.

What's going on?

What's wrong with you?

Why are you seeing these things!

Maybe if he'd hallucinated *after* the hit to the head he could understand it, at least a little bit—but that's not the way it had played out. It'd happened beforehand and that's what had caused him to get sacked in the first place.

Even though he'd smacked his head, it actually hurt less now than it had before the game. The headache, the one that'd been plaguing him all afternoon, was gone.

He realized that it was similar to when he'd fainted at the funeral—both times his headache had faded away after the vision of Emily appeared.

The mood in the locker room was dismal, a sense of collective disappointment, but the team knew better than to blame anyone in particular.

It was part of Coach's philosophy: you win or lose as a team and not as individuals. "There's no one to blame when we lose and no one to thank when we win," he'd told them more than once. "We're a team. We don't point fingers and we don't bask in glory. We go out there and fight and we take victory or defeat with dignity. We leave everything we have on the field and walk away with our heads held high. All together. As a team."

Some people might have discounted it as just typical locker room pop psychology, but Daniel got the impression that Coach Warner believed wholeheartedly in what he said.

A man Daniel had never seen before was waiting for him outside the locker room. He wore an Ohio State windbreaker.

"Hello, Daniel. My name is Coach Evers. I was hoping we could talk for a few minutes."

CHAPTER
SIXTEEN

"You alright, son?"

"I am."

"You took quite a hit."

"I'm good."

"Well," Coach Evers said, "you had a nice game out there." He took some time to note the different things that'd impressed him about Daniel's play and his awareness on the field. The compliments made Daniel a little uncomfortable, but he knew how important meeting this recruiter was and he simply thanked him.

"Listen," the scout said at last, "I wanted to ask you—I was . . . well, I'm curious. What were you looking at when you were sacked?"

"What was I looking at?"

"You were staring at a place on the field where there weren't any receivers. It was the only time during the game when I saw you do that. I was wondering what distracted you from the play."

Daniel almost said, "I thought I saw someone else on the field," but he realized how odd that might sound.

Finally, he just muttered, "It all happened pretty fast."

"Sure." Coach Evers seemed to accept that. "I understand." They spoke for a few more minutes, and at last he promised to follow up during the week to see how Daniel was doing.

He thanked the Ohio State scout, and after he'd left, Daniel hung around the locker room door for a little while, hoping that the University of Minnesota scout would talk with him too, but no one came by. The guy must not have been too excited about Daniel's performance tonight.

There's always the rest of the season. And there's always next year. You still have time to impress some scouts enough for a scholarship.

But honestly, colleges and scholarships and scouts weren't the foremost things on his mind.

And neither was the loss of the homecoming game, even though that was huge.

No, it was seeing Emily again, witnessing her pull that necklace right through her bloated neck—that's what troubled him the most.

A silver chain necklace.

A locket hanging in the middle.

She'd been wearing that in the photos at the funeral, the ones that looked like they were the most recent.

You need to do something to make these hallucinations—or whatever they are—stop.

But Daniel had no idea how to do that.

Finally, he headed down the hall, a little uncertain about

the prospect of facing the students who would most likely be congregated outside the school.

Stay on this. Seek the truth. Learn what happened.

He thought of the lake. The place where her body was found. That's where all these terrible things this last week had started.

There hadn't been a football game a week ago on the Friday night Emily disappeared. According to the news articles, two fishermen had found her body on the east side of Lake Algonquin just inside the inlet near Windy Point two days later, on Sunday afternoon.

Over the years, Daniel had been to that part of the lake a lot, mostly fishing with his dad. It was known for its wall-eyes, although a few muskies had been taken from there, including the fifty-one-incher hanging at the Antler Inn over on Highway G.

Go out there, out to the lake tomorrow. Have a look around for yourself. Maybe that'll make the visions stop.

He was debating that when he saw Nicole picking her way through the crowd of students who were milling around the parking lot.

"Are you okay, Daniel?" She didn't try to hide the concern in her voice.

"Yeah."

"You sure?"

"I'm good."

"Really? Because I . . ."

"I'm fine. Don't worry."

That seemed to reassure her. "Alright, just . . ." Then she

switched to another topic—their last conversation. "I need to tell you . . . um . . . I'm really sorry about earlier, you know, at school today. I wasn't trying to . . . Well, anyway. I'm sure whoever you ask will say yes."

"Okay," was all Daniel could think to say.

"You sure you're alright?" She looked like she was about to reach over and touch his arm, but held back. "I was worried about you."

"Really, Nicole. I am. Trust me."

Yeah, but I did see Emily again, this time during the game. Oh, and by the way, sometimes she talks to me too. So it's not like I'm losing it or anything. Nothing like that.

"So," Nicole said uncertainly, "we're cool?"

"We're cool."

Remember what Kyle said? Don't discount her. Going to homecoming with her would be—

Coach Warner caught his attention from the edge of the parking lot.

"Great." It was clear by Nicole's tone how relieved she felt. "That's awesome."

"I'll see you later."

Daniel's coach started toward him, looking frustrated, and Daniel had the sense that it wasn't just from them losing their homecoming game.

After Nicole told him one more time that she was glad he was okay, Daniel excused himself to talk to his coach to find out what was up.

CHAPTER
SEVENTEEN

"Hey, I saw you talking with the scout from Ohio State. That go alright?"

"It was good," Daniel replied. "He said he'd contact me this week, check up, see if my head's feeling better. But it already is. It feels fine."

"Glad to hear that." His gaze slipped past Daniel toward the school. "Listen, you know procedure, Daniel. Jumping through the hoops. It's all about liability issues these days. The school board, the lawyers."

"Procedure?"

Coach Warner glanced to the left. One of the paramedics had driven the ambulance around the edge of the field and was on his way to their end of the parking lot.

"No, Coach. You're not serious."

"Just bear with it. Get your head looked over, get home, get some rest. You played well tonight. Nothing to be ashamed of. Now take care of yourself. We face the Bulldogs next week and I'm going to need you on your A game."

"I will be."

Daniel took a second to mentally shift gears and get ready for this.

While he was on his way to the ambulance, Kyle jogged over and met up with him. "Dude, you got slobberknocked out there."

"Yeah. No kidding."

"You need me to give you a ride home or anything?"

He pointed at the ambulance. "They want to check me over at the hospital, but maybe you could meet me there, bring me back here to pick up my car afterward?"

Daniel's dad was on his way toward them.

"Done. Or I could just take you to your place when you're finished and we could grab your car in the morning."

"Either way works."

As Daniel was boarding the ambulance, Coach Warner and the paramedic explained to his father what was going on.

He left for his squad car. "I'll follow you to the hospital."

Thankfully, the emergency room visit didn't end up being too big a deal. The docs told Daniel he needed to take it easy for a couple days and to ice his head and take some Advil if it was still hurting.

They emphasized that he was not to drive tonight, but cleared him for practice on Monday, as long as he didn't have any recurring headaches.

Daniel's dad had to answer a call from the station, so he okayed Kyle's driving him back to the house. They decided one of them would shuttle Daniel over in the morning to pick up his car from school.

By the time Kyle pulled up to the curb in front of Daniel's house it was nearly eleven o'clock.

Daniel climbed out.

"Text me tomorrow," Kyle said.

"I will."

The night had grown colder. The air felt heavy and raw, as if winter were gnawing at autumn, anxious to move in and take its place.

Kyle left, and as Daniel was walking up the driveway to his house he saw movement in the shadows near the garage.

He froze.

A wave of apprehension swept over him as he remembered the vision he'd had on the football field, and he hoped, hoped, hoped he wasn't going to see Emily again.

The images of her sitting up in the casket, facing him, holding up that necklace, all returned to him.

In the chilled night his breath was visible when he spoke. "Who's there?"

The figure stepped out of the shadows and into the porch light.

A girl.

But it wasn't Emily Jackson.

It was Stacy Clern.

CHAPTER EIGHTEEN

"Stacy? What are you doing here?"

"I saw what happened to you at the game. I looked for you afterward, but I couldn't find you. Someone said you'd gone home, then I heard you were in the hospital. I wasn't sure if I should go over there or come here to . . ."

"But how did you know where I live?"

"Your dad's the sheriff, remember? You're not that hard to track down. Are you okay? I mean, you had to go to the hospital?"

"It's just what they always do when someone gets clonked on the head. It's no big deal."

"Oh. Good—I mean, that it's no big deal, not that you were clonked."

"Sure. I get it."

"Um . . . So I guess you probably need to what? Lie low for a couple days? Rest up?"

"They want me to take it easy, so I'm just hanging out tomorrow, mostly. I think I might go over to the lake in the morning."

"The lake?"

"Lake Algonquin."

"That's where that girl Emily was found."

"Yes."

"Why are you going over there?"

"I don't know, exactly. I mean, I guess I'm hoping to get some kind of closure."

A pause, then: "Can I come?"

"To the lake?"

"Yeah. I could use some closure too."

"Well . . ." Although her offer to come along took him off guard, the idea of hanging out with her was definitely something he was interested in. "Sure."

"It's not far from my place. How 'bout I meet you there?"

"Okay. There's a parking lot by the boat landing over on the east side. The inlet is about a ten-minute walk from there. Ten o'clock work?"

"How about ten thirty?"

"Sure."

"Alright. Boat landing. East end of the lake. Ten thirty. Got it. See you there."

After they'd told each other goodnight, she left and Daniel went inside to get changed for bed.

As he lay down, he found himself thinking about the necklace Emily had been wearing when he saw her on the field, but that she didn't have one when he saw her in the casket.

Closure.

That's what he'd told Stacy he was looking for. And that's what he was going to find tomorrow morning at the lake when they visited that inlet where Emily's body had been found.

CHAPTER NINETEEN

No nightmares haunted his sleep.

No wounds were scarring his arm when he awoke.

Yes, he had the typical stiffness and sore muscles from the previous night's game, mostly in his lower back, though his left knee was sore today too, but that was about it.

He'd been a little worried that he'd have a headache from when he was hit, but his head felt surprisingly fine.

Maybe things were finally getting back to normal.

After breakfast, his dad left for work and Daniel shuffled through the newspapers that were in the recycle bin, looking for articles about Emily.

As he read through them, he realized that he must have seen the papers before, even just in passing, maybe on the kitchen table where his dad typically left them after breakfast, because some of the details of Emily's disappearance and death seemed vaguely familiar.

Trevor was mentioned in one of the articles that contained a picture of him and Emily. Her mom had been interviewed and said she'd found the dog in the front yard late Friday night.

Apparently, her daughter had left a note that she was taking him for a walk out around Lake Algonquin near where they lived, but had never returned.

Daniel reasoned that if he had noticed these papers on the table when his dad was reading them, he could theoretically have known about Trevor, even before the funeral.

Okay, but then why didn't that register before?

Maybe it was one of those things you didn't consciously notice at first, but somehow remembered later when something reminded you of it.

He'd had that sort of thing happen when he smelled chocolate-chip cookies and remembered details about visiting his grandma's house—the layout of her kitchen, what she had on her countertop, the sound of her old clock ticking in the next room.

They were all things he hadn't necessarily noticed back when he was there last month, but when he *remembered* them happening, it all came back to him in vivid detail.

Maybe that's what was going on here—buried memories climbing to the surface, brought to light by the stress of the funeral and the homecoming game.

Paging through the newspapers kept Daniel busy until Kyle swung by at nine forty-five to take him to school to pick up his car.

They didn't talk too much about the game or the concussion or the hospital visit, but Daniel did tell him about meeting up with Stacy last night and how she was going to join him at the lake this morning.

"She just showed up at your house?"

"Yeah. She was waiting for me when you dropped me off."

"I didn't see her."

"She was standing over by the garage."

"Doesn't that seem a little weird to you? That she just came by your house in the middle of the night and then hid in the shadows waiting for you to get home?"

"She wasn't hiding."

"You know what I'm saying."

"She just wanted to talk with me."

"Okay, then how did she even find out where you live?"

"My last name's not a state secret, Kyle. There's something called the Internet."

"I hear you. I'm just . . . I don't know. Something doesn't feel right about it."

"Okay, maybe it's a little unusual, I'll give you that, but at least she cared enough to stop by." Daniel hesitated. "Anyway, I'm gonna ask her if she'll go to the dance with me tonight. You know, when I see her at the lake."

"Let me know how that goes," Kyle said vaguely.

"You don't think I should ask her."

Kyle turned onto the road leading to the school. "I didn't say that."

"No, you didn't."

Kyle took a breath. "Listen, man, I don't know her, you do. I just think it's a little strange for her to show up at your house at like eleven o'clock at night to see if you're alright when she could have just talked with you after the game like Nicole did."

"Like Nicole did."

"That's right." They arrived at Beldon High's parking lot and Kyle aimed his Mustang toward Daniel's car. "I saw you two talking."

"Ah. Well, you're right."

"About what?"

"What you just said about Stacy. That you don't know her."

Silence tightened between them.

Kyle parked. "Okay." His tone was stiff and distant. "This is your car."

"I'll holler at you." Daniel swung open his door.

"Sure."

He pulled out his keys and, after Kyle had taken off, he left for Lake Algonquin to meet Stacy.

He didn't like that Kyle was uncomfortable about her.

But he could deal with that later.

Right now it was time to meet the girl who'd waited for him after school on Thursday, and had come all the way to his house last night to see how he was doing.

CHAPTER
TWENTY

The day was languishing under a somber gray sky. Thick clouds threatened rain, but held back, as if they were waiting for some signal before dumping on the lake and the surrounding forest.

Although some of the trees were changing color, none were vibrant in the overcast day, and most of those that weren't pines were just a rubbed-out, lifeless brown, making it look like the area was already tired of autumn and ready to get on with the next season.

When Daniel parked near the boat landing, there were no other cars in the lot, but as he closed the door behind him he noticed Stacy waiting for him near the shore, wearing a charcoal gray raincoat.

When she heard the door close, she turned and smiled at him.

"Parents drop you off?" he asked.

"I decided to walk. Like I said, it's not far."

A trail encircled the lake, and as they hiked toward the inlet where Emily's body had been found, every so often they came to abandoned campsites with chunks of charred wood lying in makeshift campfire pits surrounded by hefty rocks from the nearby shoreline.

On weekends, kids came out here to party, and many of the fire pits were cluttered with glass shards from liquor bottles and scrunched, blackened, half-disintegrated aluminum beer cans that would never completely burn up no matter how hot the campfires might get.

One of the pits was still smoldering, probably from kids hanging out last night after the football game. The dull, sooty smoke wisped upward, then quickly disappeared, torn apart by the stiff breeze coming in off the water.

By the time Daniel and Stacy arrived at the inlet, the wind had picked up even more, and ragged waves were surging toward them across the lake.

They came to a sixty-foot stretch of beach that lay in sharp contrast to the rocky shoreline that surrounded most of the lake.

This area was well-known to the kids who lived in the area, and in the summertime when the lake warmed they would come here to swim in the afternoons, or at night in the moonlight, or when the northern lights were shimmering and flicking in their anxious, eerie way across the sky.

The lake bottom dropped off quickly after about twenty-five feet, and there were stories of people showing off by jumping off Windy Point there, where it was supposedly deep enough to survive a fall like that, but Daniel had never met anyone who'd actually done it. When he'd asked his dad about it, neither had he.

Daniel stood beside Stacy, and as they looked across the lake, he felt the brisk wind brushing against his face like tiny invisible claws.

A shiver slid through him. He suspected it wasn't just from the wind and the weather, but also from being here near the place where a girl had actually died.

"It was right over there." Stacy pointed toward a stretch of shallow water off to their right. "That's where they found her. I read about it. They had a photograph in the paper—I mean, not of her, but of the lake, the place where the fishermen were when . . ." She let her voice trail off.

He remembered seeing the article. "Right."

It began to sprinkle—sharp pinpricks of rain falling with unusual energy in the wind that had now started kicking up whitecaps on the lake.

Daniel gazed at the sand around him, the cattails that grew near the wind-bent grass that fringed the woods. A dead fire pit lay on the edge of the forest.

"What now?" Stacy asked.

"I'm not sure."

They both took a little time to stare quietly at the water and the untamed wilderness surrounding it. The silence that passed between them seemed appropriate to Daniel, almost like a small way of honoring Emily's memory.

Eventually, as the rain picked up, Stacy flipped her hood up over her head and Daniel turned up his jacket's collar.

"Maybe we should go," she suggested.

Stay on this. Seek the truth. Learn what happened.

"Let me look around first." He indicated for her to wait beneath one of the looming pines that lined the shore, then he paced across the beach.

He suspected that the footprints already in the sand were from people who'd been out here when they were recovering Emily's body, or maybe kids coming out to the fire pit. Other than that, he saw nothing out of the ordinary.

For a few minutes he scrutinized the area, looking for anything that might help him make sense of the events of the last few days, of the ghostly apparitions he'd seen, but all he saw were the rough waves of the lake, the distant shore, the empty swath of dark, rain-splattered sand.

No ghosts.

No dead bodies rising from the water or approaching him or speaking to him or grabbing him or pulling necklaces through their necks or beckoning for him to join them in the lake.

No apparitions at all.

Thankfully.

Go back home. There's nothing out here.

He walked to the shoreline one last time and noted a few sticks that had washed onto the sand, as well as some clumps of leaves and soggy tangles of weeds from the lake's bottom. From the line of debris it was clear that the waves hadn't reached farther up the beach in a long time.

Finally, when Daniel found nothing, he decided Stacy had been right. It was time to leave.

He'd taken two steps toward her when he noticed the pair of glasses in the sand near the woods.

Even though they were half-buried, he recognized them immediately—they were the ones Emily Jackson had been wearing in the photos at the front of the church during the funeral.

CHAPTER
TWENTY-ONE

Heart slamming hard against the inside of his chest, Daniel approached the glasses.

Emily told you to find these. When she sat up in that casket she told you to find her glasses!

Rivulets of rain trickled down the sloping beach and emptied into the lake. One of them passed beneath the glasses and had washed some of the sand away in a narrow trench, making them more visible.

He picked them up.

One of the earpieces was twisted sideways and the left lens was missing, but they were definitely the same style as the ones Emily had on in the photos, the same ones he'd seen her wearing at school before her disappearance.

"Stacy, over here."

A moment later she was beside him. "What is it?"

Daniel held them up. "They're Emily's."

"Are you sure?"

"Pretty sure. I mean, I can't be positive, but they're the same kind she wore."

"They're broken," Stacy pointed out, with a trace of uneasiness.

"Maybe someone stepped on them." But that wasn't exactly what he was thinking.

"Maybe." Stacy didn't sound convinced either.

"Well, we haven't had enough rain to raise the water level this high, so they didn't wash up onshore. And the location isn't right, I mean the distance from Windy Point—unless someone with a better arm than I have threw them off."

He suspected that the cops would have looked around here, but the glasses were near the highest point on the beach and had been half buried, so it was possible that even if his father and his deputies had investigated the area, they might have missed them.

Stacy said, "She might have taken them off and left them here if she went swimming."

As if on cue, a gust of wind slapped cold rain against them. "It's way too cold to swim," he replied. "It was even colder last week. Besides, she never would have worn her jeans and shoes if she jumped in the water on her own, would she?"

"I don't know." And then: "What do you mean, 'on her own'?"

"I mean she wouldn't have decided to go in the water dressed like that."

"On her own."

"Yes, on her own." He just went ahead and said it: "Unless someone pushed her in."

"Or held her under."

That was almost the same way Ronnie had put it the other

day when he was talking about his suspicions concerning his sister's death.

Daniel looked at Stacy oddly, unsure why she would have phrased it like that. "Yes. Exactly."

She peered at the nearby bluff towering from the water. "Remember, they were saying she might have fallen off there? The current could have carried her here into the inlet."

"But then why would her glasses be all the way up the beach, if the water hasn't risen that high?"

"But if she didn't take them off, or if they didn't get washed up onshore after she drowned . . ."

Daniel had the sense that Stacy was thinking the same thing he was. "They might have gotten broken if she was fighting with someone."

"And she might not have drowned accidentally."

"No. She might not have."

For a long time neither Daniel nor Stacy spoke. At last she said, "We should tell your dad."

"Let's have one more look around first."

"What are we looking for?"

"I guess the other lens, or maybe anything else that might show us there was a struggle." He slipped the glasses carefully into his pocket. "Or whatever looks like it doesn't belong out here."

Then a thought.

"Look for a necklace," he said.

"A necklace?"

"Yes. It has a silver chain and a locket."

She gazed at him curiously. "That's pretty specific."

"Just a hunch." He avoided eye contact. "I mean, Emily was wearing one in the pictures they had at the funeral. I'm just wondering if it might have washed up onshore."

"Don't you think maybe we should wait for your dad or the cops or whatever to get here?"

"Well . . ." He pointed to the water running off the beach and into the lake. "If the rain keeps up, it might wash stuff away before they could arrive."

"You don't just mean stuff. You mean evidence."

"Yes." It was a little unnerving to say it. "Evidence."

They spent the next fifteen minutes crisscrossing the beach and the nearby rocky shore, then examining the fire pit and the grassy areas nearby, and even the cattails, but found nothing unusual. The other lens remained missing. Nothing else indicated that there might have been a fight there on the beach.

"Okay," Daniel said. "Let's head back. I'll take these glasses to my dad, see what he thinks. Maybe he'll be able to find out if anyone else has handled them. Fingerprints, that sort of thing."

He was well aware that, though cops on television almost always tested for DNA, that didn't happen so much in real life—at least not out in a rural county like this.

Not that there were many violent crimes in the area anyway, but it was just too costly, and besides, Daniel's dad had mentioned to him one time that there was a huge backlog of DNA tests at the state level that had been requested by lawyers trying to get cases retried for people who'd already been convicted of crimes.

But maybe this time, if there was enough suspicion that

someone actually had killed Emily, they might take it seriously enough to do the tests.

As he and Stacy neared the parking lot, she shook her head. "It's really creepy, you know, to even think that someone might have killed her. It's crazy enough that she drowned, but . . . who would do that?"

Once again he remembered what Ronnie had said about his suspicions that his sister had been murdered. "I have no idea."

"Just thinking about it weirds me out."

"My dad will get to the bottom of it. For now, let's not tell anyone about the glasses. If it's even possible that she was killed instead of dying accidentally we need to let his department take care of it. Talking about it to anyone might not be such a good idea."

"Okay."

When he mentioned bringing up the glasses to anyone, he couldn't help but think about where everyone was going to be tonight—the dance—and how easy it would be to let something slip, especially about news this big.

And when the dance came to mind, he remembered telling Kyle earlier that he was going to ask Stacy to go with him.

But for some reason, it didn't seem like this was the best time to do that, not after finding the glasses and wondering about the possibility that Emily had actually been murdered instead of just drowning accidentally.

Another opportunity would come to ask Stacy.

When? The dance is tonight.

They made their way past the final abandoned campfire pit and back to the parking lot where they'd first met up. There was an additional car and a maroon SUV parked there now near the boat landing. Probably fishermen. No one was in sight.

As they were about to say good-bye to each other, their eyes met for a moment too long. Just that fraction of a second when you know you should look away, that if you don't, you're communicating something more than just passing interest.

He bit his lip and gazed past her at the water.

After the moment had lengthened into something that spoke volumes, he glanced back at her. She peered at him expectantly from beneath her hood.

He felt the urge to brush away a wet strand of hair that had curled down and lay against her cheek.

Go ahead. Ask her. It's not that big of a deal.

He was about to clear his throat and go for it, but before he could, she spoke first: "Well, let me know what your dad says about the glasses."

"I will."

"Thanks for letting me tag along out here."

"It doesn't feel so much like closure, does it?"

"Not quite." They stood looking at each other in the rain that wasn't showing any sign of letting up. "Okay." She hesitated. "I'll see you later, then."

"How about I give you a ride home?"

"It's okay. I'm already drenched."

"Seriously, I don't want you to have to walk through this rain."

"That's sweet of you, really, but I'm already pretty wet."

Time passed, flitted between them. And then it just came out. "The homecoming dance is tonight," Daniel said.

"I heard."

"Are you going?"

"No. You?"

"No."

"Okay."

"I um, maybe I could . . ."

She took care of that wisp of hair he'd been wanting to brush aside. "Yes?"

"I mean, if you wanted to, we could, you and I . . . that is, I mean unless . . . maybe—if you're not doing anything?"

"Are you asking me to the dance, Daniel Byers?"

Oh, man.

"Um . . . Yes."

"Huh."

"We could meet there, if you want?"

She looked past him toward the woods and he thought that it was definitely a bad sign, that she was going to tell him thanks, but no, thanks.

But she didn't. Instead, she gazed back at him again through the rain. "That'd be nice."

Yes, yes, yes!

"Really?"

"Sure. Yeah. Do you have my number?"

He shook his head. "No."

She gave it to him. "Call me this afternoon."

"I will."

Then she tucked her head deeper beneath her hood and walked briskly across the parking lot toward a trail that led to the closest neighborhood, which was really just a cluster of a

dozen or so homes off a dirt road that skirted the forest surrounding the lake.

Once Daniel was in the car, he called Kyle to let him know
what was up with Stacy. His friend congratulated him on being
brave enough to ask her.

"I knew you had it in you."

"Thanks, man."

"Actually, no, I didn't, but it seemed like the right thing
to say."

"Okay."

Kyle didn't even bring up the topic of how weird he thought
Stacy had been acting last night. "Maybe you guys can hang
out with Mia and me afterward?"

"I'll ask her when I talk to her this afternoon."

"Cool."

Then Daniel left for his dad's office to give him the glasses
and tell him that he thought Emily Jackson might not have died
accidentally after all.

CHAPTER
TWENTY-TWO

The sheriff's department was located next to the courthouse on Main Street.

The county didn't have enough extra money lying around to hire a full-time officer to sit in the lobby checking the handful of visitors who entered throughout the day, so there wasn't any security person posted at the entrance.

Instead, a part-time receptionist a couple years older than Daniel sat behind the counter. He'd met her before: Shawna. She was chewing a colossal glob of gum, busily texting someone.

She glanced absently at him as he entered, finished blowing a bubble that splattered across her chin when it popped, then said, "Here to see your dad?"

"Is he in?"

She nodded toward the hall. "Doing some paperwork." Her attention had already shifted back to her phone, texting with one hand while salvaging as much gum as possible for another bubble with the other.

When Daniel reached the end of the hall he found the door ajar.

His dad's office was nondescript, with a couple of chairs and a sprawling gray metal desk that'd been there as long as Daniel could remember. Papers lay strewn across it, with an intimidating pile of files waiting in the in-box. A shelf packed with policy manuals stood between the window and the locked gun case.

Gun culture in Wisconsin is different from a lot of areas in the U.S. Here, especially in this part of the state, it's expected that you own a gun, that you hunt, that you have firearms on hand and readily available to protect your family, or, in this case, the community at large. It wasn't a big enough department to have an extensive gun vault, so his dad stored the assortment of rifles and shotguns right there in his office.

Daniel gave the door a slight knock, entered. "Hey, Dad."

He looked up from his work. "Dan. How's it going?"

"Good." He took a seat in the stiff chair facing his father's desk.

Gesturing toward Daniel's drenched clothes, his dad said, "Got caught in the rain, huh?"

"Yeah. Out by the lake."

"The lake?"

"Lake Algonquin."

He looked at Daniel curiously. "Really?"

"Yes."

Daniel sorted through how to explain what was on his mind. "Listen, I need to talk to you."

"Sure."

Just tell him. See what he says.

"Actually, it's about Emily Jackson."

"Okay."

"I . . . um . . . I think she might not have died by accident."

"What are you talking about?"

"I think maybe she was murdered."

His dad put down his pen. "Murdered."

"Yes."

"What makes you think that?"

Daniel set the glasses on the desk.

"What are those?"

"Emily's glasses."

His father studied them, but refrained from picking them up. "How did you get them?"

"They were in the sand near the inlet where she was found."

"Why did you go out there?"

"I wanted . . ." He ended up using the same word he'd used with Stacy. "Closure."

"So you found these on the beach?"

"Yes. Near the woods."

"Kids go out there to party all the time. What makes you think these were Emily's?"

When his dad said *were* instead of *are* it just reminded Daniel again that Emily was gone and was not coming back, which only served to make this even harder to talk about.

"She had them on in the photos that were at the front of the church at the funeral. And I remember seeing her wearing 'em at school."

"But they might be someone else's who wears the same style."

"I mean . . ." Daniel hesitated. "It's possible, but—"

"Dan, the coroner did an autopsy Sunday night. There's no reason to believe that Emily Jackson was murdered."

"The glasses are broken, Dad. And I found them up the beach away from the water. If she was fighting with someone, they could have gotten knocked off. Maybe that's how they got broken."

"Fighting with someone."

"Yes."

Daniel doubted that bringing up the vision of Emily's ghost at the funeral asking him to find the glasses was going to help his case, so he kept that to himself. "Besides, the water level hasn't risen enough to have carried them that high up the beach."

"How do you know that?"

"I checked the waterline. It's too cold to go swimming. And if she fell in accidentally, how would she have had the foresight to take off her glasses beforehand and leave them there by the edge of the woods?"

His father was silent. "There are any number of reasons these glasses could be broken. They might not even be Emily's at all, and who knows how long they were out there in the sand."

"But if it's even possible that they're hers, that she didn't die by accident, don't you think you should look into it? Maybe search for fingerprints or DNA or something?"

He drummed his fingers against the desk twice. "Does anyone else know about these?"

"Just Stacy. She was out there with me."

"Stacy?"

"This new girl at school. We're going to homecoming tonight together. To the dance."

"I didn't know you had a date."

"It's not officially a date, it's just going to the dance."

"Gotcha."

"It's sort of last-minute. I asked her this morning."

His father thought for a moment. "Alright, listen: I'll look into it. But I don't want any rumors going around that Emily Jackson was murdered. Don't bring this up to anyone. No texting. No tweeting. Nothing like that."

"Don't worry, I won't."

"And the same goes for Stacy. I don't want her talking about this with her friends."

Daniel was glad he'd already covered that with her. "I'll make sure. Thanks, Dad."

He leaned back in his chair. "So what's your plan for the rest of the day?"

"Head home, I guess. Dry off. Grab some lunch. Probably work out. Hang out until the dance."

"And your head, it's feeling alright after last night?"

"Yeah, it's good."

"If you do work out, I don't want you doing anything intense, not until you've given that head a day or two to recover."

"I'll be careful."

A nod. "Well, I'm not sure when I'll be back home. If I don't see you before you leave for the dance, I want you back by midnight."

"Right. No problem."

Daniel waited for the rest—"No *partying afterward. Don't*

do anything stupid"—but his dad left that part unsaid. Apparently, he trusted that Daniel would know the ground rules by now.

"Okay." His dad's attention had gone back to the glasses, and as he spoke he seemed distracted. "I'll catch up with you later."

Daniel left his father's office feeling both encouraged and a little uneasy.

He was thankful his dad had agreed to follow up on all this, but just the fact that he was doing so told Daniel that there was a chance, even if it was only a slight one, that Emily's death had not been accidental.

He tried calling Stacy to let her know how the meeting with his dad had gone and to remind her not to tell anyone about the glasses, but she didn't pick up and it went to a generic voicemail, just telling him to leave a message. He told her to call him, and then texted her in case she wasn't checking her messages.

Back at the house, while he was throwing some leftovers together for lunch, he got a text. Thinking it might be Stacy, he checked the phone right away, but saw it was just from one of the guys on the team, asking how his head was. He replied that he was fine.

A little later in the afternoon, while he was finishing lifting weights in the basement, his dad called and explained that he'd sent the glasses by courier to the FBI office down in Milwaukee.

It wasn't something he was obligated in any way to share with Daniel, but putting things into play that quickly on a

Saturday told him that his dad wasn't fooling around; he really had taken Daniel's concerns seriously.

He texted Stacy again, tried calling her. Nothing. He kept the phone close by, but an hour later, he still hadn't heard anything from her.

Daniel thought back through their conversation at the lake and couldn't remember if she'd specifically agreed to meet him at school tonight, or just agreed in a more general sense to go with him.

Regardless, she had told him to give her a call this afternoon. That much he remembered for sure.

At five, when he still hadn't heard from her, he reassured himself that she must have meant that he was supposed to meet up with her at the dance.

That's all it was.

A slight miscommunication.

Just something for them to clear up when they connected tonight at school.

As he considered things, he couldn't shake the thought that there'd been a fight out there on the beach, a fight that had resulted in Emily's death.

At least now the FBI was looking into the glasses.

He wanted to talk to someone about it, but he couldn't bring it up to anyone.

Except for Stacy.

Well, he could do that when he saw her in just a couple hours.

CHAPTER TWENTY-THREE

At seven, Stacy hadn't returned his calls and hadn't texted him back.

The dance started at eight.

She'd told him she lived near the lake but hadn't said exactly where—although it had to be within walking distance, and it was most likely in that neighborhood near the lakeshore.

However, he didn't know what car she drove, so it wasn't like he could just cruise the roads in the area looking for her car parked in front of a house or anything.

He and Kyle had poked around online to see if they could find out more about her, but had come up dry. So there wasn't an address he could work from.

Daniel felt like if he left any more messages for her, it would have made him seem desperate. And driving around looking for her house would have definitely come across as stalkerish.

In the end, he couldn't think of any way to get in touch with her, and when he called Kyle to tell him what was going on, his friend told him he should just show up at the dance and look for her there.

"Since you didn't get a chance to talk to her this afternoon, she's gonna assume you'll meet her at school. I mean, since it came up in your conversation anyway, right? Make sense?"

"Unless I got the wrong number and now she thinks I changed my mind and don't want to take her after all."

"Did the texts go through?"

"My phone said they did."

"Then maybe she changed her mind and is just ignoring you."

"Thanks."

"Sure. Well, there's only one way to find out what's going on."

"Show up at the dance."

"Mia and I will meet you guys there."

Daniel wanted to tell him about the trip to the lake and the glasses, and about how the FBI was even going to be involved, but knowing how important confidentiality with all this was to his dad, he said nothing.

Ty Bell and his buddies were loitering outside the school when Daniel arrived.

Smoking wasn't permitted on school property, but they were being discreet about it and taking puffs only when no teachers or chaperones were passing by. From the smell of it, at least one of them was smoking something other than just a cigarette.

They leered at Daniel as he entered but said nothing. However, Ty dropped his cigarette butt to the ground and roughly stomped the life out of it with his heel.

There were two dances at Beldon High every year—homecoming in the fall and prom in the spring. In contrast to how formal prom was, homecoming was a lot more a come-as-you-are deal. A few people always dressed up, but most of the students didn't bother.

The theme this year was "Under the Stars," and the glee club had all these sparkling aluminum foil stars hanging from the ceiling throughout the school entrance and in the cafeteria, which was open in case students wanted to hang out there instead of dancing in the adjoining gymnasium.

Daniel found Kyle and Mia near the cafeteria's doorway to the gym.

Mia was a slender, pale girl with straight black hair and a pierced lip and studded tongue. Under her jeans jacket, she wore a retro cutoff T-shirt that revealed her slim midriff and her pierced navel. Not typical fare for an autumn dance, maybe, but not unusual at all for Mia.

She had one arm tucked around Kyle's waist. "What's up, Daniel?"

"Mia, good to see you. How's the book coming along?"

"Smokin'."

Daniel had never met anyone who was trying to write a novel before, let alone someone his age who was doing it, but Mia was nearly as gifted at English as Kyle was, and that's probably one of the things that attracted them to each other.

Her book was going to be a ghost story, which, given everything that was going on this week, Daniel found ironically appropriate.

When Mia saw how some of the girls were glancing toward Daniel, she said, "Lots of moths here tonight."

He looked at her curiously. "Moths?"

"Yeah. And you're the flame, Señor Quarterback."

"Ah."

"So where's this Stacy girl?"

"I'm not sure. I'll introduce you as soon as I track her down."

Daniel wasn't sure where to start looking for Stacy, but she wasn't outside or in the cafeteria, so he figured she had to be in the gym.

Even though they'd lost the homecoming game last night, it didn't seem to have dampened the mood of the dance too much.

Balloons and homecoming banners hung throughout the gymnasium. Last spring some kids had spiked the punch at prom, so even though there'd been talk about not having any at the dance tonight, a table had been set up near the bleachers and a clutch of chaperones and teachers stood close by to keep an eye on things.

Daniel had the sense that the people who would be into spiking the punch would just see it as more of a challenge with all the adults around and would still find a way to get booze into the bowls.

Coach Jostens was stationed with a few teachers by the table, scanning the crowd of students as if he were looking for someone. He acknowledged Daniel with a small gesture and Daniel replied in kind. Miss Flynn and Mr. McKinney stood talking with each other near some parent chaperones.

Mr. Ackerman, the photographer who'd been at the game, had a place set up in the corner to take the pictures of kids who wanted them professionally done. There was no line.

A few people, those who actually knew how to dance, were on the floor, but most of the girls were clumped up together along one wall. The guys had set themselves up along another.

Things would loosen up. They always did.

Daniel had no idea how dances used to go before cell phones, but lots of kids were texting and checking their messages to make it look like they were engaged with something, when they were actually either not into dancing, didn't have anyone to dance with, or were too anxious to ask anyone onto the dance floor.

Sports were huge at Beldon High and nearly everyone recognized their local football star, Daniel Byers. Guys greeted him or stepped out of his way; the moths fluttered and flirted, especially when they saw he wasn't with a girl. He tried his best to politely ignore them.

He passed through the crowd looking for Stacy, but didn't see her anywhere. Not even in the groups of girls who were now forming on the dance floor.

A strobe light hung somewhat precariously above them. For some reason there was even a fog machine.

A huge screen hung at one end of the gym with music videos of the songs that were playing. Once things got started it would actually help some kids who were having a hard time knowing how to dance.

Earlier in the year it'd looked like Kyle and a couple of

his friends who were trying to put a band together were going to play for the dance, but for some reason that had fallen through—probably because their music wasn't so much high school dance fare, but had more of a college-coffeehouse vibe going on.

A senior whom Daniel had seen around but didn't really know was DJing and was choosing mostly pop and electronica trance tracks. Whichever song he'd chosen must have been popular, because kids flooded the dance floor.

The music became intense. Students in the middle of the gym, where no chaperones opted to go, started grinding against each other crazily in the erratic, pulsing light.

Stacy was nowhere to be seen.

Trying not to be too conspicuous, Daniel made his way across the gym searching for her, but if she was here she was also invisible, because he couldn't find her anywhere.

He checked his phone, then the punch table again.

Nope.

Nothing.

But he did see Nicole standing by herself at the far end, holding a plastic cup.

He could hardly believe that a girl as popular as Nicole wasn't dancing with someone, and the only thing he could think of was that whatever guy she was with had just stepped away for a minute.

Leaving her alone.

Like Emily was.

Before she died.

For a moment he thought back to the beach, to the glasses, to what Ronnie had told him the other day about his suspicions that his sister had been killed.

Nicole looked a little embarrassed when she saw Daniel, but nodded a greeting. When he asked her how she was doing, she gave him a somewhat forced smile. "Good. I'm good. You? Having fun yet?"

"I pretty much just got here." The music throbbing around them made it a little hard to carry on a conversation and they had to lean close to each other to talk.

She gazed past him and he guessed she was trying to figure out if he was here with anyone. For a moment he thought about telling her that he was looking for his date, but then decided against it.

A few seconds later one of Nicole's friends came by, so she excused herself, and he went to look for Stacy again.

Ten minutes later he still hadn't found her or gotten any messages from her.

As he was leaving the gym to search by the front doors once more, he ran into Kyle and Mia. Neither of them looked too into the DJ's choice of music. When Kyle saw that Daniel was still alone he raised his hands palms up: *Well?*

Daniel shook his head and joined them. "I'm not sure how long I should wait for her."

Kyle turned to Mia. "A girl's perspective. What do you think?"

"You want honesty or politesse?"

"Honesty."

"I think it sucks—and that's way toning down my honesty." Then she said to Daniel, "Leaving you hanging like this? Very uncool. Especially not even returning your texts."

"Give it a few more minutes," Kyle suggested. "Then we can bail. Chill at my place."

Even though Daniel was good friends with both Kyle and Mia, truthfully, he did sometimes feel like a third wheel when it was just the three of them hanging out together. On the other hand, it was really awkward being here at the dance without a date.

Just head home. If Stacy doesn't show up, take off. You don't need to stay.

The song ended and when the DJ threw on a slow dance, Mia took Kyle's hand. As she led him toward the dance floor he called back to Daniel, "Hey, we'll see you in a bit, okay?"

"Sure."

Daniel's eyes followed them into the gym and he saw Nicole standing by herself again, this time near the door to the visitors locker room. Ever since he'd spoken with her earlier he hadn't seen her dancing with any guys.

Maybe she'd come alone after all.

Or maybe her date stood her up, just like yours did.

For a couple seconds he was tempted to ask her to dance, but in the end he figured that wouldn't fly too well with Stacy if she did happen to show up.

He went to the parking lot to look for her and checked his messages again.

Still nothing.

The night had cooled, and gray tendrils of fog were snaking out of the nearby woods.

His thoughts trailed back through the unusual and tragic events of the last week, and his frustration over Stacy's not showing up shifted unexpectedly to concern.

Could something have happened to her?

Something bad?

No, that was just ridiculous.

She was fine.

For whatever reason she'd just decided not to show.

Okay, he was a big boy. He could deal with that. There was no reason to start getting paranoid.

He was about to text Kyle and tell him that he was heading home when Nicole stepped out of the building.

She held up her hand. "Honestly, I'm not stalking you," she said. "I just needed some fresh air."

"You waiting for someone too?"

"Actually, Brent Beslin was supposed to meet me forty-five minutes ago." She shook her head. "Jerk." A much stronger word might have been in order, but just the fact that she held back from using it said something about her.

Daniel knew Brent, and if he was supposed to be here with Nicole, he was definitely dating out of his league. Not at all the kind of guy Daniel would have guessed Nicole would come to the dance with, but since she still hadn't had a date yesterday when he spoke with her at school, Brent obviously hadn't been her first choice.

You were.

"Yeah," he said at last. "Jerk."

Daniel knew that, personally, he wouldn't have left Nicole hanging if he'd been the one to ask her here. No, there was no way that would have happened.

For a moment he remembered Emily, her funeral, the fact that she was the kind of girl that people ignored and—

"So, do I know her?" Nicole asked him.

"Do you know her?"

"The girl you're waiting for, silly. Coming to something like this by yourself isn't your deal at all. You're more private than that. Besides, you've been looking for someone ever since you got here."

"You know me pretty well."

"Yes, I do."

"Stacy."

"Stacy?" She looked a little confused.

"The new girl."

"Oh."

"She was supposed to meet me here."

"Of course."

Ty and his friends were still lurking nearby. They'd stopped smoking, but were joking around about something among themselves. Every once in a while one of them would glance over at Nicole and smirk and whisper something to the guy next to him.

Daniel didn't like the way they were leering at her. Not at all.

She got a text, checked it, then shook her head. "So I was gonna head home, right? But Gina gave me a ride here, and now she's decided to stay." A sigh. "Perfect."

Nicole had worked together with Daniel on a project last year for biology and their study group had met at her house. It wasn't far from his place. "So," he said, "you don't have a ride home?"

"Not till later."

That meant Daniel had a choice to make.

He could wait here for Stacy, he could take off for home, or he could offer to give Nicole a ride to her house.

Yeah, and if he did that, he could just imagine Stacy showing up right in the nick of time to see Nicole climbing into his car. Oh, that would be brilliant.

But Stacy wasn't here, hadn't been in touch all day, had obviously changed her mind about coming.

So, stay?

Leave?

Offer a ride?

Nicole seemed to be waiting for him to say something.

And finally he did: "I could drop you off at your place, if you want?"

"Naw, I'm . . . well . . ." She faltered, obviously reconsidering. "Seriously?"

"It's no big deal. I was about to leave anyway."

"Is that alright? I mean, since . . . ?" She left the rest unsaid, but he could anticipate that she was thinking about how he was supposed to be meeting Stacy.

"No. It's fine."

"That'd be awesome, actually. Let me go tell Gina. I'll be right back."

She slipped back into the building, Daniel texted Kyle that

he was taking off, and when he looked up from his phone, he saw that Ty and his friends had left.

A few minutes later Nicole returned, walked with Daniel to his car, and they left school together to head to her home west of town.

CHAPTER
TWENTY-FOUR

The farther they drove into the country, the thicker the fog became.

It was almost as if they were passing into another realm, a bleary, unexplored world that was slowly unfolding before them from nowhere as they drove into it.

"So your head's okay?" Nicole asked.

While he appreciated everyone's concern, he was getting a little tired of people asking him how he was. "It's a good thing it's as hard as it is."

"I'll say."

"You weren't supposed to agree with that."

"Well, like you said earlier, I know you pretty well."

"I guess you do."

But that's not exactly what was running through his mind. Instead, he was wondering if his head really was okay.

He kind of wanted to tell her, "You know, the more I think about it, the more I think I passed out at the game not because I got smacked on the head when I was tackled, but because I saw Emily's ghost, just like I did at the funeral. So I really don't know if I'm okay at all."

No, it probably wouldn't be the best thing in the world to be quite that open and honest with Nicole tonight.

On the other hand, maybe she would be good to talk to, at least if he wasn't quite that forthcoming.

"I know this is sort of out of nowhere, but do you believe in ghosts?" he asked her.

"Ghosts? Have you been talking to Mia about her book?"

"No, just thinking about them."

"I don't know. What about you?"

I might be starting to.

"I'm not sure." He recalled the blog entry Nicole had read yesterday in class. "In that prayer you wrote for Teach's class, you mentioned demons. Was that for real? Do you believe in them or was that all symbolic?"

"No, I do."

"But not ghosts?"

"Well . . . maybe." She gave it some thought. "I mean, when I was working on that assignment, I found this story, in the Bible, you know, about a guy named Saul—he was the king of Israel. Anyway, he found this medium and had her try to summon back a prophet named Samuel from the dead to talk to him."

"What happened?"

"It worked. Samuel appeared—or at least his ghost did. I'm not exactly sure which it was."

"But Samuel was dead when he appeared to Saul?"

134

"Yes."

"Sounds like a ghost to me."

"Yeah," she admitted. "Me too."

"So it's possible, then, for dead people to communicate with the living?"

"At least in that case it was."

Daniel had heard about people doing what Saul did—trying to consult with the dead. For just an instant he wondered if that might be a way to get some answers.

But just for an instant.

Because, really, the last thing he needed to do was ask dead people to show up and start talking to him. They were doing that pretty well on their own.

At least one of them was.

"And," Nicole went on, "Jesus apparently believed in ghosts. Twice his disciples mistook him for a ghost and he told them he wasn't one, proved it the second time by letting them touch his hands and his side."

"How does that show he believed in ghosts?"

"Well, he said, 'A ghost does not have flesh and bones.' But if ghosts weren't real, why would he have put it that way?"

"Oh, I get it. If ghosts didn't exist he would've just told his friends they were being idiots—because how could he be a ghost when they weren't even real?"

"Yeah—instead of proving to them that he wasn't one." She looked at him questioningly. "Why the interest in demons and ghosts?"

"Just wondering."

Ghosts. Demons. What a great conversation to be having when you're driving through the countryside on a fog-enshrouded night.

They were only a couple miles from Nicole's house when they came around a curve and Daniel saw something ahead of them, lying in the middle of the road.

At first he wasn't sure what it was, but as he slowed down he realized it was a toddler's plastic swimming pool. The road dipped slightly and the headlights revealed that it was a little crunched on one side and partially filled with murky water.

It was directly in the middle of their lane.

Daniel stopped.

Let the car idle.

The fog fingered through the night, and taking into account what he'd been talking with Nicole about only a few minutes ago concerning whether or not his head was okay, he had a thought that he did not like.

Maybe the pool wasn't really there at all. Maybe he was just imagining it, and Emily's ghost was going to rise out of the water and walk toward his car.

He waited, hoping Nicole would say something about the pool to prove that it was there, because if it wasn't, that would mean he definitely was starting to lose touch with reality.

Daniel studied her face in the dim, greenish glow cast from the dashboard lights. She was still staring in front of them at the road. He anticipated that if she didn't see the pool she would've most likely been looking at him instead, trying to figure out why he'd stopped the car. So he took her intense gaze out the windshield as a good sign.

The silence went on until it became uncomfortable, then she said, "Drive around it, Daniel. Just go through the other lane."

Well, that was good. At least she saw it too.

"I think I should move it."

"Just leave it. I don't like this."

He reached for the door handle and felt her hand on his other arm. "Something's not right. It couldn't have just fallen out of someone's truck or something. It wouldn't have water in it then."

"I know. Wait here. Lock the doors behind me."

Daniel stepped out of the car.

The cool night wrapped around him. Some kind of owl he couldn't identify shrieked in the distance, and slight rustling sounds in the darkness told him he might have disturbed an animal hidden in the shadows along the side of the road.

Tendrils of dreary mist curled through the night, filtering eerily through the headlights' beams.

No stars. No moonlight.

Daniel didn't hear the doors lock so he opened his again. The car was still running. "Lock them, Nicole. I'll be right back."

"Daniel, let's just—"

"Trust me."

He closed the door, and after a moment, she hit the lock button.

Fog encircled him as he paced forward.

The pool was ocean blue and had pictures of happy cartoon dolphins and small green fish imprinted on it. The left side was crinkled enough for some of the water to have seeped out.

When he was about fifteen feet away, he heard movement again out of sight along the edge of the road. Something large crunching across the leaves.

"Hello?"

No reply.

He came to the toddler pool and grabbed its edge to drag it off the road. The water made it a little hard to tug, but as he lifted one side, some of it sloshed out the other, and he was able to drag it along the pavement toward the ditch.

He'd made it about halfway there when he saw the first figure step out of the darkness and into the headlights, right next to the car.

Ty Bell.

And since he almost always had his three buddies with him, Daniel couldn't imagine that he'd come out here alone.

CHAPTER
TWENTY-FIVE

Even though Ty was mostly backlit, his face was partially visible and he was giving Daniel a steady, unflinching gaze. "Byers."

Daniel dropped the edge of the plastic pool. "Get away from the car, Ty."

He appraised Daniel as, one by one, his three friends emerged from their hiding places along the edge of the road.

If Daniel remembered correctly, one of the boys had a pickup; they could have easily transported the pool in that.

They must have overheard you talking to Nicole at school, offering to drive her out here.

But were they really close enough to hear you? How long were they planning this? Was—

Right now all that mattered was getting Nicole out of here.

Ty nodded toward his three friends, who approached the car.

"Step back," Daniel ordered them.

But one of the guys tried the driver's-side door and cursed when he found it locked.

Daniel started toward them. "I said, get away from the car."

But the other guys just circled it, unsuccessfully trying all the doors. Daniel heard Nicole call out for him from inside the sedan.

Alright.

That's it.

He rushed Ty, who flicked out an automatic knife as soon as Daniel made his move. "Uh, uh, uh. Be a good boy." While Daniel slowed to evaluate things, two of the other guys flanked Ty while the third pounded on the car windows, yelling for Nicole to open the doors.

Daniel's hands balled into fists. "You really do not want to do this."

Ty glanced toward his friends, who edged in closer to him, then eyed Daniel. "I think it's you who doesn't want to do this."

Whether he got benched next week or not, Daniel was going to do whatever it took to protect Nicole, even if he had to take on all four of these guys.

From his years of playing football, he knew he could take a pounding, but Ty had a knife. Getting into a fight with him tonight might very well mean getting sliced up or stabbed.

But if that's what it took to keep Nicole safe, that's what he would do.

Daniel realized that if he were on his own it wouldn't have been worth it to stick around and he probably would have just walked away, left the car, made his way home to get his father and bring him back to pick up the car.

But he wasn't alone.

Nicole's being here changed everything.

The boy who'd been banging on the windows stepped into the darkness and clicked on a flashlight. A moment later he said, "Aha." When he returned, he was holding a large angular rock. "This should do the trick."

He eyed the side window.

"Drive away!" Daniel called to Nicole. "Go!"

But she didn't.

Time to move.

The guy with the rock seemed to pose the biggest threat to Nicole, so Daniel went for him first.

He sprinted toward him, and as he lifted the rock, Daniel tackled him hard, sending him hurtling off the road, into the underbrush.

Somehow the boy managed to hold on to the rock as they landed, and he tried to smack Daniel with it, but Daniel stopped him and was able to get it away from him.

As he was about to toss it into the woods, he felt two guys grab him under his armpits and pull him backward toward the road. He tried twisting to the side, but they were holding him with a fierce grip and he couldn't wrench free.

They threw him onto the pavement.

Rolling to the side, he was on his feet in an instant.

Daniel held the rock high. "Whoever goes any closer to the car is going to regret it. Now get out of here before someone gets hurt."

The boy that Daniel had tackled was climbing out of the ditch cursing, but his eyes were on the rock and he didn't seem quite as aggressive as before.

However, Ty, who was still holding the knife, took two steps toward Daniel until he was standing only a couple paces away. His knife's blade gleamed wickedly in the headlight beams.

Fog swirled around them both like anxious smoke.

"Nicole," Daniel shouted. "Drive away. Now."

She called out something to him, but he couldn't understand the words and she didn't leave.

Ty and Daniel each held their weapon. Neither backed down. Neither looked away.

Daniel cocked his arm back. "I can throw a football through a tire at thirty yards. I won't miss you from ten feet."

A flicker of uneasiness crossed Ty's face. He screwed his mouth into a sneer. "Did you hear what they found in Emily's notebook?"

Daniel didn't answer.

"Word gets around."

"What are you talking about?"

Ty shook his head slowly. "I can't believe you don't know. I was at the lake. I saw you there."

"When? What? This morning?"

"Right." But it was more of a scoff than anything else. He signaled for his buddies to follow him, and then the four of them slowly retreated and merged into the misty darkness.

Daniel guarded the car until a pickup truck that'd been pulled off the road about a hundred feet ahead of him roared to life, and Ty and his buddies sped off. Then he went for the door handle as Nicole hit the unlock.

Opening the door, he asked if she was okay. She nodded, but her breathing was rushed and ragged.

"Did you call 911?"

"I didn't think to," she said. "I was . . ."

"Okay. I'll be right back." Daniel quickly moved the pool the rest of the way off the road and then joined her in the car.

When she reached for his hand, her fingers were trembling.

"It's alright. Let's just get out of here, okay?" He felt her fingers intertwine with his. He didn't pull away.

She nodded again. "Yeah."

After a moment, he let go of her hand, pulled the car forward, and they drove in silence until Nicole asked, "What was all that about a notebook?"

"Just Ty being Ty."

But Daniel wondered if there was some way Ty actually had found out what was in Emily's notebook.

"What did he mean, he saw you at the lake?" Nicole asked.

"I was there this morning. I didn't see him, but there were a couple cars in the parking lot when we got back to it. I didn't recognize them, but he must have been there somewhere, watching us."

"Us?"

He hesitated. "Stacy was there with me."

"Oh. Sure," she said softly. "That makes sense."

"Listen, I'm not—"

"Don't worry, no, no, I get it. Seriously, it's okay."

He wanted to explain everything: that he'd asked Stacy to the dance, but she'd blown him off and not shown up or even texted him to tell him she wasn't coming, but he couldn't find the right words.

A few minutes later they arrived at Nicole's house, and

Daniel waited until she was safely inside and had texted him that the doors were locked before he backed out of her driveway and headed home, all the while wondering about what exactly might be in Emily's notebook.

And why Ty might have been at the lake this morning too.

CHAPTER
TWENTY-SIX

Inside the house, Daniel's dad was sitting in the living room on the couch. A CNN news show quietly droned on in the background from the television mounted on the wall. He asked him how the dance had gone.

"Okay."

"You're home a little early."

"Things wrapped up sooner than I thought they would."

"But you had a good time with that new girl, Stacy?"

Daniel couldn't think of any reason to hide the truth from his dad. "Actually, she never showed."

"Oh. I'm sorry to hear that."

So am I.

I think.

"Yeah."

Daniel decided not to bring up driving Nicole home or the confrontation with Ty and his friends. "So when do you think you'll hear from the FBI lab?"

"Depends how many tests they end up doing. I told them

to put a rush on it, but I'm not really expecting to hear anything until the middle of the week at the earliest."

Ask him. Go ahead. What could it hurt?

"Hey, did you hear anything about Emily's notebook? The one from school, the one that was found in her locker?"

Now his father muted the TV and gave Daniel his full attention. "I don't know anything about a notebook."

"Okay."

Daniel headed for the stairs, but his dad called, "Hang on a second."

When he turned to face him, he saw that his dad's expression had hardened.

"What's going on here?"

"What do you mean?"

"All this interest in Emily and her death."

I keep seeing her appear to me. . . .

"I just . . . She knew how to swim."

"She knew how to swim?"

"Yeah. I talked to her brother at school the other day. He told me."

"Her brother told you."

"Yes. Everything points to her not drowning by accident."

His father took a deep breath. "Listen, I don't want you poking around this anymore. If the FBI finds anything unusual we'll handle it, but I don't want you doing any more snooping around."

"I'm not snooping."

"Yes. You are." He leaned forward. "I want you to promise me you'll leave this alone."

"Dad, I—"

"Promise me."

Daniel was quiet.

"Daniel?"

He remembered the words he'd heard as he was waking up on the football field yesterday: *Stay on this. Seek the truth. Learn what happened.*

"Okay," he said at last. "I promise."

"Alright. Good. Goodnight."

"Goodnight."

As Daniel headed to his bedroom, he berated himself for lying to his father.

No, he couldn't leave this alone, not when Emily—or her ghost or whatever—kept appearing to him. Somehow he had to make it all stop.

And now, apparently, he needed to do that in a way that wouldn't attract the attention of his dad.

CHAPTER TWENTY-SEVEN

Daniel got ready for bed.

Who would know what's in that notebook?

Ty did, or at least he thought he did.

One other person came to mind—Ronnie, Emily's twin brother, the boy Ty and his friends had shoved into the locker the other day at school. He would probably know.

Daniel didn't have Ronnie's phone number, but he found his Facebook page, clicked to the message link, and stared at the empty text box that popped up on his screen. All he had to do was leave a question for Ronnie and he could untangle this, finally get some answers, finally nail down what was going on.

As he was trying to figure out what to write, his phone buzzed with a text.

He checked the screen.

Kyle: he had something he needed to talk to Daniel about and asked if they could get together tomorrow; lunch at Rizzo's?

They agreed on noon.

Even though no notifications were showing up on his phone's screen, Daniel checked again for any messages from Stacy.

Nope. Nothing.

Okay, well, that relationship looked like it was over before it had even begun. If he didn't hear from her tomorrow he would try to find out what was going on when he saw her at school Monday, but honestly, that was one conversation he was not looking forward to having.

His thoughts shifted back to Nicole, to those brief moments when she'd held his hand after Ty and his friends took off.

Nicole.

Stacy.

He was starting to feel caught in the middle of something that was going to end up hurting someone no matter how things turned out, and he didn't like that prospect one bit.

Going back to the message box on Ronnie Jackson's page, he tried to decide what to do, whether or not to contact him.

As he evaluated things, he reviewed what he knew.

At the funeral, Emily had told him that Trevor was in the car, but that he shouldn't have been. Later, he realized that Trevor was her dog. But since that information had appeared in an article in the paper, it was something that he might have been aware of, at least subconsciously, before the funeral.

She'd told him to find her glasses, which he ended up locating near the spot where she died.

Broken. Away from the water.

She knew how to swim.

From her casket, she'd grabbed his arm and left a mark. If

Nicole was right about ghosts not having flesh and bones, that you couldn't touch them, then it wasn't likely he'd encountered a ghost.

But if not that, what?

The next clue, if that's what these apparitions really contained, was Emily's necklace. Sure, she was wearing it in some of the photos, but why would she have held it up to him during the game? Was she trying to tell him something?

And if so, what?

It was like they were all things that he didn't consciously remember, but afterward realized were lodged in some secret part of his brain like those memories of his grandmother's kitchen were.

And then there was the notebook and Ty's comment the other day about Kyle and Emily.

Honestly, Daniel had no idea how all this fit together, except that it was looking more and more like Emily had not died by accident.

Also, it seemed like she wanted something from him, and he had the sense that it was a lot more than just having him find her glasses on the beach.

Yes, he'd promised his dad that he would stop looking into this, but how could he do that, how could he leave it alone, when there were so many weird things going on, so many coincidences that couldn't possibly all be coincidences?

At last he decided he needed to go ahead and take a specific step to resolve things, even if it was just a small one.

He slid the cursor into position in the message box on Ronnie's page and typed, "I have a question for you. Can you text me tomorrow?" Daniel left his name and number and hit send.

Tomorrow morning he could spend some time sorting through everything, then meet up with Kyle for lunch and find out what was up.

Hopefully, he would also hear from Ronnie and Stacy.

And he could begin to resolve the things that were going on, the things that felt like they were ripping though the fabric of his sanity.

The fabric of your sanity?

Another phrase that sounded like something Kyle would have come up with, not Daniel.

Just like the one about the vultures picking away at your dreams.

He needed to get a grip on himself.

Yes, he did.

Before the fabric ripped all the way through.

CHAPTER TWENTY-EIGHT

Daniel dreamt of death.

He knew he was only dreaming, that it wasn't real, but that didn't make it any less terrifying. When you're awake, you can close your eyes to the horrors of life. You can turn away, run, hide, change the channel.

Not so when you're asleep.

Even if you know you're sleeping, you're still at the mercy of your dreams. People who are asleep can't simply decide to wake up. Nightmares don't let you off that easily. They hold you in their clutches until they decide, in their own good time, to let you go.

And so.

The dream.

It's sunset and he's pulling into the parking lot at the lake. The oil-dark water is rimmed with pines, the sky is streaked with the muted colors of the dying day.

It's only when he gets out of the car that he realizes he's not alone. It's a dream, and dreams work under their own set of rules, so it doesn't surprise him. A girl he hadn't noticed before is in the car with him, and now she steps out to join him.

Emily.

But she doesn't look like she did the last few times he saw her in the waking world. Now her hair is combed and clean and not tangled with weeds from the lake bottom. Her skin is normal-colored, not grayish blue. Her neck isn't bloated. Her eyes aren't glazed over and pale with the washed-out color of death.

She's wearing her necklace, the one with the heart-shaped locket. She has her glasses on.

He hears a scuffling sound from inside the car and notices that her dog is in there now, in the backseat. Maybe he was there before, maybe he just appeared, it's impossible to tell. She wants to bring Trevor along, but he convinces her to leave the dog there. "We won't be long," he tells her. "This way he won't run off."

"He'll be good," she protests. "He won't run away."

"We won't be long."

They crack the window open, lock the doors, and then the two of them walk together toward the beach near the base of Windy Point.

All goes well until they reach the stretch of sand near the inlet. They begin to argue.

It's a dream and it doesn't need to make sense: They argue about something stupid, it's not even clear what. Something that happened at school. Something to do with the locket.

They're near the woods, near the fire pit. He grabs her arm.

She tries to pull free, to fight him off, to wrestle away, but he's stronger and he's able to drag her toward the water. She screams but they're too far from any homes. No one can hear her.

He entwines his hand in her hair and thrusts her head forward, holds it under the water.

She thrashes.

Yes.

And tries to pull away, tries to get her mouth to the surface, but soon enough, her struggling stops and she becomes limp in his hands.

He lets go, his heart racing with fear and a horrible realization of what he has done. He backs up and turns to rub away the evidence of their scuffle, to draw his foot across the sand to erase the drag marks from when he pulled her to the water.

There on the sand he sees a glint in the moonlight, because then it is night, and it's a dream, so somehow that makes sense.

The glint is a lens from her glasses.

Knowing that it's a dream, he tries to wake up. He tells himself that this isn't real and wills himself to open his eyes, but the nightmare just wraps more tightly around him like it's never going to let him go.

He picks up the small rounded piece of glass and searches for the frames but can't find them in the dark. Even using his phone as a flashlight he doesn't see them and finally gives up the search.

Her body lies motionless and facedown in the water.

He unclasps her necklace, removes it, pockets it, then tugs her deeper, to where the current will carry her away.

No one will ever find out. No one will know.

No one.

Will ever.

Know.

Daniel woke up shaking, staring at the ceiling.

Waking up this morning wasn't like it was sometimes for him—a slow transition from the dreamworld, the images fading one by one into the murky realm of his unconscious.

No, this time he woke up all at once. And the images didn't fade, just remained stark and vivid in his mind.

Trevor.

The lake.

Emily Jackson.

And, though it was frightening to dream of her like that, he felt compelled to find out more, to see what would happen next.

He closed his eyes again and tried to return to the dream to see how it would unfold.

But it was like trying to climb into someone else's thoughts—everything was indecipherably smudged and marred around the edges and he wasn't able to reenter the story.

At last he gave up and opened his eyes.

And thought about the dream.

He'd seen the events of that night through the eyes of someone who'd killed her. A nightmarish version of what might have happened. An explanation for the broken glasses, the missing lens, the words Emily had told him at the funeral about Trevor being in the car. The way she might have died.

But she might have just fallen in the water.

Or jumped. Or been pushed.

Or it might have happened just like Daniel had dreamt it had, as his mind tried to make sense of everything that was going on.

It'd all seemed so terrifyingly real.

But that's the nature of nightmares. Sometimes you think you're awake when they happen. Sometimes you know you're asleep and you want nothing more than to wake up, but when you're experiencing them they seem to be actually happening.

Just like the visions you've been having.

For some reason he'd pictured Emily alive again. And her dog Trevor was in the car. It was as if his mind was sorting through the facts and then filling in details no one would have known unless he was there.

Still, it was chilling to discover that the dead girl who was haunting him during the day was also starting to pursue him in his dreams at night.

When he finally got up, it was after nine.

His dad usually took Sundays off, but it hadn't worked out that way this week, and when Daniel made it to the kitchen he found a note from him saying that he'd be back at four, that there was some fresh OJ in the fridge, and that he loved him.

Daniel was processing the dream and pouring some milk in his cereal when he got a phone call.

It was from someone he hadn't heard from in over a month.

His mother.

CHAPTER
TWENTY-NINE

"Daniel. How are you?"

"Good." Getting a call from his mom was unusual enough, but getting one at this time on a Sunday morning was even more out of nowhere. It made it hard to figure out what to say.

"Your father told me you've been having headaches. That you actually passed out at that church—at the funeral. And then at the game Friday night? You were hit so hard you got knocked out?"

"I'm okay, Mom. Don't—"

"But is that true?"

"I blacked out for a few seconds at the game, that's all. It's not that big of a deal. And the funeral was a fluke. I don't know. The headaches are over now. I'm fine."

"Your father said they took you to the emergency room after the game."

"It's just what they always do when that happens to someone." He figured that saying the phrase "gets a concussion" would make her worry more, so he left that part out. "They looked me over and didn't find anything wrong."

He poured himself some orange juice, then stuck the pitcher back in the fridge.

"I want you to see a doctor."

"I told you, Mom, I'm fine."

"I've spoken with your father about it. He agrees with me."

His dad hadn't mentioned anything about that to him, and it seemed like something he definitely should have filled him in about.

"They looked me over at the hospital already. I'm fine."

"I'm thinking of coming back. To visit."

"What? Back here?"

"Yes."

"When?"

"This coming weekend. That way maybe I can see your game on Friday night."

He plopped down at the table. "Did you talk to Dad about any of this? About coming back?"

"Not yet. I wanted to talk to you first, see if it was alright with you if I came."

"You want to come to my game."

"Yes."

This was the first time all year she'd expressed interest in coming to any of his games. "So you're asking if it's okay with me if you come to my game Friday night?"

"That's what I was wondering." She sounded a little taken aback that he was pressing her like this. "Yes."

"And you want me to be honest?"

A small pause. "That sounds like a no."

"It is."

"You don't want to see me?"

"That's not what I said."

"Then what are you—"

"I don't want you to come back unless you're going to stay."

"That's not possible, Daniel. Your father and I, well, we—"

"My father and you what? What is it? It's been six months and you still haven't told me why you left."

"It's complicated."

"No, it's not. You married Dad. You had a son. Then one day you moved out and left them. What part of that is complicated? What am I missing here?"

"This isn't the time to talk about it." Irritation had edged into her reply.

"It's been six months. When exactly were you planning on explaining yourself? I'm just asking because I want to make sure I'm ready for it when the big day arrives."

"Your father and I have our reasons for why we're separated. When the time is right we'll explain them to you."

As far as Daniel knew, his dad didn't have any reasons for why the two of them were separated. It was only his mom who had hers.

He felt his hand tighten around the phone. "When did Dad call you? I mean about the doctor."

"Friday night."

"He called you on Friday night and you waited until now to check up on me?" Daniel didn't even try to remove the barbs from his words.

"Don't use that tone with me, Dan. I—"

He hung up.

And stared at the phone, waiting to see if she would call him back.

She did not.

He ticked off the seconds.

A minute passed.

Still nothing.

He wasn't sure if that disappointed him or not.

When he looked at the bowl of cereal he'd set on the table he realized he'd lost his appetite.

Shoving back his chair, he dumped the cereal into the sink and, even though it was only soggy flakes and he didn't really need to, he turned on the garbage disposal and listened to the harsh blades work their way through his breakfast.

They spit up churned bits of cereal and splatters of milk, which he washed back down the drain.

He wasn't supposed to meet Kyle until noon, and he wasn't in the mood to work on his homework in the meantime, so he went online and searched for information about hallucinations instead. At least it was a way to get his mind off the conversation with his mom, and the fact that she wanted him to see a doctor.

Something Dad agrees with her about.

Daniel scoured the sites that talked about hallucinations— the different types, their causes and treatment strategies. He printed out some articles, scanned others, took notes on what he read.

Evidently, sometimes people saw things, others heard voices speaking to them, and sometimes people also felt things that weren't there, particularly having the sensation that they had bugs crawling all over them.

Well, at least he hadn't had to deal with that.

Yet.

Just burn marks on your arm.

But how was that only a hallucination? He'd felt Emily actually grab his arm, had undeniable evidence of it when he went to bed that night and woke up the next morning.

Seeing. Hearing. Feeling.

He was three for three.

What caught his attention the most wasn't the types of hallucinations as much as what caused them. Something was affecting him, something was wrong with him, and when he read about the reasons people had hallucinations, none were very encouraging.

It's just in your head.

No.

Leave out the *just*.

It was in his body too.

The first articles he came across listed what seemed like obvious enough reasons: alcohol and drug use. Meth, coke, crack, LSD, ecstasy—any hallucinogenic, even marijuana, could make you see things.

But Daniel wasn't on drugs.

Withdrawal could also do it, but obviously he wasn't going through that.

Sometimes the line between reality and fantasy got blurred when you were falling asleep or waking up; hypnagogic and hypnopompic hallucinations, they were called.

It was like this shadowy mental state that scientists didn't fully understand but that could cause people to believe they were seeing or hearing things that weren't actually there.

That might possibly explain the weird dream he'd had this morning, but the times he'd seen Emily he hadn't even been close to falling asleep. In fact, the second time it was just the opposite—he was in the middle of playing a football game.

Sometimes hallucinations were caused by a cranial injury—although, apart from getting knocked around a little on the field over the years, he couldn't think of anything along those lines that might have happened to him.

Seizures sometimes caused hallucinations. So did migraines.

So that could possibly account for his headaches, but they didn't fit the typical pattern of migraines, and the detailed, elaborate things he was seeing and hearing wouldn't have happened with simply a migraine, or even a minor seizure.

Stress, exhaustion, sometimes sleep deprivation could cause people to be unable to distinguish between dream states and reality.

He hoped maybe that was it.

Not enough sleep.

But that didn't explain the marks on his arm.

Maybe he had a brain tumor—particularly one in the temporal lobe. Apparently, there were parts of your brain that processed your sense of sight and sound. If there was pressure on them, or impulses sent to them that weren't supposed to be, you could end up seeing or hearing things.

One website Daniel stumbled onto told how some scientists had done research on people in surgery and made them laugh, made them hear voices that weren't real, made them see things just by triggering different parts of their brains with mild electrical currents.

Brain disease could explain the headaches he was having.

There weren't a lot of other possibilities left.

Except the major one: schizophrenia.

Slowly going insane.

Even though headaches weren't usually a precursor to schizophrenia, he was the right age and he had other symptoms, or whatever you wanted to call them: visual and auditory hallucinations, disorganized thinking, delusions. . . .

So. Schizophrenia.

Or maybe a brain tumor.

Two really thrilling prospects.

When he got a text from Kyle asking where he was, Daniel realized it was already quarter after twelve and he was late for his lunch meeting with his friend.

Last night Kyle had texted that he had something he needed to talk about.

Daniel replied that he was on his way, and left for the restaurant.

CHAPTER THIRTY

Rizzo's had a faux-Italian look going on, with checked table-cloths, Italian music in the background, pictures of the Sicilian countryside on the wall. Next to one of them hung a framed dollar bill that was apparently the first one Rizzo had earned back in 1989 when he opened the restaurant.

If Rizzo wasn't Italian himself, he sure fit the stereotype— thick boned, black haired, a bushy mustache, prone to talking wildly with his hands. He was one of those dough throwers, and part of the experience of eating at his restaurant was watching him spin and flip the pies.

The smell of fresh dough inside the place was amazing and was almost worth the price of a pizza.

Daniel and Kyle ordered an extra-large pepperoni-and-jalapeño pie and went to the soda machine for their drinks.

"You ever think about North Dakota?" Kyle said.

"North Dakota?"

"Rizzo. It's where he's from."

"Really."

"Yup. I don't know why it just struck me, but most states

have something they're famous for. Even South Dakota has Mount Rushmore. I think North Dakota might be the only state that's not unique."

"Wouldn't that make it unique?"

"Ah. True. So maybe their motto should be: 'The only thing that sets us apart is how nondescript we are.'"

"The people of North Dakota might not like hearing you say that."

"They're good-natured folks. They won't hold a grudge." Then he added, "Besides, they can claim being the birthplace of Rizzo, world-famous pizza-dough thrower, at least, world-famous within a ten-mile radius of his restaurant."

They took a seat in a booth at the back of the restaurant.

Kyle set down his Pepsi, then said soberly, "Well, it's officially one week."

"Since Emily's body was found."

"Yeah."

"In a way it seems like it was a lot longer and in a way it seems like it just happened."

"I know what you mean." Kyle gulped down some soda. "It's weird."

"Grain by grain."

"What?"

"That's what you wrote the other day for Miss Flynn's class about how, grain by grain, the sand erodes through our moments."

"Slipping down the fragile slopes of our days," he said reflectively. Then he quoted the rest of his poem word for word: "'And I wonder, as I tumble down the side, who will change the weather and give my life another shot at glory?' Yeah, I did."

"Man, you have a good memory."

"Well, you remember numbers, I remember words. Especially phrases I make up."

Daniel decided that before he asked his friend why he'd wanted to talk with him today, he would fill him in on what had happened the previous evening.

"Hey, listen, last night I ended up taking Nicole back to her house. On the way, Ty and his friends tried to attack us."

"What do you mean, tried to attack you?"

"They'd left something in the middle of the road. When I stopped to drag it out of the way, they stepped out from where they were hiding. One of them went for a rock. I think they were going to try to break through the window of the car, maybe go after Nicole."

"That's crazy. What did you do?"

"I got the rock from the guy. Ty had a knife. I thought he was gonna come at me, but in the end he backed off."

"I'll bet Nicole was freaking out."

"She was rattled; she'll be okay. But before they drove away Ty said something about Emily's notebook, about what was in it. Have you heard?"

Kyle shook his head. "Uh-uh. Did he say?"

"No. I've been wondering why he even brought it up. Also, he must have been out at Lake Algonquin yesterday morning when I was there with Stacy. He mentioned he saw me by the lake."

"Well, I doubt he was out there to go fishing."

"What do you mean?"

"You know him. He's not exactly an outdoorsman."

"Why do you think he went out there?"

"To drink. To party. Who knows."

"At that time of day?"

He shrugged. "Why did you go out there?"

"I guess to . . ." He didn't exactly want to bring up the hallucinations. "Well, process what's been going on. I thought I might find some answers."

"Maybe it was the same with him."

Daniel didn't know what to say to that.

They sat for a while, and he tried to mentally sort things out, replaying what had happened the night before—Stacy not showing up, Nicole meeting him outside school, Ty and his friends waiting for them beside the road.

"What are you thinking?" Kyle asked him.

"Well, for one thing I'm thinking that I have no idea what I'm gonna say to Stacy when I run into her at school tomorrow. I mean, she invites herself to come to the lake with me, then when I ask her to go to the dance, she accepts, tells me to call her, and then doesn't answer the phone or show up. She doesn't call, doesn't text. Nothing. I mean, how am I supposed to take that?"

"How do you want to take it?"

"What do you mean?"

"I mean do you want an apology or excuses or what? What could she tell you that would make you happy?"

Daniel absently pulled off the paper covering his straw. "I don't know. I guess just the truth."

"Sometimes the truth hurts."

"Sometimes it's all we have."

"A good reply, sensei. I will be your pupil forever."

"I'll remember that."

The conversation shifted to stuff that was going on at school and the events of the last week. Kyle still didn't bring up the reason why he'd texted that he wanted to meet today, and the whole time they spoke Daniel wondered about it.

He also wondered how much he should tell Kyle about the weird things he'd been seeing, hearing, and feeling—how reality had become obscured to the point where it was hard to know what was real and what wasn't.

Time passed, the pizza came, and they dove into lunch.

Eventually, Daniel realized that if he couldn't tell his best friend about some of the things he was experiencing, he couldn't tell anyone.

Still, anxiety twisted through his gut as he tried to figure out the best way to bring it up.

"Hey, listen, Kyle . . ."

Man, he did not want to do this.

"Yeah?"

But he also did want to do it, did want to talk to someone about what'd been happening with him and what might have been causing the hallucinations.

"What is it?" Kyle had a mouthful of pizza.

Here goes nothing.

"I've been seeing things."

"What do you mean?" Kyle swallowed. "What kinds of things?"

"Ones that aren't there."

"Bro, that's usually what people mean when they say they're seeing things. I'm wondering what kinds of things that aren't there are you seeing." He reached for one of the three remaining slices.

"Ghosts. I've been seeing ghosts. Well, one ghost, actually. Emily Jackson's."

Kyle stopped short when he heard the words. He stared at Daniel. "You've been seeing Emily Jackson's ghost?"

"I've seen it twice now. Once at the funeral, the second time at the football game, right before I got sacked. That's why I didn't throw the ball, why I hesitated on that play. Either it's her ghost or . . . I don't know. I guess I'm hallucinating."

There.

Now.

It was out in the open. He'd told someone and at last things would change.

Kyle would either believe him or he wouldn't believe him, but either way things were going to be different. And at least the secret wouldn't be trapped inside Daniel any longer. At least there was a possibility that he might get some answers about what was going on.

His friend didn't say anything for a long time, just worked his way through the slice of pizza he'd picked up. He looked deep in thought.

The fact that he didn't reply made Daniel anxious. "I think she's trying to tell me something, Kyle."

"Emily is dead, Daniel."

"I know, but—"

"There's no 'but.' She's dead and ghosts don't exist."

"You don't believe in ghosts?"

"No," Kyle replied. "I don't. Revenants and eidolons, any of that."

"Revenants and eidolons?"

"Different kinds of ghosts."

"What about all the stories you tell when we go camping, on road trips, that sort of thing?"

"They're stories—just like you said. Urban legends, campfire tales, that's it. You know that."

"But what about all the things people see, spirits, specters, hauntings? You don't really think they're all just figments of their imagination?"

"Just because people see things doesn't mean those things exist. Sometimes our eyes play tricks on us."

"This is a lot more than my eyes playing tricks on me."

Kyle was quiet.

There really weren't very many possible explanations for what was happening. Either he was seeing ghosts or he was seeing something that wasn't there.

Either seeing the dead, or hallucinating.

Great options there.

Normal people don't have hallucinations. Only people who are losing touch with reality do.

Only people who are going crazy.

Kyle covered another slice with crushed red pepper to the point where it looked almost inedible. "So talk me through it. You're seeing ghosts, and at the game you didn't pass out because you were hit? That's what you're saying?"

"I don't know exactly. All I can say is that I saw her walking toward me on the field."

"Emily."

"Yes."

"Alright." He took a bite of the red pepper–ified slice. It would have put most people's mouths on fire. It didn't seem to faze Kyle. "Lay it out. Details."

Daniel talked through the events that had preceded each of the two blackouts.

He recounted Emily's words about Trevor and her request for him to find her glasses, then he told Kyle about the necklace and how she'd tugged it through her neck and held it up for him to see.

He finished by saying, "I don't think this is going to stop until she gets what she wants."

"And what is that? What does she want?"

"The truth."

"The truth about what? Her death? Her drowning?"

"Yes."

"Like in that movie *The Sixth Sense*? When the ghosts kept appearing? That kid who saw dead people?"

"Yeah, I guess."

"Why you?"

"I have no idea."

Daniel wanted so badly to tell him about the broken glasses that he and Stacy had found at the beach, but he knew he couldn't. "If there's no such thing as ghosts, you're telling me I'm having hallucinations? Is that it?"

"Maybe. Yeah. I don't know. I'm just saying I don't think you're seeing Emily Jackson's ghost."

Daniel remembered his research on hallucinations earlier in the morning. He didn't really like considering the possibility that he had some type of brain tumor or was beginning to go insane, so he stayed on the topic of ghosts. "She grabbed my arm at the funeral. There was still a mark there the next morning."

"Show it to me."

"It's gone. It healed."

"Okay."

"I'm not making this up, Kyle."

His friend stared for a moment at one of the pictures of Italy hanging on the wall, then looked back at Daniel. "Did I ever tell you the story of the doll in the window?"

"I don't think so."

"Well, I don't know for sure if it's still there, but when we lived in Minnesota, we would drive through Janesville to get to our place. If you took the old Highway 14 through town, as you're heading west, just as you cross Main Street, there's this old two-story house on the right-hand side of the road."

"What happened?" Daniel anticipated where this was going: "Was someone killed there?"

"No. But if you looked up at the attic window you'd see a doll hanging there. It was one of those old-fashioned dolls made of wood and it was hanging from a rafter with a noose around its neck."

"Okay, that's disturbing."

"No kidding. Well, there are all these stories about the doll and why it's there. Some people say it moves; others say some-one died in the house and the place is haunted. The way I heard it, there was a girl who lived there and the other kids made fun of her because she was the sort of kid that adults call 'special,' and kids call all kinds of other things. You know what I mean."

"Sure," Daniel said quietly.

"Anyway, the other kids in the town were relentless, mak-ing fun of her, calling her names, all that. The story goes that even when she was a teenager she carried that doll with her everywhere—which only made them make fun of her more. One day her mom was looking for her and couldn't find her anywhere."

He paused, as if to accentuate how long the girl's mom searched. "Eventually she went outside to look for her and when she turned around toward the house, she saw her daughter hanging in the attic window where she'd killed herself—hung herself off one of the rafters. And they say that after the funeral, her parents took the same rope that their daughter had used and they hung that doll up there in the window as a con-stant reminder to the townspeople of what they'd driven their daughter to do."

Daniel was silent.

"So, last month I was doing this contemporary-issues assignment and I thought I'd try to find out what really hap-pened. I came across this newspaper article from 1975 that said that one time, years ago, the guy who lived in the house was looking through a *National Geographic* magazine and saw a picture of a house in Pennsylvania that had a doll hanging in the window and he basically said, 'Huh. Wouldn't it be cool if we had a doll hanging in our window too?' So he hung it up there."

Daniel waited. "That's it?"

"That's it."

"No suicide? No girl getting made fun of? Nothing like that?"

"Nope. Just a guy paging through a magazine."

He evaluated that. "I don't think I get it. What's the point?"

"Before my dad died he told me there's this saying in Africa: 'Something happens and then a story comes along and finds it.' That's what happened out there in Janesville. Some guy hung the doll in the window and then a bunch of stories came along and found it."

"And that's what you're saying is going on here?"

"This girl died. Emily did. Okay. It's terrible. Stories are going to come along to try to explain it. It's normal, you know? Just like how people at school are saying something up there at Windy Point might have pulled her off the edge—a ghost, I'm not sure; I don't know what all that's about. Sometimes there's no way to make sense of something. There's just the plain old everyday facts and that's all."

"So you don't believe me."

"I believe what you're telling me—that you saw what you say you saw, that you heard it, but . . ."

"But you think it's all in my head. So what about the wound on my arm, the one in the shape of her hand, the one that felt like it'd been burned onto my skin—that was all in my head as well?"

"You say it healed?"

"Yeah, the next day. Before football practice."

"A mark that looks like it was branded onto your arm—a mark the size of a hand—heals in just over twenty-four hours?"

"I'm telling you the truth."

Kyle was silent. "Let's get out of here. I gotta think about this."

He rose and, without another word, grabbed the last slice of pizza, then went to pay Rizzo, who was tossing an extra-large circle of dough into the air.

Kyle held up a twenty.

"Punch the button and grab your change," Rizzo called to them in his robust Italian—but now Daniel noticed, also slightly North Dakotan—accent.

"Keep it, man."

"*Grazie.*"

When they got outside Daniel said, "That was a nice tip."

"That was my mom's money."

"Ah."

They headed toward their cars.

"Listen," Kyle said, "when the mind believes something it affects your body. People get sick and get healed by their thoughts—placebos, you know. Using 'em, soldiers on the battlefield can make it so people don't even feel amputations. And then there's that weird thing about phantom pain, where a person who's lost a limb can still feel it hurt. I've heard they can even feel the limb that isn't there bump against stuff. It's wild."

"So the mark on my arm just appeared because I believed Emily grabbed me?"

"I don't know. I guess, yeah—that or I'm totally wrong

about all this and ghosts are real and this one is gonna haunt you until it gets what it wants—whatever that is."

"Sometimes you're a little too honest."

Daniel's phone vibrated.

"Sometimes the truth is all we have."

Daniel checked the screen and found a text from Ronnie Jackson: "Can u come ovr to my house @4? need to talk to u."

"What's up?" Kyle asked.

"It's Ronnie, Emily's brother. He wants to meet up this afternoon at four. You should come too."

"Ronnie texted you?"

"I asked him to. I wanted to talk to him about Emily."

"Because you think she was murdered."

"Yes."

"My mom's showing a house today. I have to watch Michele."

Kyle's four-year-old sister had been a surprise baby to everyone in his family. Ever since his dad died in a car accident two years ago, Kyle, his mom, and Michele had been on their own.

A lot of times his mom had to work on weekends, and Kyle helped watch Michele whenever he needed to. Though he sometimes complained about it, Daniel knew he really didn't mind, that he fiercely loved his little sister and would do anything for her.

Kyle hit the unlock for his car. "Let me know what Ronnie says, and if you see anything else, you know, any eidolons."

"Eidolons. Right. Hey, last night you texted me that you had something we needed to talk about. That was the whole reason we met for lunch. What's up?"

"It can wait."

"Don't do that."

"It's okay."

"Tell me, Kyle."

"I'm saying—"

"Kyle. Go on. What is it?"

"Yeah. Okay, you're right. You should probably know." But he didn't continue.

"Know what?"

"Well, I heard people are putting stuff on Emily's grave. If you really think she was murdered, maybe the killer returned there, you know, like they do on TV shows when they go to the funeral of the victim or the cemetery—leave stuff at the grave, take souvenirs, that sort of thing. I was wondering if you wanted to go out there, have a look around, see if there's anything out of the ordinary."

"You mean anything that might tell us who the killer is."

"What could it hurt, just taking a look around?"

Probably nothing, except Daniel had told his dad he was going to stop poking around, looking into this.

Oh, and is that why you're going to go over to talk to Emily's brother?

The graveyard.

Yeah.

If there was ever a place to see a ghost, it was out there.

"I don't know."

"Listen"—Kyle swung his door open—"call me and tell me how it goes with Ronnie. We can talk about the cemetery thing later."

They said good-bye and Kyle took off.

Daniel had a couple hours before he needed to leave for the Jacksons' house, so he went home to read up on killers. It didn't take long to find out that often, they really did return to the scene of the crime, as well as attend the funerals and visit the graves of their victims, just like Kyle had suggested they did.

He looked into hallucinations again for a little while, especially tactile ones, to try to figure out how that burn mark had actually appeared on his arm, and how it had healed so fast. However, even after an hour, he didn't dig up anything helpful or encouraging.

Basically, if you start seeing things that aren't there, or hearing or even feeling things that aren't there, there's almost always something seriously wrong with you.

Maybe his mom and dad were right. Maybe he did need to see a doctor—a shrink maybe—to figure out what was really going on.

He texted Ronnie to get his address and found that he lived near Lake Algonquin, probably in the same neighborhood Stacy was from.

Daniel left home deep in thought about their suspicions that Emily was murdered, and the possibility that a killer might have visited her grave and dropped something off there or taken a memento with him when he left.

CHAPTER THIRTY-ONE

Daniel arrived at Ronnie Jackson's house a few minutes before four. For some reason he was nervous. Even though he didn't want to be rude, he realized he needed to swing by the bathroom as soon as he got inside.

After parking at the curb and walking up the driveway, he knocked on the door.

A dog was barking inside the house.

Trevor.

A few seconds later he heard someone's footsteps.

It took a moment for whoever was there to unlock the door, but finally it swung open and a man appeared.

Daniel recognized him as the person who, at the funeral, had told him he was thankful that he'd come, that it meant a lot to him. From Daniel's online research into Emily's life, he knew this was her dad.

"Yes?" Mr. Jackson didn't seem to recognize Daniel from seeing him at the funeral, but Daniel suspected he might not remember very much at all about that day. Emily's shaggy, shedding golden retriever, Trevor, stood by his side, staring at Daniel, panting, his tail wagging.

Daniel introduced himself, then said, "I'm here to see Ronnie. I know him from school." He added, "He asked me to come over."

"Well, Ronnie's with his mother right now running errands." Mr. Jackson hesitated, as if he were trying to figure out what to say next. "They'll be home in just a few minutes. Please. Come in."

A piano sat at one end of the living room. Surprisingly, there was no TV, just a brown-striped couch, two recliners, a couple of floor lamps, and a coffee table with four magazines arranged neatly on its glass top.

The couch and chairs were covered with dog hair. It must have been quite a chore to keep them clean with Trevor around. An open doorway at the other end of the room led past the dining room to the kitchen.

Alright, here came the embarrassing part. "Um, may I use your bathroom?"

"Sure. We're remodeling the one down here; just go upstairs, second door on your right."

"Thank you."

When Daniel reached the top of the stairs and saw the stickers on the first door to the right, his heart seemed to come to a stop. A sheet of paper was taped to the door. Written in a girl's flowery handwriting were two words: "Emily's Room."

Daniel stood there staring at the door. A flurry of images and questions swarmed through him. The funeral, the football game, Ty's cryptic comments, the horrifying dream last night.

And then, as if out of nowhere, he heard a voice inside his head: *Go in. Look around.*

No, there was no way he was going to do that.

But the voice persisted: *Just take a look, that's all.*

He heard Mr. Jackson putting dishes away in the kitchen, which was out of sight of the stairway. From there, he wouldn't be able to see Daniel enter the room.

But despite that, he didn't open the door. Instead he strode toward the bathroom.

However, when he got there, he couldn't quell his curiosity and he went back and pressed gently against the door to Emily's room and eased it open.

Just for a minute. Just to see where she lived.

Then Daniel stepped into Emily Jackson's bedroom.

CHAPTER THIRTY-TWO

The pink walls had posters of boy bands, horses, and kittens. There was a calendar hanging above her desk with days neatly crossed off, ending on the day before she disappeared.

Emily didn't have space for all her books. The shelves were jammed and there were books piled on the floor and even stacked horizontally on top of the ones that were shelved.

She liked fantasy—Tolkien, Rowling, Paolini, and others, and preferred hardcover to paperback. The shelves looked sturdy, but sagged under the weight of the heavy volumes.

Her bed was meticulously made, with a neat pile of stuffed animals positioned, just so, beside the pillow.

The small polka-dot garbage can beside her closet was empty and the only things on the desk were a closed laptop, a spiral-bound notebook, a propped-up photo of her and Ronnie with Ackerman's Studio logo imprinted on the corner, and a pencil holder with seven items in it—a highlighter, two mechanical pencils, three pens, and one red Sharpie.

The room was neat. Too neat. The kind of neat a mom might go after when she's getting ready for company.

Or maybe when she's trying to tidy up and preserve the memory of her daughter.

Daniel stood motionless just inside the doorway.

He wasn't about to go rooting through Emily's things, shuffling through her dresser drawers or digging through her closet. He felt weird enough just being here looking around her room, but there was one thing he wanted to do before leaving: take a look inside that spiral-bound notebook on her desk.

As he stood there, he wondered if this was the notebook people were talking about—the one that'd supposedly been in her locker at school, the one Ty had mentioned.

Daniel leaned toward the hall and listened intently. It sounded like Mr. Jackson was still in the kitchen.

It wouldn't take much time at all to flip open the notebook and just take a peek at what was inside, then get out of her room, hit the bathroom, and head downstairs.

Finally, Daniel reassured himself that he would have enough time to glance through it before Mr. Jackson would get suspicious of the toilet not flushing, so he walked to the desk.

As he picked up the notebook, a loose sheet of paper slipped out and glided to the floor.

He knelt to replace it and saw that it was written in the same script that appeared on the sign on her door.

Quickly, he scanned it.

It's right after second hour. All around me, people are talking and laughing and getting snacks from the steel-and-glass vending machines.

I watch the Popular Kids talk. I watch them and

I despise them and I envy them and I hate myself for wanting to be like them.

Then one girl shifts to the side and leaves a small opening in the circle, so I step in.

But they don't notice me. They just keep talking and laughing in their cool-student-sort-of-way and I don't know what to say. I don't have anything to say. The conversation goes on without me.

I'm invisible to them.

Every time I think of something to add, they're already talking about something else.

The rest was written with a different-color pen, as if she'd paused and then picked up the entry later to finish it:

So, finally, I step back and the circle closes up again . . . like a wound healing itself . . . and I go to the window, unwrap my candy bar, and watch the geese fly south for the winter.

As I eat something sweet.

Next to the steel-and-glass machines.

The words were so sad, and Daniel couldn't help but think again of dreams and death and the story Miss Flynn had read in English class—the one about the girl who wanted to be a movie star and never got up enough courage to leave her hometown.

He remembered what he'd been thinking on Tuesday when he went to Emily's funeral—that she was the kind of girl everyone walked past at school, ignored at lunch, never really had time for.

Until she was dead. Then all the students made time for her funeral.

Some things about the world were just tragically upside down.

He slid the paper back into the notebook, and began paging through it.

And immediately felt uneasy.

One name appeared dozens of times, scribbled in the columns and margins. A name with hearts drawn beside it.

The name of his best friend.

Kyle Goessel.

CHAPTER THIRTY-THREE

Daniel stared at the words, then flipped forward and backward through the notebook. No other boys' names were written in the columns next to the English notes and algebra equations, just Kyle's.

Emily obviously had a crush on him, but the other day Kyle had said he didn't even know her.

But he does know where her locker is.

And he did act a little strange when you asked him about her.

Also, when they'd shown up at the locker that Ty had shoved Ronnie into, Ty had said he knew about Kyle and Emily. What did all that mean?

But Kyle was with Mia, and he wouldn't have led Emily on. He wasn't that kind of guy. And for as long as Daniel had known him, he'd never dated younger girls—let alone those who were two years younger than him.

Whatever it meant, there was something more going on here, another whole level of meaning, like in a puzzle or a riddle where what you see isn't what you get, where looks are deceiving, and things aren't what they appear to be.

And he couldn't shake the feeling that this all had to do not just with Emily herself, but with her death.

Her murder.

As Daniel was thinking about that, he realized that he didn't hear sounds coming from the kitchen anymore.

Out the window, movement on the street below caught his attention.

A car turning into the driveway.

Quickly, he closed up the notebook and set it back on the desk, trying to make sure it was in the same position as when he'd found it.

Downstairs, footsteps were crossing the hallway leading to the stairs.

Daniel hurried out of the bedroom, closing the door softly behind him. He rushed to the bathroom, quickly used the toilet, flushed it. Rinsed his hands.

When he left the bathroom, Emily's dad was at the top of the stairs, as if he were standing sentry in front of Daniel's only exit. "He's here. Ronnie is. I told him you'd be right down."

"Thanks." Daniel tried to read his face to tell if he had figured out what he'd done.

Before Mr. Jackson turned around to head back down the stairs, his gaze flicked toward Emily's room. Daniel felt a sweep of nervousness.

Mr. Jackson studied the door longer than he needed to, but in the end he said nothing about it and simply led Daniel to the living room.

Daniel breathed a quiet sigh of relief as he followed Emily's father down the stairs.

Ronnie was hanging his jacket on a hook near the front door. "Hey, Daniel."

"Hi, Ronnie."

"Thanks for coming over."

"Sure."

Mrs. Jackson appeared in the doorway, introduced herself, and Daniel shook her hand. She looked at him curiously. "So you know Ronnie from school?"

"He's the quarterback," Ronnie told her. "On the football team."

"Sheriff Byers's boy?"

Daniel nodded. "Yes."

"Aren't you the one who passed out at Emily's funeral?"

Not the question he'd expected, and not one he was excited to answer. "I felt dizzy. I'm sorry. I—"

"Maybe it would be best if you left," she cut him off.

"Mom," Ronnie objected. "It's okay."

Daniel wasn't sure why she would want him to leave just because he was the guy who'd fainted at Emily's funeral, unless she thought it had disrupted things too much or that it was some kind of stunt he was pulling.

"Dear," Mr. Jackson said to her, "let Ronnie and his friend talk, they're just—"

She glared at him harshly, then spun on her heels and headed to another room. Daniel couldn't even imagine what this family was going through right now, and whatever Mrs. Jackson's reasons, he wasn't about to stay if she didn't want him to.

"It's alright," he told Ronnie and his father. "I should probably be going anyway."

"But you just got here," Ronnie objected.

Daniel wanted to talk with Ronnie, but he really did not want to get in the middle of this. "We can catch up at school tomorrow. Cool?"

Mr. Jackson was looking toward the room his wife had stormed into. He set his jaw and left to find her, leaving Ronnie and Daniel alone.

"Can I talk to you on the way to your car?" Ronnie asked.

"Sure. Come on."

As they left the house Ronnie said, "My parents, you know. My mom, she's just . . ."

"Yeah, no. I get it. Don't worry about it."

Daniel remembered the photo Emily had taken of herself and Trevor at Windy Point. "Hey, I read in the paper that Emily had left home to go on a walk out by the lake. Did she do that a lot?"

"Not all the time, but it wasn't that unusual. She left a note that she was taking Trevor for a walk before she, well . . . you know."

Daniel thought of how Emily had told him that Trevor was in the car. He wanted to ask Ronnie about it, but couldn't think of any way of doing it that wouldn't sound weird. After all, how could he have possibly known about her dog being in a car—if that was even the case?

Instead, he took the conversation in another direction: "Do you know what was in the locket of her necklace?"

Ronnie looked at him curiously. "How did you know about that?"

"She was wearing it in a couple pictures at the funeral. I guess I just thought she must have liked it, worn it a lot."

"Yeah, um, I don't know. I think it was a picture of some guy she liked. But here's what I really wanted to talk to you about: her cell phone."

"What about it?"

"She didn't have it on her when she was found."

"So she didn't carry it in her purse?"

"No, her pocket, mostly."

Would her cell phone really have fallen out of her pocket if she just went into the water?

No.

Unless she fell off Windy Point, maybe—but then what about her broken glasses up on the beach?

Daniel wondered if the fact that she didn't have her phone with her had raised any red flags with law enforcement, or if his father had looked for it. He hadn't mentioned anything, but then again, his dad wasn't really allowed to fill him in on the details of his cases.

Bringing up the broken glasses might have helped Daniel get information from Ronnie, but he knew his dad was against his sharing anything about them. And, honestly, the last people in the world Daniel wanted to get worried that Emily might have been murdered were her family members.

Ronnie already thinks that.

Regardless, he held back from saying anything about the

glasses. Instead, he asked Ronnie about what he'd brought up the other day at school. "So, your sister knew how to swim?"

"Not just knew how, she swam all the time at the YMCA back in Madison before we moved here. She was really good."

"Is there anything else?"

"She was thinking about going out for Mr. McKinney's math club thing next semester." Ronnie paused. "To try and make some new friends."

"Okay."

"Are you going to find out what happened out there at Lake Algonquin? What really happened?"

Don't make a promise you can't keep.

But Daniel did anyway.

"Yeah. I am."

CHAPTER THIRTY-FOUR

Once he was in the car again, Daniel texted Kyle to call as soon as he had a chance.

Then he took off for home.

Clouds had blown in.

A storm was on its way.

Daniel caught up with his dad in the garage cleaning his Glock at the workbench.

Partly he was tempted to bring up something about the missing phone, but he realized his dad wouldn't be at all happy to learn that he was still looking into Emily's death.

"Mom called me this morning."

His father set down the cloth he was using on the gun's barrel. "She did?"

"Yeah. She wants to come to my game on Friday. She told me you called to tell her I blacked out at the homecoming game."

"She's your mother, Dan. She has a right to know how you're doing. Can you imagine what she would have said to me if she found out later that you'd gone to the emergency room and I hadn't told her about it?"

"Why did she leave?"

His dad was silent.

"I asked her and she wouldn't tell me. I mean, anyone could tell you guys were having some problems, I get that, but—"

"I don't really want to talk about this right now, Dan."

"Sure, I know, but—"

"Not right now."

But Daniel didn't give up. "Was there . . . is there another guy?"

"When the time is right I'll explain everything."

"You know, that's what she said too. That it wasn't the right time."

"There you go."

"I asked her when it was going to be the right time. She didn't tell me. Maybe you can."

"No—there wasn't another guy. She just preferred being alone rather than with me."

And with me, Daniel thought. *She preferred being alone to having her son around.*

He wasn't sure his dad's answer really satisfied him, but he accepted it for now. Rather than dwell on the reasons, he said, "She wants me to go see a doctor. She said you did too."

"We think it might be best. I was going to bring it up to you, but we haven't had much of a chance to talk. I scheduled an appointment for you tomorrow up in Superior."

"What? I have school and then football practice tomorrow afternoon. I can't miss that."

"I'll call the school to get you an excused absence, and I'll talk to Coach Warner. I'm sure he'll understand."

"Dad, listen, I don't want to go see a doctor."

"I understand. But in this case I'm not asking."

"We have a game Friday and—"

"Daniel. We're going to get you checked out."

"Checked out." Then it struck him. "Why Superior? It's not our doctor?"

"I got a referral. It's a specialist. A neurologist."

"I can't believe you didn't at least talk to me about this before setting it up," Daniel exclaimed. "That's not right."

Tension drew tight between them.

His father was the first to speak. "We leave at eight tomorrow morning."

There was a rule at their high school that if you missed classes for the day, you weren't allowed to practice with your team or play in any games that night. So, going to the doctor tomorrow would also mean missing practice.

Also, if he missed school tomorrow he wouldn't be able to find out from Stacy why she hadn't shown up at the dance, or talk with Kyle about Emily and whether or not he knew she had a crush on him.

Sure, okay, he could call or text them, but both of those things seemed like they'd be better discussed in person than texted back and forth. Besides, Stacy wasn't replying to his messages anyway.

Daniel said nothing, just headed to the kitchen. He felt like slamming the door to make a point, but left it open instead.

For some reason it seemed to make more of a statement than banging it shut behind him would have.

However, when he got to his bedroom he let loose on the door.

Anger gripped him, anger from everywhere and nowhere.

He squeezed his hand tight and aimed it at the wall beside the window.

His fist left a dent in the drywall.

He stared at it.

This isn't like you.

What's wrong?

You're changing. You're losing it.

A little frightened by what he'd just done, by what was happening to him, he moved a Mavericks poster to cover the hole, and then dropped onto his bed.

Checked his texts.

Nothing from Kyle or Stacy.

He went to the desk and tried to put everything else out of his mind and focus on his homework.

That turned out to be useless.

Without getting any assignments done, he put his books away. After lifting weights until his arms and chest were pretty much wasted, he threw together a sandwich and some leftover spaghetti for a very late supper.

He checked his phone again, and this time he did have a text: Nicole, thanking him for taking her home last night and asking if he might have found one of her earrings in his car.

It didn't take him long to locate the earring between the

seats. He texted her back that he was going to be gone tomorrow, but would bring it to school with him on Tuesday.

She replied that that'd be cool and she'd see him then.

He got ready for bed, lay down, and closed his eyes to try to get a full night of much-needed sleep.

But that's not what happened.

Instead, he woke up at 3:14 a.m. in his clothes, chilled, and completely drenched.

CHAPTER
THIRTY-FIVE

Daniel opened his eyes.

His room was still steeped in darkness, with only a faint smear of light coming through his window from the streetlights down the block.

A storm had blown in and at first he thought he might have been awakened by the thunder rolling through the night.

Yes, he confirmed he was still in bed. When he looked down, he could see that he was wearing his clothes and lying on the sheets and everything was soaking wet—his shirt, his pants, his socks, the blankets.

What on earth? Why are you wet? Why do you have your clothes on? Could this all be a dream?

Daniel blinked, then squeezed his hand into a fist and felt the pain from when he'd smacked the wall earlier.

Yes.

He was awake.

He felt the bed.

Yes, absolutely, it was wet.

He half expected Emily to appear there in his room or at his window, scratching at the glass like in that old *Salem's Lot* movie, when the vampires show up at the kid's house and drag their fingertips against the window, trying to get invited in.

But she did not.

Nothing out of the ordinary appeared.

He checked the time. Quarter after three.

He would've thought that getting wet like this would have awakened him right away, so nothing really made sense—not why he was wearing his clothes, and certainly not why they were drenched.

Daniel sat up.

It was pouring outside.

He had to have been out there, out in the storm.

Flicking on the bedside light, he looked around the room and noticed his boots lying discarded beside the dresser.

The soles were covered with mud.

Muddy tracks and a trail of dribbled water led from his room to the hallway.

Sleepwalking? He'd never done that before, not that he was aware of, at least, but he couldn't think of any other explanation for what was going on.

Really? Sleepwalking? You went outside during a storm and didn't wake up, and then you took off your boots and climbed into bed? All while you were asleep?

It seemed utterly unbelievable, but not any crazier than the other things that'd been happening to him all week.

Daniel swung his feet to the floor. Even though he felt apprehensive about following the tracks, about seeing where they might lead, he also felt the need to do so. He'd been outside. Why?

If you were sleepwalking in the storm, the rain would have woken you up.

But it had not.

He couldn't remember anything about getting dressed, leaving his room, or returning to bed, and he had no idea how long he'd been lying there before he woke up a few moments ago.

Whether or not he'd been walking in his sleep, somehow he had been out in the rain, and there was no way he was going to be able to fall back asleep without knowing where he'd been.

He was already wet, so it only made sense to go back outside without changing clothes, but he didn't want to trudge more mud through the house, so he decided to put on the boots when he reached the front door.

Picking them up, he left his room and walked quietly down the hallway, following the muddy tracks.

If his dad came into the hallway, he had no idea how he would explain why he was soaking wet or why he'd left a trail of water and mud in the hall—or what he'd been doing outside in the first place.

At the end of the hallway, enough light from the neighborhood seeped through the living room windows and crawled down the hall to make the tracks on the wooden floor visible.

The wind battered the roof, and a thick drumbeat of thunder rattled the windows, but as far as Daniel could tell, his dad was still asleep in his bedroom.

Apart from the storm outside and the hum of the refrigerator in the kitchen, the house was silent.

Trying not to wake his father, Daniel crept as silently as he could down the hallway, especially as he passed his dad's bedroom door.

He'd never known him to be a light sleeper, but he heard the bed squeak softly as his father turned over in his sleep— either that or got up.

Daniel froze and listened for the bedsprings to creak again.

His heart pounded and squirmed like it had a life of its own.

He listened, waited for the door to open, for his father to appear, but nothing greeted him except an anxious, expectant silence.

The water dripping from his clothes pooled slowly around his feet.

It seemed like an eternity passed, but it was probably little more than a minute or two. When Daniel heard no more sounds coming from his dad's bedroom, he started down the hall again, following the muddy tracks and splats of water.

His eyes were becoming accustomed to the dark, so it was getting easier to distinguish where the hallway ended and merged with the kitchen on one side and the dining room on the other.

He'd thought the tracks might lead to the front door, but now he could see that they did not. Instead, they went toward the back door—the one that led to the deck overlooking the garden and the swath of woods that lay behind the house.

They disappeared outside.

When he opened the door to the night, a slash of lightning illuminated the yard and he noticed a shovel leaning against the side of the house. It was positioned beneath the overhanging gutter, which protected it from the driving rain.

The blade had clumps of fresh, wet soil stuck to it.

So, he'd either been digging something up.

Or burying something.

For some reason, probably because of the rain, the night held the damp, earthy smell of spring rather than autumn's odor of slowly decaying leaves—but that only seemed to add to the disorientation Daniel was feeling.

It was almost like he'd slipped out of his normal life and landed in a place where time was fluid and could wander back and forth, wavering its way through the seasons, taking him with it.

He tried once again to remember being out here earlier, hoping that he might be able to recall something—a wash of images, an impression, a fragment of a memory, anything that might give him a clue as to what was going on or why he'd left the house.

But it was no use; he wasn't able to remember anything.

The nearby streetlights cast a bleary glow over the neighborhood, but their light was dampened and obscured by the sheets of rain.

He was able to make out the faint outline of the woods looming before him, as well as the vague, dark forms of the neighbors' houses, but that was all. He doubted it would be enough light for him to find what he might have been digging up—or burying—out here in the dark.

Another flash of lightning ripped through the night.

The muddy boot prints ended at the edge of the deck.

The garden lay fifty feet ahead of him.

The forest rose just beyond that.

He didn't want to risk waking up his father by turning on the outdoor deck light.

Slipping back inside, he grabbed the flashlight he used when he went caving, a headlamp that he typically left stashed in a clutter drawer in the kitchen in case the electricity went out.

He returned to the deck, turned on the headlamp, laced up his boots, and drew the door softly closed behind him.

Then he grabbed the shovel and headed into the storm.

CHAPTER THIRTY-SIX

Fierce rain sliced through the night, and the wind beat against him like it was trying to drive him back into the house.

He directed the headlamp's beam at the ground in front of him, then used one hand to shield his eyes from the rain.

Even though he'd raked the leaves a couple days ago, the wind had brought a fresh layer of them down and they lay plastered against the grass. The sound of rain pat-splattering against them filled the night around him.

The storm had erased any evidence of boot impressions on the leaves.

Turning around, he saw no sign that anyone had been digging in the autumn-dead flower beds that lined the back of the house.

He aligned himself with the direction of the muddy prints that left the deck, tried to guess where he might have gone earlier when he ventured into the storm, and then angled his light toward the woods in a straight line from where the boot prints ended.

The garden lay between him and the woods. It was the one that his mom used to keep, the one that was overgrown now, the one that the footpath through the woods began at and—

No.

A thought came to him. One that he did not want to consider.

When his mom took off six months earlier, she'd left her puppy with his dad and him, and when Akira got out of the house and was hit by a car three months after that, Daniel and his father had buried her out here, about twenty feet past the garden, just off the trail through the forest.

The two of them had placed a large rock over the puppy's grave to mark the spot and to keep scavenging animals from digging up the corpse.

Daniel tipped the headlamp up and, at the edge of the light's beam, saw that the ground was disturbed where Akira had been buried. A mound of dirt lay beside a gaping hole. The stone had been moved aside and leaned against a tree near the pile of soil.

Someone had dug up Akira's grave.

He had.

From where he stood he couldn't see into the open grave.

Carrying the shovel, and peering uneasily through the headlamp's streak of rain-smeared light, Daniel approached the hole.

CHAPTER THIRTY-SEVEN

Empty.

So where was the carcass, or bones, or whatever would actually be left of her by now?

You must have put Akira's remains somewhere.

As that thought gripped him, the storm raged around him in the night.

He spent a few minutes studying the area, but found nothing—no bones, no desiccated corpse, no sign that there had ever been a dead puppy lying in this hole. He even explored along the trail that led through the woods, but didn't find any evidence of the dog's remains.

At last, convinced that there was nothing more out here to see, he refilled the hole with soil and patted it down as best he could with the shovel's blade, then scattered leaves across the area and rolled the rock back in place.

If someone knew what to look for and came to this exact spot, he might be able to tell that it had been dug up, but Daniel couldn't imagine any reason anyone would be coming out here to examine Akira's grave.

Where did you put the corpse, Daniel? What did you do with those bones?

The question felt like a solid weight crushing down on him.

Once again he tried to remember what had happened earlier in the night when he should have been asleep in his bed, but he came up blank.

After finishing disguising the hole, he returned to the house, wiped off the shovel, and put it away in the garage. He changed out of his clothes, then tossed them into the washing machine.

As silently as he could, he cleaned up the mud that lay smeared in the hallway, sopping up the water with rags and old towels.

As he did, he thought of the conversation he'd had with Kyle about going to take a look at Emily's grave.

A visit to a graveyard to look for clues.

Maybe that's what was on his mind, at least subconsciously.

Maybe that's why he'd done this tonight in his sleep.

A couple of times as he was cleaning up, he thought he might have awakened his father, but he never came out of his bedroom.

Finally, Daniel rinsed out the muddy towels and rags and tossed them into the washing machine with his clothes, figuring he could do the wash first thing in the morning, rather than now, when it would wake up his dad.

After stowing the headlamp, Daniel found his way to his bedroom, removed the sodden sheets from his bed, and dropped them into the washing machine as well.

Since his mattress was still wet, he left it uncovered so it could start to dry. Instead of sleeping on top of it, he spent the rest of the night on the floor in his sleeping bag, trying to grab as much sleep as he could.

It didn't go so well.

With Akira's missing remains on his mind, he kept waking up and fluctuating into and out of a tired, dream-encrusted haze until his alarm rang at seven thirty.

They were leaving for the doctor's office in Superior in thirty minutes.

Yawning, he got dressed. Even though he normally didn't drink coffee, some caffeine was probably in order or he couldn't see himself making it through the morning without crashing and burning.

He was about to punch the button on the washing machine when his father walked in on him. "You're getting an early start on that."

"I had some clothes I needed to throw in."

"They're not going to finish before we leave. We won't be able to dry them until we get back this afternoon. Why don't you just wait until then?"

The tension from last night's conversation in the garage hadn't disappeared yet, and everything both of them said was marked with a cool, objective distance.

"I already put the soap in. Might as well get it done now."

His dad mulled that over. Daniel had the sense that he was going to press things, but he changed the subject instead. "Did you get breakfast yet?"

"No. I'll be right in."

"Alright. Remember, we need to leave by eight if we're going to make the appointment."

"Yeah. I'll be ready."

His dad left for the kitchen, and Daniel leaned a hand against the washing machine and let out a long breath.

He had no idea what he would have said if his dad had looked into the machine and seen the muddy towels.

You dug up Akira.

You did it in your sleep.

Even though it was some weird type of sleepwalking and wasn't officially a hallucination, his research on their causes came to mind.

A brain tumor.

Some kind of head injury he wasn't aware of.

Or maybe, based on how he seemed to be losing touch with reality, schizophrenia.

Maybe he really was going crazy.

Honestly, the thought of going insane frightened him even more than the possibility of having a tumor growing in his brain.

Instead of digging up the grave, what if he'd walked into the middle of the road as a car was approaching? Or gotten into his own car and driven off the road into a ditch or off the embankment into Pine River?

He'd heard about people who'd actually killed family members in their sleep. What if he'd attacked his father?

No, this couldn't go on. The visions, the nightmares, the sleepwalking. He needed some answers before something serious happened.

Though he didn't like admitting it, the sooner he could get checked out to see what was wrong, the better.

After starting the wash, he grabbed some coffee and a bite to eat, packed his laptop so he could work on his U.S. History report in the car or while he was waiting to be seen at the doctor's office, and then he left the house with his dad.

And saw what he had done with Akira's corpse.

He'd left it on the hood of his dad's car.

CHAPTER
THIRTY-EIGHT

His father stared at the rain-soaked carcass of the dog, then gazed at his son.

"What do you know about this, Daniel?"

Why would you have left Akira's body there? What is wrong with you?

"I don't know why anyone would've done that." Daniel felt limp and somewhat dizzy, like he was standing on ground that was made of sand and he was slipping down into a world where he would no longer be able to tell what was real from what was not.

Languishing in a nightmare. Trapped forever in a dream.

The words came to him just as the phrases for his blog had come the other night when Kyle was over: *Dark birds that feed on the flesh of his dead dreams. Picking them clean until only the bones remain.*

Yes.

They are.

And they're ripping through the fabric of his sanity.

Of your sanity.

Thankfully, the corpse was old enough that the area didn't reek of rot and death, but there was a faint odor of decay, probably made more distinct by the damp morning air.

"How many people know where Akira was buried?" his dad asked.

"Just us and Kyle."

He threaded things together. "The laundry, huh? But why would you do this? What's going on with you?"

Daniel might have felt more reassured somehow if his dad had been angry, but he didn't sound mad at all. Just deeply worried.

"I don't know," Daniel said. "I don't remember anything."

"But it wasn't Kyle, was it?"

A long pause. "No."

Here it comes.

"Go on, get in the car."

His father went for a garbage bag and retrieved the shovel from the garage, then used it to carry the dog's remains to the backyard. When he returned he said simply, "We'll take care of it when we get back home."

"Honestly, Dad, I don't know what happened. I woke up wet. I must have sleepwalked."

"Alright." But from his tone it didn't sound like he thought things were alright. "A headache? Did you have one when you went to bed last night? Do you have one now?"

"No. Have I ever sleepwalked before? Maybe when I was little or something?"

"Only once."

"When was that?"

"When you were five. After your grandfather died. Your mother and I were in the living room and you walked past us on your way to the front door."

"Where was I going?"

"We asked you that. You said you were going to find him."

"To find who? Grandpa? But he was dead."

"Yes." He started the car. "He was."

The conversation pooled off into stillness like water trickling into a stagnant lake.

Then the two of them left for Superior to find out what was really wrong with Daniel.

CHAPTER
THIRTY-NINE

The morning was spent in a series of tests—an MRI, a CAT scan, and some other ones Daniel had never even heard of. It was nearly noon when the neurologist finally met up with him and his father to talk through the results.

She was a petite woman with stark brown eyes, wire-rimmed glasses, and short hair. She had a somewhat uneasy smile, probably from trying to put a positive spin on the bad news that she had to share all too often with her patients.

Daniel could see a storm of worry on his dad's face and it spoke volumes as to how much he really did care about him.

He guessed that his dad was probably thinking about more than just the two times in the last week that his son had blacked out. Undoubtedly, the incident with Akira's corpse was also on his mind.

The two of them took seats in the doctor's office on the pair of leather chairs facing the desk. Diplomas hung from the walls, and thick medical textbooks filled the shelves. The window behind the desk faced a small park that lay across the street where two little kids were playing with their mom in the sunlight.

The doctor sat facing them. "Well, from what I can see, we can rule out a tumor, and that's something we can be thankful for." She paused as if she were expecting them to agree, but they were quiet, attentive, waiting expectantly for her to tell them what was actually going on.

She took a little time to summarize the test results, then concluded by saying, "The truth is, I can't find anything physically wrong with you, Daniel. That's good news." The way she phrased that made Daniel think that maybe she was about to share some bad news.

Nothing physically wrong. So it must just be in your head, that's what she's saying.

And that was bad news in itself, because if there was no tumor, there weren't that many reasons left for why he was having hallucinations. Pretty much just one thing: schizophrenia.

"And so," Daniel's dad said, "where does that leave us?"

"Well, there's another doctor you might want to see. Actually, he's right there in Beldon." She sounded like she was trying a little too hard to sound nonchalant as she spoke.

"A second opinion?"

A slight pause. "In a sense. Yes."

Daniel had a feeling he knew what kind of doctor she was about to recommend.

"But you did the tests already," his dad said. "You said we can rule out a brain tumor. Are you saying you think we need another set of eyes to interpret the results?"

The silence that followed made Daniel uncomfortable, and

he expected that by now his dad must certainly have pieced together what was going on. Maybe he was just waiting for the doctor to spell it out to them.

At last she replied, "That's not exactly what I'm suggesting. I'm saying that physically there's nothing wrong with Daniel."

"Physically." The way he said that made it clear that he was thinking along the same lines as Daniel.

"Yes." She sounded like she definitely did not want to be having this conversation. Reaching into her pocket she produced a business card. "I've written his cell number on the back. He's experienced at this sort of thing."

"And what sort of thing is that?" His father's voice had become sharp.

"Um . . . Well, you told me what happened with the sleep-walking last night and—"

"What are you saying? A shrink? That my son needs to see a psychiatrist?"

"From what you've shared with me, Daniel has been under a lot of stress lately—the funeral of the girl from his school, the pressure of performing well at the football game in front of the college scouts—"

"It's not stress," Daniel told her. "That's not what's causing any of this." He didn't bring up the hallucinations. That definitely would not have helped matters.

Daniel's dad shook his head. "My son doesn't need to see a psychiatrist."

She was still holding the business card out for them. "There's no stigma to—"

"Thank you for your time." Daniel's father rose.

"He's very good," she assured them. "Meet with him once. If it doesn't go well, at least you gave it a shot."

"Thanks, but we'll be alright." He indicated for Daniel to follow him out of the office.

It looked like the doctor was about to pocket the card, but she extended it one more time. "If you change your mind."

Although Daniel had the sense that his father had no intention of calling the psychiatrist, in the end he accepted the card and stuffed it into his pocket.

Then, with what seemed like somewhat forced politeness, he thanked the doctor and led his son out of her office.

Daniel puzzled over why his dad was so set against him seeing a psychiatrist. He could think of only one reason: right before their separation, Daniel's parents had seen a counselor a few times and that hadn't turned out exceptionally well.

Psychologist, psychiatrist, it didn't really matter.

Either one is going to look for the same thing—something wrong with your head.

Something that's not just physically wrong.

Once they were outside, his father tossed the business card into a nearby trash can. "Let's get some lunch."

"Sure."

When they were in the car and on their way, Daniel said, "What are you going to tell Mom?"

"Exactly what that doctor said."

"And that is?"

"That there's nothing wrong with you."

Of course, that wasn't *exactly* what the doctor had said,

but Daniel had the sense that pointing that out would not be such a good idea.

"What are you hungry for?" his dad asked.

"Doesn't matter. Anything is fine."

"Subs, then. I saw a place on the way."

Apart from mentioning it to the doctor, they hadn't spoken at all about the incident involving the puppy's remains since they'd left home earlier that morning, and Daniel expected that at any time his dad would bring it up.

But he did not.

They were about fifteen minutes from Beldon when his father turned off the highway and steered the car onto one of the little-used county roads near the national forest and the trail leading to Wolf Cave.

"Where are we going?" Daniel asked.

"There's somewhere I'd like you to take me."

"Where's that?"

"I want you to show me exactly where you found those glasses on the beach at Lake Algonquin."

CHAPTER
FORTY

Daniel led his father along the trail that skirted around the lake and eventually they came to the stretch of beach where he'd brought Stacy.

The storm from the previous night had cleared out, and in contrast to Saturday, when it'd been cold, overcast, and rainy out here, today the sky was stark blue with only a few tendrils of sparse clouds dragged in thin lines along the horizon.

It looked more like a summer day than one in the heart of autumn.

Again, just like last night when it'd smelled springlike outside, the seasons seemed to be fluctuating in a random way around him.

"Right over here, Dad."

His father joined him at the spot where he'd found the glasses.

He was silent as he studied the area, and Daniel had the sense that he was looking for something specific, though what it might have been he couldn't say.

His dad kicked some sand aside, noted the position of the campfire pit and the distance to the trail that led up the bluff to the top of Windy Point.

As patiently as he could, Daniel waited for him to say something, and finally, when he didn't, Daniel asked, "What are you thinking?"

"You were right about the distance from the bluff and about the water not rising this high up the beach. You're sure you found them right here?"

"Positive."

He knelt and dug through the sand near the spot, most likely looking for the missing lens. A few minutes later, when he didn't find anything, he stood. "You told me you came out here for closure."

"Yes."

"Closure for what?"

"What do you mean?"

"I mean, what were you trying to settle in your mind? What were you hoping to find?"

"It was about Emily's death. I was trying to figure out a way to deal with it."

That was partly true.

It was also true that he was trying to deal with the fact that after Emily died she'd started appearing to him.

"And how would coming out here do that?" his dad asked. "Bring closure for you?"

Daniel struggled with deciding how much to tell him about what was happening. If he confessed what he'd been seeing, his dad would almost certainly think he was going nuts—especially after what had happened this morning with Akira.

He already knows something is up. I mean, you wander outside in the middle of a storm, dig up your mom's dead puppy and lay it on the hood of the car . . . Seriously? And then you have no memory of it ever happening?

His dad waited for him to answer.

"I've been seeing things."

"Things?"

"Emily. She appeared to me, twice. Asked me to find her glasses. Told me Trevor was in the car."

"Trevor?"

"Her dog."

Daniel expected his father to respond as Kyle had, with a comment about how Emily was dead and couldn't possibly be talking to him.

But instead he was silent.

He had to be thinking that something serious was wrong with his son. Something very serious. He had to be.

Now that Daniel had brought up the hallucinations, he thought he might as well just lay everything out there. "I saw her sit up in the casket when we were at the funeral, and I saw her walking across the football field in the homecoming game."

"And you thought that coming out here would make those visions stop?"

He studied his dad's face to try to discern what he was thinking.

"I didn't know," Daniel said. "I was hoping it would."

"You say she appeared to you before your concussion at the football game?"

"Yes. That's what made me hesitate. That's why I got hit in the first place."

There was a long pause.

"Do you think I'm going crazy?"

"No." But he hadn't answered immediately, and that made Daniel wonder how honest he was being.

"Are you thinking about that other doctor?" Daniel asked. "The psychiatrist?"

This time he did reply right away. "Regardless of what's going on here, we need to make these visions—or whatever they are—stop."

I agree.

"So you think I should see him?"

"I won't lie to you. After what happened last night I'm . . . Well, it can't hurt anything. Talking things through with someone."

"In Superior you didn't like the idea."

"In Superior I didn't know a dead girl was talking to you."

Daniel didn't bring up the mark that'd appeared on his arm. "Okay. I'll talk to him."

"I'll give him a call in the morning."

"You threw out the business card."

"I remember his name." He started down the trail. "Dr. Fromke."

"And his number?"

"And his number."

You have to be paying pretty close attention to memorize a phone number when you just glance at a business card. So, maybe his dad had considered having Daniel see the shrink back when they were leaving the doctor's office that morning after all.

Daniel was deep in thought all the way home.

When they arrived his father told him that he would take care of Akira, that he didn't need to worry about it.

Daniel wondered if he was burying the dog by himself so his son wouldn't know where the remains were and wouldn't be able to find them if he did happen to get up in the middle of the night again.

It seemed like the trust they'd established over the last few months was beginning to erode. And it was all because of things that were out of Daniel's control.

After supper he realized he still hadn't spoken with Kyle, Stacy, or Nicole, and he felt like he needed to touch base with all three of them.

He evaluated things.

Kyle. Nicole. Stacy.

He decided to try Nicole first.

CHAPTER FORTY-ONE

"Hello?" she said.

"Hey, it's Daniel."

"Hey. Where were you today?"

He'd informed her last night that he would be gone from school today, but hadn't told her where he was going to be. "I had a doctor's appointment."

"Everything okay?"

"Yeah. It's good. I'm good."

"I took down the assignments for you," Nicole told him. "I mean for the classes we have together."

"Thanks."

"Miss Flynn was asking about you. I thought that was a little odd, I mean, kids get sick or miss class all the time. But she asked me where you were."

"Huh."

Why did she ask Nicole? She knows you're best friends with Kyle. Why wouldn't she have asked him?

At last he got to the reason for his call. "I wanted to make sure we met up tomorrow so I can give you your earring."

"Oh. Sure, whenever, that'd be great." Then she said, "Daniel, I need to tell you something."

"Yeah?"

She took a deep breath. "So, about the other night. When you were taking me home. When I was in the car and Ty pulled out that knife and those guys were surrounding me, pounding on the windows . . . I was . . . Well, I was really scared."

"I can understand."

"Were you?"

"Yes."

"I couldn't tell."

"Sometimes I'm good at hiding things."

"Oh." She didn't seem to know what to make of that. "But also, you made me feel safe. I trusted you. I mean, when you were ready to fight off all four of 'em to protect me. It was pretty awesome."

"I wouldn't have let anything happen to you."

"I know."

And I won't let anything happen to you.

"Anyway, thanks."

"Of course."

"See you tomorrow."

"Meet you after fourth hour?"

"After fourth hour," Nicole said. "Perfect."

Next, Kyle.

Emily had written his name all over her notebook, and Daniel hadn't had a chance to talk to him about it yet. He'd been hoping to discuss it with him in person, but he didn't want to wait any longer, so he called his friend.

When Kyle picked up, they whipped through some filler talk, the kind of stuff that gives you the context for a conversation about the things that really matter:

"Why were you gone today?"

"I was at the doctor's."

"What for?"

"My head."

And so on.

Daniel concluded by sharing about his sleepwalking and what he'd done to Akira's body.

"Okay, I have to say, dude, that's very disturbing. You know that, right?"

"Here's the scariest thing: I did all that—put on my clothes, dug up the grave, moved Akira's body, then climbed back into bed—and I don't remember any of it. I was wondering if I did it because of what we'd talked about the other day when you mentioned visiting the graveyard."

"Yeah, I don't know. I guess that makes sense—I mean, if that's what was on your mind. Or maybe you dug up your mom's dog because you've been thinking of that other dog, Trevor."

Daniel hadn't considered that.

"Hey, listen," Kyle said, "when I was watching Michele yesterday I was thinking about what we were talking about— ghosts and everything. She has this imaginary pet kitten, Toni, that she talks to all the time and it got me wondering about stuff people see that isn't there, you know, what's real and what's not. I'm still not sure I believe in ghosts, but I went online yesterday and did some research. Have you ever heard of daymares?"

"Daymares?"

"They're like nightmares, only you have 'em during the day—obviously. They're like daydreams, only horrifying. Similar to nightmares, but you have them while you're awake."

"So, hallucinations?"

"I guess; I'm not sure what the difference is. I'm wondering if maybe that's what's going on with you."

"I'll read up on 'em. Tomorrow my dad's calling a shrink to see if we can figure out what's wrong."

"A shrink?"

"Yeah."

Ask him about Emily. Tell him about her notebook.

But Kyle spoke before Daniel could: "So you told your dad? About the visions and everything?"

"Well, finding Akira's body on the hood of the car was a pretty good indicator that whatever's going on with me is not good."

"And it sounds like it's getting worse."

"Thanks for that little reminder."

"Anytime, bro."

Daniel stared at the journal on the edge of the desk in front of him. "Remember how I wrote that blog entry for Teach on how my thoughts were wandering out of formation?"

"Yes."

"Another image came to me when we were driving home from the doctor's today."

"What's that?"

"Well, it's like flakes of paint breaking off when I rub my hand against what appears to be real, and I end up rubbing one layer of reality away."

"Did you just say 'flakes of pain'?"

"Paint."

"Gotcha."

Daniel thought back to the headaches he'd been having.

Flakes of pain.

That might not be such a bad description after all.

"You seem to be coming up with all sorts of wild images—flakes of reality rubbing off, vultures picking away at the corpse of your dreams. Where do you think all this is coming from?"

"I honestly don't know."

"It's like a part of your brain that's never really been active is waking up."

Maybe that's why you're seeing things, sleepwalking, all of that.

Maybe that has something to do with the headaches.

"That's possible."

But why?

And why now?

Kyle asked, "So how did the meeting with Ronnie go yesterday?"

"Okay. He told me Emily's cell phone was never found."

"By your tone of voice I can tell you're thinking that's suspicious."

"He said she normally carried it in her pocket, not her purse. I doubt the current would have been able to snatch a cell phone from her pocket."

And based on the location of the broken glasses, it doesn't look like she fell off the cliff anyway, he thought, but didn't bring that up.

"I wonder," Kyle reflected, "who the last person was who she talked to or texted?"

"No kidding. If she was killed, it might tell us who she was with out at the lake."

As the conversation paused, Daniel decided it was time to get to the reason he'd called.

"Kyle, did you know that Emily had a crush on you?"

"What are you talking about? Ronnie told you that?"

"No. I saw her notebook while I was at their house. She wrote your name over and over in it. Drew hearts next to it, you know, like girls do."

Silence. "I had no idea it was that serious."

"So you knew?"

"I mean, I'd heard she liked me, but I'm with Mia. Besides, Emily was a freshman and it wasn't like I would've asked her out."

Those were the same things Daniel had thought of earlier. "But you told me you didn't know her."

"Yeah, no, I mean, I said hi to her a few times in the hall. That's all. Her locker was just down from mine. I was just trying to be polite." He paused. "She must have gotten the wrong idea."

"She must have. I think Ty might have seen the notebook."

"That's why he brought it up with you on Saturday?"

"Yeah, and also why he said that he knew about you and Emily—back when we first met up with Ronnie when they were bullying him."

"So you really think someone might've killed Emily?"

"Yes."

Kyle reflected for a moment. "You think it might have been Ty?"

So far Daniel had simply been entertaining the possibility that Emily had been killed. He hadn't thought of anyone in particular doing it. "I don't know."

"It would explain how he knew what was in her notebook."

"There could be a lot of explanations for that."

"Maybe."

"My dad doesn't want me looking into her death anymore. He thinks I'm snooping around. He wants me to leave it all to him."

"So what did you tell him?"

"I promised I wouldn't keep investigating things."

"Aha. So no trip to the cemetery?"

"Well, we'll see. I've started seeing and doing really scary things—digging up Akira is just the latest one. I need to find some answers, and I need to find them fast before I go off the deep end and do something dangerous or that I would really regret."

"And you think solving this will do that?"

"I sure hope so."

"Well, I'll help in any way I can, but for now, if she really was murdered, it could have been just about anybody. I don't think you should trust—"

"Please don't tell me not to trust anyone," Daniel said.

"Why not?"

"In the movies, it's always the guy who warns the main character not to trust anyone who turns out betraying him in the end."

For a moment Kyle didn't reply. "Okay. The last thing I'd want is for you to get suspicious of me."

"Or you of me."

"I'll see you tomorrow, man."

"I'll see you then."

Flakes of pain.

Really, not such a bad image.

Daniel turned to the journal and wrote down the impressions about the flakes of reality, then went on:

> The boy was not always this way, not always slipping into grayland.
>
> He could remember the way it used to be. That was the hardest part—knowing that once he hadn't been losing his grip on reality. Back then he used to think he was normal, well, as normal as normal is.
>
> But now things were different. He'd moved from the world of ordinary to the fringes of insanity.
>
> All in a matter of days.

How much does it take to push you over the edge? There's always a tipping point, like with an avalanche—always that seemingly inconsequential matter of a few snowflakes that makes all the difference.

And then, once the avalanche starts, there's no holding it back.

Daniel couldn't help but wonder if one of these visions would do that, push him over the edge in a way that he wouldn't be able to recover from.

Once you slip into madness, can you ever climb out of it again?

Grayland.

Caught between black and white.

Between good and evil.

Now there was a scary thought.

He surfed the Web for info about daymares and nightmares and found that normal people typically have a few disturbing nightmares a year. Artistic and extraordinarily creative people—painters, sculptors, composers, novelists—might have several of them a month.

Schizophrenics might have several vivid, disturbing dreams every week.

Some while they're awake.

It seemed that the barrier between reality and fantasy was thicker for some people than for others. And for him, it was becoming thinner and thinner.

Or maybe it wasn't even there at all anymore.

With that on his mind, he went to take the garbage to the curb and found the front door locked and dead-bolted shut.

Dad did that to keep you in. So if you sleepwalk you won't get outside.

Of course, it would have been possible for someone who was sleepwalking to unlock a door just as easily as it might have been for him to open it. Still, as far as Daniel knew, his dad never dead-bolted that door, and the fact that he had done so tonight just confirmed how concerned he was.

Back inside the house, after taking care of the trash, Daniel tried texting Stacy.

No reply.

His mattress was still damp from last night, so he pulled out his sleeping bag again.

Before climbing in, he took a moment to slide his dresser in front of his door. He didn't know if it would help, but just in case he did try to leave during the night to look for Akira's corpse, it might slow him down.

CHAPTER
FORTY-TWO

No problems with sleepwalking last night.

Thankfully.

At school, Kyle asked him again to introduce him to Stacy, and Daniel promised that he would, even though it was going to be an awkward conversation because she'd stood him up on Saturday night.

"Remember how we were talking about visiting the cemetery?" Kyle asked.

"Yeah."

"I think we should go after your football practice this afternoon. I work for a few hours at Rizzo's after school, but I get off at six."

"In the middle of the supper rush?"

"He has someone else coming in."

"You really think we'll find something at the graveyard?"

Kyle shrugged. "Who knows. Maybe it'll bring you some of those answers you've been looking for."

Daniel remembered that St. Andrew's Cemetery was listed

in the bulletin from Emily's funeral as the place where they were going to hold the graveside service.

"And," Kyle suggested, "maybe it'll help you not to sleep-walk if you go out there. You know, if thinking about going to the graveyard caused you to do that the other night with Akira."

They agreed to meet at St. Andrew's at six thirty.

After third hour, Daniel checked his texts and saw one from his dad. He'd been able to set up an appointment with the psychiatrist next Wednesday at four o'clock. "I'll talk to your coach if you want me to, get you cleared to miss practice," he wrote.

Daniel had missed football practice last night, and the prospect of missing another one next week was not thrilling.

"What about tmrw?" he texted his dad back. "No school."

"Tried that. This is the earliest he can get you in."

"I'll tell Coach myself," Daniel typed.

He met up with Nicole after fourth hour and returned her earring. They spoke for a few moments about Saturday night. She thanked him for finding the earring, and after she left for class he checked his phone. Still no texts from Stacy. He hadn't seen her all day. Maybe she was sick. Or maybe she was purposely avoiding him.

He had the inclination to search the halls for her some more, but in the end he decided that he'd looked for her, texted her, called her enough. If she wanted to talk to him, she had his number. At this point it was up to her.

The rest of the afternoon and football practice went by in

a refreshingly normal way. It was good to have things not slide any further through the barrier between fantasy and reality.

After practice, Daniel told Coach Warner that he was going to miss practice next Wednesday because he had to see a doctor.

"You went to a doctor yesterday," Coach said ambiguously.

"This is . . ." Daniel didn't want to get into trying to explain why he had to see a shrink. "Well, it's sort of a follow-up."

"Anything I should be concerned about?"

"No. I'm good to play this week. Don't worry."

"Keep me posted."

"I will."

On the way to the graveyard to meet Kyle, he got a call from the Ohio State recruiter who'd been at the game Friday night. He asked Daniel how he was; he told him he was fine, thanked the guy for following up, and they set up a time next week to connect again.

The road leading into St. Andrew's Cemetery hadn't been maintained well and morphed from pavement to gravel almost as soon as it left the county highway and entered the cemetery grounds.

When he arrived, he saw Kyle waiting for him with both Nicole and Mia beside him.

CHAPTER
FORTY-THREE

When they greeted each other Daniel found out Kyle had asked Mia to come and she'd asked Nicole.

"Reminds me of girls always heading off to the bathroom together," Kyle observed. "I mean, can you imagine a guy being like, 'Dude, I gotta pee. Wanna come along?'"

"Ew, that would definitely be wrong," Mia agreed. "But it's a different deal for girls, right, Nicole?"

"Absolutely."

Still, it seemed a little uncharacteristic for Mia to have invited her, and Daniel figured it might've just been because he was going to be there.

All four of them had been at this cemetery before, for a school project back in eighth grade.

They'd had to do grave rubbings, holding a piece of paper against a gravestone and then using a charcoal pencil to rub against the paper to transfer the indentations of the dead person's name and their dates of birth and death onto it.

It was sort of a macabre assignment, and some of the kids really freaked out about it.

Daniel had rubbed the stone of someone who'd died in 1924. It was a baby boy who'd lived only seven days.

Emily Jackson had lived 5,250 days longer than that baby.

Now, counting back, Daniel realized he'd lived 6,103 days longer.

Numbers.

He just couldn't help but notice the numbers.

Yeah, Miss Flynn was right when she'd commented about Kyle's blog entry last week, the one about time sliding down the slopes of his days. "The sand tumbles down quickly for us all," she'd told the class.

Grain by grain.

Moment by moment.

Slipping away.

"Do you know where Emily's grave is?" Mia's question to the group drew Daniel out of his thoughts.

"No," Kyle answered. "I say we spread out to look for it. Pairs. Mia, you're with me."

"You good with that?" Daniel asked Nicole.

"Yeah. Sure."

"The grave will be fresh," Mia noted grimly. "It's just a week old."

The same as that baby's entire life.

Man, that was a lot to process.

The graveyard was sprawling and hilly, so Daniel figured it might take a little searching to find where Emily was buried. The pines that grew throughout the grounds were going to make it even harder to find the grave.

Twilight.

The sun was low and the shadows long.

Which seemed appropriate for being in a graveyard.

As they searched, Daniel got to talking with Nicole. He didn't tell her about the disturbing visions he'd been having, but he did share that he and Kyle were starting to have their suspicions that Emily had been killed. "Her brother, Ronnie, told us she knew how to swim."

"Before you drove up, Kyle said you two wanted to come out here to see what stuff might have been left on her grave," Nicole said quietly. "Maybe by someone who'd been with her when she died."

The way she phrased that struck him: *Been with her when she died.* Not, *Killed her.*

"Yes."

"That's sort of creepy."

"I'm with you there."

"You really think we'll find anything?"

Earlier, when Kyle had suggested coming here, the idea had made sense to Daniel, but now as he thought more about it, he wondered if the odds were really in their favor after all.

Probably not.

"I really don't know."

When he brought up Emily's notebook and confided in Nicole that Kyle's name had been written in the margins, she told him she'd heard that a freshman girl had a crush on Kyle, but hadn't known who it was. "Jessica Tray's sister saw Emily drawing hearts in her notebook one time. Must have been for him."

They walked over a small rise and found the grave.

Emily's name and the dates of her birth and death were on a temporary marker, as well as the inscription, "Born to Be Loved." They must have still been engraving the actual granite gravestone.

Seeing the grave, Daniel thought again of Ronnie's mom and how strangely she'd acted when he was at their house.

She gave birth to this girl.

And then had to bury her.

It was impossible to imagine how hard that must have been, and despite how tersely the woman had spoken to him, his heart went out to her.

Lying beside the grave marker were several bouquets of flowers, drooping and wind-whipped from the storms that had savaged the area over the last week.

The flowers made Daniel recall seeing the comments on Emily's Facebook page, and how he'd thought of that as the twenty-first-century way of remembering someone.

Apparently, both ways were still around.

And that was okay.

Somebody had stuck a small pinwheel in the ground, but it was motionless in the still dusk. Beside it were a few framed smiling photos of Emily with Mr. Ackerman's photography studio logo in the lower left-hand corner. They were in plastic bags to protect them from the weather, but Daniel saw the necklace draped around her neck in each of them. A couple of stuffed animals had been left by the gravestone and were damp and mud-splattered from the rain the other night.

For a moment neither he nor Nicole spoke. Finally, they called Kyle and Mia over to join them.

Together, the four of them stood mutely around Emily's grave.

"Hang on a minute," Mia said. "Those flowers—I saw some just like 'em over by this other grave."

She led them across the cemetery.

Lying on a grave near the road, resting tranquilly beside the gravestone, was a bouquet of flowers identical to one of those that was on Emily's grave.

The name on the gravestone: Grace McKinney.

Mr. McKinney the freshman math teacher's wife.

She'd died two summers ago.

The inscription read: "Beloved wife, taken too soon."

"That's a little bizarre, don't you think?" Mia said. "That these flowers are fresh, just like the ones on Emily's grave."

"I don't know," replied Kyle. "Mr. McKinney probably came out here to put flowers on Emily's grave and just brought some for his wife's grave as well. Or vice versa."

"Emily had him for a teacher," Daniel reminded them. "There's nothing too weird about him leaving flowers on her grave."

No one had brought up how Grace McKinney died, but now Daniel did. "She didn't just die. Remember? She drowned."

Nicole stared at the gravestone. "Yeah. In their swimming pool, wasn't it? Dove in, hit her head on the bottom?"

"Yes," Mia replied. "At least, that's what they said."

"You don't think . . . ?" Nicole began.

"I don't know."

Daniel led them back to Emily's grave, and Nicole and Mia

attempted to brush the mud off the stuffed animals that'd been left there.

"Should we say something?" Nicole cradled the teddy bear gently in her arms. "Maybe a prayer or a few words or . . . I don't know. It just seems like we should . . ."

Mia turned to Kyle. "You go."

He thought for a moment, then said softly, "When I walk in the ways of the night I breathe in gasps of ragged darkness; when I step into the melody of dawn the shadows begin to recede." He paused. "I hope you stepped into the melody of dawn, Emily. I really do."

Grain by grain.

Our moments pass away.

And then we do.

Nicole set down the teddy bear. "Wouldn't they have been able to find out if Emily fell off the cliff? I mean, you'd think she would have broken some bones when she hit the water or have a lot of internal injuries."

"I think we would've heard about it if she had any broken bones." Daniel recalled that his dad had told him they did an autopsy that hadn't turned up anything unusual. He chose not to mention the location of the broken glasses that indicated Emily had most likely not fallen off Windy Point.

Back at their cars, Kyle asked Daniel if he could talk with him for a minute, and the two of them stepped away so the girls wouldn't hear them.

CHAPTER
FORTY-FOUR

"I don't think it's like the doll," Kyle said.

"What's not like the doll?"

"What's going on here. I don't think it's like the doll in the window over in Minnesota. You know—from the story I told you about."

"I'm not sure I'm following you."

Kyle pulled out his phone. "I mean, about something happening and then a story coming along and finding it." He tapped the screen, brought up the calculator app.

"No, seriously, Kyle, not today. This isn't the time."

"No, I just wanted to remind you of what you can do."

"I know what I can do. Put it away."

He held up the phone just to show Daniel the screen. "Listen, your mind, it calculates stuff no one else can. It does it subconsciously, in ways even you can't figure out. Remember? Like me with music."

"Sure, but what does that have to do with what's going on here?"

"I think somehow you're threading clues together, things no one else is noticing, like with Trevor, going out to the lake, the necklace Emily wears in all those photos."

"But how?"

Kyle pocketed his phone. "You're seeing this stuff, I don't know, in the paper, from tweets, remembering it from when you saw her around school, I'm not really sure, but your brain is integrating it all." He tapped the side of his head. "You're solving things up here, but then you have these visions. The deal is we just need to decipher what your mind is trying to tell you."

"What about Akira? Why do you think I did that?"

"To get us out to the graveyard."

"But that was originally your idea."

"True," Kyle acknowledged. "But maybe somehow it jarred something in your head and you realized coming out here would help us. Or, like I said earlier, maybe it had something to do with thinking about Trevor."

"But why? And why would all this start now?"

Kyle shook his head. "To solve how Emily really died? I'm not sure. You said it felt like flakes of reality were falling away. What's it like when that happens? When you see these things?"

"Reality gets blurred. I can tell something's happening that shouldn't be, but everything else is the same. It looks completely real. Sounds real."

"And it feels real: like when your arm was burned."

"Right."

"So this is different from daymares or hallucinations. And I don't necessarily think it has to do with ghosts." Kyle thought for a moment. "Call 'em blurs—I mean when you see these things."

Even if they were some sort of hallucinations, Daniel was glad to refer to them as something else. "Blurs sounds good to me."

"I think we should look more into how Mrs. McKinney died."

"So do I," Daniel agreed. "As soon as we can."

"You mean tonight?"

"Why not? Meet at my house?"

Kyle considered that. "Let's cruise over to my place. That way your dad won't accidentally walk in on us and find you still looking into all this."

"Good point."

Since Daniel had told his father he wouldn't keep investigating things, he felt a small sting of guilt, but moving forward on this, finding out the truth of what had happened to Emily, seemed to trump everything else, even the promise he'd made.

Before leaving the graveyard they told Mia and Nicole what was going on and the girls asked to join them at Kyle's. "We're part of this now too," Mia reminded them firmly. "We need to find out answers just as much as you two do."

"Okay," Kyle said, "give me a chance to help tuck my little sister in—I need to tell her a bedtime story. Let's meet at my place in an hour."

CHAPTER
FORTY-FIVE

The walls of Kyle's attic bedroom were plastered with posters of his favorite bands. His electric guitar sat propped on its stand in the corner beside his impossibly cluttered desk.

Mia was already there when Daniel arrived, but Nicole was still taking care of a few things at her house.

"Well," Mia said. "What's the plan?"

All three of them had their laptops open.

Daniel got things started. "We need to find out whatever we can about Mrs. McKinney's death. Also, there are stories about other people drowning at Windy Point. I want to know if those are just the kinds of things kids say, or if there really have been other cases of people who've died out there."

"I'll search for stuff about Windy Point," Kyle offered.

"I'll take Mrs. McKinney," Mia said.

"Alright." Daniel contemplated things. "I'll look into Mr. McKinney's past, see what I can learn about him, if there's anything suspicious that pops up."

They worked in relative silence. After a little while Mia asked them to fill her in more on what was going on. "I mean, what's *really* going on. There's something you two aren't telling me."

"That's either presumptuous or perceptive," Kyle said.

"Perceptive. I'm a girl. Go on."

When she pressed them, Daniel finally ended up explaining about the hallucinations.

Mia took it all in. "Sort of like macropsia."

"What's that?"

"When I was doing research for my novel on inexplicable things people see, you know, for the ghost-sighting parts, I came across this really bizarre disorder: macropsia. Rather than seeing things as they really are, people who have it see certain objects as if they're enormous. A girl's brush might appear bigger than the girl. Or it might look like her doll is the size of a house, or her folded-up blanket is as big as a mountain. Micropsia is the opposite. You see stuff as way smaller than it is."

"How is that like what's happening with me?"

"Well, it's about perspective and differentiating between what your mind is telling you is real and what actually is real."

"So," Kyle said, "how do you tell if your eyes are playing tricks on you?"

"See, that's the thing. Our eyes don't play tricks on us; it's our mind that does. We see what our brains tell us to see, not what our eyes do. It's why optical illusions work. Your brain is trying to make sense of things, but ends up getting confused."

Yup.

That was a pretty good way of describing what was going

on: his brain was trying to make sense of things, but was getting confused. Very confused.

Nicole arrived, and since Daniel had just told Mia what was happening, he brought Nicole up to speed as well.

She listened in silence. It was hard to tell what she was thinking. "That's why you were asking me about ghosts and demons the other day?"

"Yes."

For a moment no one spoke.

"You know," Daniel said at last, "the flowers weren't the only thing on Emily's grave. There were stuffed animals, that pinwheel, and some photographs from Mr. Ackerman's studio. He's the guy who takes pictures at all our football games. You see him in the hall sometimes getting photos for the yearbook. He was set up to take portraits at the homecoming dance."

"Are you thinking what I think you're thinking?" Mia asked.

"I don't know. I saw him at the funeral. If we're going to look into Mr. McKinney, we should probably find out what we can about Mr. Ackerman too."

"I'll check the website for his studio," Nicole offered, "see if there are any pictures of Emily or Mrs. McKinney, anything like that."

They searched.

Time passed.

Mr. Ackerman?

Mr. McKinney?

Was it really possible that one of them might actually have killed Emily?

But what about Grace McKinney? Is her death connected to Emily's?

Too many questions, too few answers.

Finally, they gathered in a circle to share what they'd found out.

"Well," Mia said, "from what I can see online, Mrs. McKinney was swimming alone when she drowned. Her husband was downstairs doing some kind of woodworking project—at least, that's what he told the police. He said that, through the window, he saw her dive in and never come up. By the time he got out there it was too late to save her."

Nicole looked at her inquisitively. "Let's say he's lying. What possible motive could he have had? Was there some sort of life insurance policy or inheritance if she died?"

"It didn't say. It doesn't look like he was ever a suspect."

"But then what about Emily?" Kyle asked. "If he really did kill them both, he would've needed some other motive to drown a girl from his class, right?"

"I guess," Mia acknowledged. "Yeah, that makes sense."

"Motives are pretty much like eels," Daniel said, remembering something his dad had told him one time. "They're twisty and slippery and as soon as you think you have one in your hand, it slides away from you. Was it greed? Was it anger? Hate? You'll always come up short when you try to nail down the motives people have—and there are almost always more than one in there swimming around."

Kyle didn't come across any evidence that anyone else had died at Windy Point. As far as he could tell, the rumors and legends were just that—the kind of stories kids make up and that eventually end up with a life of their own, just like the stories about the doll in the window in Janesville, Minnesota.

"Okay." He turned to Daniel. "What do we know about Mr. McKinney?"

"Well, not much that's very helpful. From what I can see—his profiles on social media sites, that sort of thing—his hobbies are deer hunting, fishing, and caving, he likes country music and Jason Statham movies, and he moved to town three years ago. He's a member of Whitetails Unlimited, lists himself as not being in a relationship, no kids, graduated with honors from UW–Madison twelve years ago."

"So, nothing earth-shattering," Mia said.

"No."

With nothing more to share about Mr. McKinney, Daniel took the conversation in a different direction. "I still want to know how Ty found out what was in Emily's notebook."

"That's not that big of a mystery," Mia replied. "I think one of those guys who hangs out with him has a brother who's a freshman. Even if Emily wasn't popular, it would've been easy enough for him to overhear something."

Nicole reported on Mr. Ackerman—no pictures of Mrs. McKinney or Emily on his site. Nothing else really struck her as unusual there. No link between him and Mrs. McKinney, apart from having his home studio near their house.

When Nicole finished, they all processed things for a moment, then she noticed the time and told them she needed to be heading home.

"I'll walk you to your car," Daniel offered, and grabbed his windbreaker.

The night was chilly and brisk.

He offered his jacket to Nicole and she draped it over her shoulders. "Thanks."

"Sure."

"It must have been terrifying to see those things," she said. "Ghosts, whatever."

"Blurs."

"Blurs?"

"It's Kyle's term. Seems to fit. It's when the line between what's real and what couldn't possibly be real becomes fuzzy to me."

Or actually doesn't exist at all.

"Listen," she said, "remember when I said Jesus proved to his disciples that he wasn't a ghost? How he told them to touch him because ghosts don't have flesh and bones? That's what convinced them he was a real person after he rose. Touching him."

"But what if the ghost touches you? At the funeral Emily grabbed my arm. It left a mark. So, according to what you're saying, I shouldn't have felt that, right?"

And if they're just hallucinations, would you feel anything anyway?

Well, you felt her hand on your arm.

It was hard to know what to make of things.

"Hmm . . ." Nicole seemed to be thinking aloud. "I can't say I understand how it all works, but it's worth a try, isn't it? I mean, the next time you see Emily, reach out and try to touch her."

"You have no idea how unappealing that suggestion is."

"Now that I think about it, I see your point."

The night eased in around them.

He couldn't quite figure out how to say good-bye. A small hug might have been in order, but his nervousness around girls swept over him again, and instead of a hug he just laid his hand gently on her arm. "If someone really did kill Emily, we're going to find out who it was."

"Yeah."

Mia stepped out of the house. "Hey, you two."

He realized he still had his hand on Nicole's arm and lowered it again. "Hey."

Nicole took off the jacket and handed it back to him.

Daniel held back on the hug, they all said goodnight, and then he returned to Kyle's room to touch base before taking off.

CHAPTER FORTY-SIX

"Tomorrow is a parent-teacher conference day," Kyle said. "Is your dad taking you to meet with any teachers?"

"No. My grades are good enough."

"Me too. My mom's cool with how I'm doing. So, what are you up to?"

"Well, we still have football practice at three thirty, but that's it."

"Mr. McKinney will be at school before that." There was a hint of mischievousness in his voice.

"And?"

"And that means he won't be home."

"Obviously, so what are you . . . Oh, you're not suggesting that we—"

"Yeah. Go to his house, have a look around outside, you know, check out the pool where his wife drowned, see if we find anything."

"That was two years ago. I doubt that at this point we're going to find anything that would implicate him."

"But what about the basement window? We could check

the sight lines to make sure he wasn't lying about seeing her dive into the pool."

"What if the neighbors see us?"

"Maybe all we need to do is walk past his house. There's nothing illegal about that. Maybe from the way it's positioned, if the angle's right, we'll be able to see into the backyard from the road. He'll be at school anyway, meeting with parents. If he really did kill Emily—kill his wife too—we need to find out as much as we can about him before going to your dad."

Telling his father about what was going on made sense, but right now all they really had was conjecture. They certainly needed something more solid if they were going to go to the sheriff.

"I suppose walking by and having a peek at his place wouldn't hurt anything," Daniel said. "What time are you thinking?"

"Well, I have to work later in the afternoon and you need to be at school to change for football practice. What, a little after three?"

"Yeah."

"How about one o'clock?"

"That should work."

They found Mr. McKinney's address online.

"I know that neighborhood," Kyle said. "There's a strip of forest behind his house over near Mr. Ackerman's place— Mia's friend had her senior pictures taken there at his house. We could just slip through the woods, have a look around, and be gone. In and out. Fast and clean."

"Fast and clean?"

"I read it in a book somewhere. Something this one FBI agent likes to say. So, what do you think?"

"Yeah, the woods sounds better than walking by the house. Besides, there might be a fence around the pool and we wouldn't be able to see it from the street out front."

"Alright."

"And there's a road on the other side of that forest?"

"Yeah."

"We can leave our cars there," Daniel said.

"Sweet."

This was probably not a good idea in any way, shape, or form, but as Daniel drove home, he figured that just walking through the woods and having a look around wasn't that big of a deal.

Especially if this guy really had killed two people.

CHAPTER
FORTY-SEVEN

All the lights in the house were off when Daniel got home. He figured his dad had already gone to bed, so he was careful to be quiet as he went to his bedroom.

He was about to change for bed when he heard a light rap on the window.

Then again.

Someone tapping on the glass.

The only person he could think of who might be there was Kyle, but that would be strange; he would have texted first.

And would he really have gotten here so fast?

Could it be Emily?

Another blur?

He wasn't too excited about the idea of pulling back the curtains, but he knew he needed to see who—or what—was on the other side.

On his way to check it out, he heard it a third time.

Apprehensively, Daniel drew back the shades and saw Stacy Clern on the other side of the glass.

He slid the window open.

"Sorry if I startled you," she said.

"What are you doing here?"

He was surprised to see her—yes, he was—but she did have a history of showing up at his house late and unannounced, so he wasn't completely shocked.

"I need to talk to you. Can I come in?"

His first impulse was to tell her no.

"What is it?"

"I don't really want to talk through the window." Her voice was hushed. She gestured toward the windowsill. "May I?"

He didn't like the idea of letting her in, but this chatting-through-the-open-window thing wasn't ideal, and the living room wasn't great either, since they might easily wake up his dad.

He slid the window all the way open. She waved off his help and climbed through on her own.

"I like your room."

"Thank you. So, what is it? What's so important that you came over here at this time of night?"

"I wasn't sure what else to do, since you seem to be avoiding me at school."

"What are you talking about? I haven't been avoiding you."

"I thought maybe it was about the dance."

"No, I'm . . . The dance?"

"I thought you were gonna call me Saturday. When we were at the lake you told me you were going to call me in the afternoon."

"I tried to. I texted you a bunch of times. You never returned any of my messages."

"You did?" She looked confused. "I didn't get 'em."

"None of them?"

"Uh-uh."

He took out his phone and verified that he had the right number.

"Yeah, that's it," she told him. "I don't understand. That's so weird."

"Are you getting other people's messages?"

"Yeah. Maybe it's something with the phone company."

"Let's try one right now."

"My phone's at home. Send me a text. I'll check it when I get there."

He did.

Honestly, being in his bedroom alone with Stacy felt a little uncomfortable, especially since it seemed like things were sort of moving forward with Nicole: friends, sure, but it felt like they were edging closer to something more than just a casual friendship.

"I've been thinking a lot about the glasses," Stacy said. "Did your dad find out anything?"

"Not that I've heard. No."

"Did you think of checking when Emily went to the lake? Maybe we can find out who else was there at the same time."

"My dad doesn't want me looking into things anymore," he told her truthfully.

"Oh." A pause. "So how are you? I heard you were at the doctor's yesterday."

Man, word got around.

"Everything alright?" she asked.

"Yeah."

Actually, I'm not sure. I've been having these blurs.

"What was the appointment for? Because of the game? Because of your head?"

"Sort of."

"Sort of?"

He weighed how to respond, how much he should share with her. "Some stuff has been happening."

She gazed at him with concern. "Are you alright, Daniel? I mean really alright? It seems like something's . . . well . . . What's going on?"

He didn't want to tell her about the blurs, per se, but he decided to fill her in a little bit on what was happening, at least indirectly why he'd needed to see the doctor yesterday.

"It's the way I see things."

"The way you see things?"

"What's real and what isn't."

"What do you mean?"

Trying to think of how to explain things, he gazed around the room and finally had an idea. Daniel held up a blanket so that it hung vertically above his bed. Stacy stood beside his desk, her back to the wall. He noticed that she was tapping her fingers nervously against her leg.

"Alright," he said. "Imagine that everything on your side of the blanket is reality. Those are the things you can see, taste, feel, whatever. The things that are really there. Everything on my side of the blanket is . . ."

"Just imaginary." She finished his thought for him. "All in your head."

"Right. Now, from what I've found out in the last week, most people have a pretty thick blanket—barrier—that's in their minds that helps them know which side they're on."

She was watching him carefully; if he didn't know better, he'd say warily.

"So we can tell what's real and what's not," she said.

"Exactly. But now imagine that the blanket is a shower curtain or something and you can see through it, but everything on the other side is blurry. So you'd know the other side is there—"

"But you'd be able to tell which side was which." Stacy sounded slightly relieved. "You'd see the difference."

"Yes."

"And that's you?"

A pause. "No. Not quite." He dropped the blanket. "It's gone."

"The blanket is?"

"Yes."

"Completely?" She'd moved almost imperceptibly farther from Daniel.

He nodded. A moment passed.

Stretched thin.

"Does that scare you?" he asked her.

She didn't answer but said instead, "But can you tell this is real? That I'm really here, in front of you, right now?"

"Yes," he said.

But he wasn't sure. He wasn't sure about anything.

Not since realizing he was going insane—at least, that was the only explanation he could think of, since according to the neurologist there was nothing physically wrong with his brain.

But he wasn't about to get into all that with Stacy tonight.

"Maybe I should be going." She seemed to have suddenly become uneasy being here with him.

"Don't worry, it's just . . . I guess I'm trying to sort a lot of things out right now."

"Yeah." She edged closer to the window.

He offered to help her climb out, but she looked at him strangely and told him that no, she was fine and that she would see him tomorrow, and then she was gone, leaving Daniel to evaluate whether he should've told her what he had, and what the next step needed to be in unraveling what was going on.

The stuffed animals and flowers at the graveyard, the broken glasses, the necklace, the clues that pointed toward Mr. McKinney—all of it intrigued and confounded him.

Maybe you do need to try to find out who might've been at the lake the day Emily disappeared, like Stacy suggested.

How?

He didn't know.

Once again he heard, from somewhere inside of him, *Stay on this. Seek the truth. Learn what happened.*

Yes.

Tomorrow.

Visit Mr. McKinney's house.

He and Kyle would seek the truth, learn what they could, and then slip away before anyone knew they were there.

CHAPTER
FORTY-EIGHT

Even though there was no school today, Daniel woke up at his normal time and was frustrated he hadn't been able to catch up on any sleep.

Maybe his sleeplessness was causing all this.

Blurs.

Daymares.

Trapped forever in a dream.

He made it to the kitchen just as his dad was getting ready to leave for work.

"Are you gonna be able to take a day off this week?" Daniel asked him.

"Hopefully tomorrow morning, at least. Hey, I thought I heard you talking with someone in your bedroom last night. Was Kyle over?"

"No, I was . . ." He almost lied, almost said that there was a speech he was supposed to give at school, that he was practicing, but this time he gave his dad the truth instead. "It was Stacy. The girl I told you about the other day."

"In your room? At that hour?"

"It's not like that. We were just talking."

"I don't like you having girls over late. You know that. Not alone in your bedroom."

"Yeah, I know. Sorry. It just sort of . . . Well, it came up out of nowhere."

"So when do I get to meet her?"

Daniel realized that the last his dad had heard, Stacy was supposed to be going to the homecoming dance with him but had never shown. "Um . . . I'll introduce you. The next time she's around."

"But not at that time of night."

"Right."

"By the way, the FBI e-mailed me early this morning. The only prints on those glasses were some partials they couldn't identify, and yours."

"From when I picked them up."

"Right."

"So how did they have my prints on file?"

"I did. From that criminology project you guys did last year for your political science class. I included them when I sent the glasses down."

"Oh."

Another dead end.

Since Daniel had missed school on Monday, his homework had piled up, and he spent the morning finishing some of it for tomorrow so he'd be free this afternoon for his trip to Mr. McKinney's house with Kyle.

He'd gotten his assignments from Nicole and now read the two chapters Miss Flynn had assigned for Friday.

Poetry.

Honestly, Daniel didn't even get what some of the poems were about. However, rather than analyze them, Miss Flynn usually chose to just let the poems speak for themselves and didn't offer analytical explanations like other teachers seemed to be into doing. So at least he wouldn't be expected to dissect them.

Considering what he'd been going through lately, however, one of them really struck him.

> There is a moment beyond this moment
> I finger it, fragile and delicate and hopeful,
> torn sweetly from the fabric of
> the robe of time. I touch it, glancing
> my fingertips across its promises.
> And something stirs deep within me
>   wondering,
>   buoyant,
>   and wild.
>   *Could it be that*
>   *everything really matters?*
> The wind tastes like
> spring-flavored freedom
> this time of year.
>   —Alexi Marënchivek

When he read it, he didn't try to take it apart word by word, but rather tried to "drink in its essence," as Miss Flynn put it. "Stop trying to understand poems," she'd told them one time in class, "and try to understand yourself better after reading them."

Well, he understood one thing: he hadn't tasted spring-flavored freedom in a long time, at least not since hearing about Emily's death.

Afternoon came quickly, and at one o'clock he met up with Kyle on the street that ran along the far side of the woods that lay behind Mr. McKinney's house.

"Are you sure you want to do this?" Kyle asked.

"Not really. But I want some answers. And if we can find out anything while he's gone, we can tell my dad and have him look into things. But I think we need to confirm that Mr. McKinney isn't home before we do anything."

"I'm not exactly sure how we can do that without knocking on his door, and that might be a little counterproductive."

"How about this," Daniel offered. "We call school, ask if he's there, say we need to change a parent appointment with him this afternoon, something like that."

"Cool." Kyle drew out his cell and without hesitation found the number and phoned the school's office. "Hello?" He tried to disguise his voice but sounded more like he had something stuck in his throat than like someone's dad. "Is Mr. McKinney there? I need to reschedule a meeting about my son later this afternoon."

He waited for a reply, then said, "Wait, that's our baby crying. I'll call you back. Thanks."

He hung up.

"He's there."

"Alright," Daniel said. "Let's go."

CHAPTER
FORTY-NINE

As they made their way through the woods toward the house, Daniel said, "Stacy stopped by my house last night after I got home."

"Really. Stacy showing up in the middle of the night at your place. What a shocker that is."

"She came by to ask me about the glasses."

Daniel hadn't intended to say that. It just came out, and only when Kyle asked him what glasses he was referring to did he realize what he'd said.

He took a deep breath and explained everything about the broken glasses he'd found on the beach, about the missing lens, about how the FBI had looked them over for fingerprints and had only been able to identify his.

"Why didn't you tell me any of this earlier?"

"I guess it was at least one promise I made to my dad that I was trying to keep."

"Well, it makes her death even more suspicious."

"I know. Anyway, like I was saying, Stacy asked me about 'em. Apparently she thought I was avoiding her, since she didn't get any of my messages Saturday—you know, when I was trying to contact her about the dance. I guess something's going on with her account or the phone company or something."

When he said that, he realized he still hadn't heard back after texting her last night, so maybe she hadn't gotten that one either.

Daniel went on, "She suggested we try to find out who else was at the lake when Emily went out there."

"Makes sense. But how?"

"Ask around, I guess. I'm not sure."

"Well, what are you thinking about her?"

"Stacy?"

"Yeah."

"What do you mean?"

"I mean, do you still want to go out with her?"

"As opposed to Nicole?"

"Pretty much."

They were almost to the other end of the forest, and Daniel could see the back of Mr. McKinney's house. It looked like there was a wooden fence maybe four feet high surrounding his pool.

"I don't know. I'm not really sure. I thought Stacy was blowing me off, but now I find out she wasn't. With everything else going on, it's actually a hard week to sort things out."

"I hear that."

After scanning the area to make sure no one was around, they stepped onto Mr. McKinney's property, approached the pool, and saw that it was empty.

It was apparently drained for the winter and gaped before them like a giant mouth, open and hungry and waiting. No diving board. A mildewed waterline ran around its inner edge.

Looking at the house, Daniel saw that one of the basement windows did face this direction, so it was possible that Mr. McKinney had been telling the truth. However, with the fence encircling the pool it didn't look like the angle was right for him to have seen his wife dive in.

Kyle must have been thinking the same thing. "Maybe he put up the fence after she drowned?"

"Maybe."

Daniel imagined the pool filled with water and what Mrs. McKinney's body might have looked like lying at the bottom. For a moment the image became terrifyingly real—not quite as distinct as the blurs when he'd seen Emily, but the water, the body, even summer sweeping across the forest all appeared before him and—

"You okay, dude?"

He looked away from the pool. "What?"

"You. Are you okay? I was asking you about the cellar."

"The cellar?"

Kyle pointed to an outside entrance to the basement, one of those angled sets of double wooden doors that opens outward so you can access a set of basement stairs. A padlock was threaded through the hasp, but it hadn't been snapped shut.

"What exactly were you asking me?" Daniel said, but he thought he already knew.

"What do you say? Just have a peek?"

"Inside?"

"To check the angle, you know, from the basement window to the pool."

Daniel and Kyle stared at the cellar doors for a long time.

Mr. McKinney's wife was dead.

Emily was dead.

But there was no proof either had been murdered.

Maybe he has something noting that he was out at the lake; maybe he had a fishing trip or something on the day Emily died. That might be enough for your dad to start looking into this.

"He's at school. We could slip in," Kyle said. "He'll never know."

You looked around Emily's room. This isn't any different.

Yes, actually it is.

Sneaking into a guy's house was a lot more than just opening the wrong door on your way to the bathroom.

"There's not nearly enough evidence pointing to him yet." Kyle was eyeing the open padlock. "There's no way your dad could get in there, get a search warrant, whatever. We're here, Mr. McKinney isn't. This is our chance to get some answers."

Daniel scanned the neighborhood. It looked like only a couple homes had a view of the back of Mr. McKinney's house, but no one was outside. The shades appeared to be drawn.

The only way to stop these blurs is to figure out what's going on.

And the only way to do that is to eliminate Mr. McKinney as a suspect.

This might be their only chance to do that.

They approached the house and Daniel slipped the padlock out of the hasp.

He flipped the doors open and started down the steps into Mr. McKinney's basement.

CHAPTER FIFTY

The cellar air was musty and damp and smelled faintly of rotten fruit.

Kyle tipped the doors shut behind them.

A thin slit of sunlight managed to leak through the space between the doors. That, along with two small grimy windows on opposite sides of the cellar, gave them enough light to see.

They descended the stairs.

The concrete blocks forming the walls were crumbling in places, leaving bare dirt poking through and sliding into small mounds on the floor.

An old wooden shelf holding jars of preserves and pickled fruit lined one wall.

A thick layer of dust had settled across them, and they must have been sitting there for a really long time, because the metal screw tops on most of them were rusted or covered with some kind of corrosion.

A water heater sat at the far end of the cellar, a workbench beside it. Above the bench, there was a pegboard holding an array of hand tools: screwdrivers, pliers, hammers, and so on. Some of them appeared old-fashioned, maybe decades old.

"That window is just off to the side," Kyle noted.

"Yeah."

They walked over to look at the pool.

Yes, the fence was visible, but seeing someone dive in the pool? That might have been a stretch.

Half-finished woodworking projects lay strewn across the workbench. A pile of sawdust nearly a foot high had formed beneath a vise that was attached to the bench and must have been used to hold the boards Mr. McKinney cut through with the handsaw he'd stowed nearby.

Scattered throughout the cellar were pieces of discarded furniture, cardboard boxes stacked in piles five or six feet high, shelves with dusty books covered in mildew.

A small potbellied stove squatted near the wall closest to the stairs.

Daniel recognized caving equipment—ropes, knee pads, a helmet, headlamps, a first-aid kit—on one of the shelves. Two tackle boxes and a few fishing rods lay beside it.

He listened carefully for any movement above him in the house, but heard nothing. However, he did hear one thing in the cellar: a faint scratching sound near the shelf containing the preserves.

When he took a step closer to investigate, a rat scurried out, skittered along the wall, and disappeared into a jagged hole in a concrete block.

Then all was silent.

Daniel wasn't about to go through all the boxes piled on the floor, but he did walk the perimeter of the basement to search the shelves for disturbed dust or any items that might be there that shouldn't have been—specifically grim mementos a killer might keep, like a girl's clothing or jewelry. He found nothing.

Go upstairs. See if there are any clues about his schedule.

No!

Yes. You're already in his house. What's the difference? You're here. Take advantage of it. Learn what you can.

Maybe he was ready to go up there.

Maybe he wasn't.

In either case, he wanted to make sure no one had arrived or was on their way in.

The window they'd already checked out was located at the back of the house. The other one was across the basement, high on the wall. It would make sense that he should be able to get a view of the front yard and the driveway if he could just get up close enough to see out of it.

Daniel positioned a wooden crate beneath the narrow, filthy window and stepped onto it.

He brushed away some of the cobwebs that laced his side of the glass and peered outside.

Though he couldn't see much, he was able to make out the empty gravel driveway.

"Let's take a quick look upstairs and then get out of here," he said.

"Right on."

Daniel replaced the crate where it'd been and they crossed the cellar to the wooden steps that ascended to the main part of the house.

Then he and his friend started up toward the lip of light that eased beneath the door at the top of the stairs.

CHAPTER FIFTY-ONE

Even though Daniel was confident the place was empty, he took it slowly and made as little sound as possible, just a natural response from being in someone else's home like this.

The sixth step from the bottom creaked as he put pressure on it.

When he reached the top step, he felt a flicker of uneasiness as he turned the knob and pressed the door open.

The kitchen.

Dishes in the sink, a table with four chairs, cupboards that were all closed. The lights were off, but the window above the sink let in the afternoon sunlight.

The refrigerator door had an array of magnets posting a shopping list and a variety of photos, to-do lists, comic strips, and reminders.

In the brief span of a moment, he counted twenty-eight magnets holding up nineteen objects.

He checked for any to-do list items that mentioned fishing on the day Emily disappeared, but found none.

The stove had a frying pan on one of its burners, a kettle on another.

They closed the door to the basement. Daniel didn't notice anything out of the ordinary. He tried the door near the refrigerator and found that it opened to the empty garage.

Kyle scrutinized the pictures and notes on the fridge.

"See anything?" Daniel asked.

"Nothing incriminating. Not yet."

The living room looked typical as well. All was quiet. All normal.

A clock on the wall ticked away the seconds. It was one of those sounds that someone living in the house would probably get used to, but to Daniel it seemed magnified a hundredfold.

It was sort of like the rattle of the train that passed through town—he'd gotten so used to it that he didn't even notice when it happened—unless someone actually pointed it out.

But if you were new to the area, you would hear it.

Tick.

He looked down the hallway, at the photos that lined the wall.

Tock.

Starting down the hall, he studied the pictures.

There was a wedding photo as well as one of Mrs. McKinney standing next to her husband on a mountainside. Beside it were two pictures of underground caverns. From the times Daniel had been in Wolf Cave with his dad, he recognized them as two of its main chambers. In one of the cave photos, the math teacher was with the school photographer.

The final picture showed Mr. McKinney and Daniel's offensive coordinator, Coach Jostens, beside a lake holding up a muskie that one of them must have caught.

So, they were friends.

Daniel hadn't known that.

As he looked around, his heart seemed to find a new rhythm, pumping in sync with the clock on the wall.

Tick . . . Tock . . . Tick . . . Tock . . .

The doorway to the bathroom at the end of the hallway was partway open. The door beside it—

Tick.

Was probably the master bedroom—

Tock.

As he waited for Kyle, he swung through the master bedroom and looked around. When Kyle arrived, Daniel went into the room across the hall while his friend headed toward the bedroom closet.

In Mr. McKinney's home office, Daniel found three shelves of books in a semicircle around a handmade wooden computer desk with an older-model laptop and a printer. A swiveling office chair faced it. A wastebasket half-full of crumpled papers sat beside it.

A dozen high school yearbooks were stacked on one of the shelves—the last three from Beldon High. The others were from Roosevelt High and Coulee High, both schools in their conference. Mr. McKinney must have taught at Coulee first before spending one year at Roosevelt and then moving to Beldon. A photo of a math club with the emblem of a coiled snake and the name of the team "The Adders," from the year he was at Roosevelt High sat on the desk.

A gun rack held a shotgun and two hunting rifles.

There were no calendars with clues about being at Lake Algonquin. After a brief internal debate, Daniel sorted through the balled-up papers in the wastebasket, but found nothing.

Unlike Emily Jackson's bedroom, the office didn't look overly neat.

Just normal.

Everything seemed utterly, remarkably normal.

"Hey," Kyle called from the bedroom. "Come here. I found something."

When Daniel joined his friend, he saw that the closet door was open and Kyle was kneeling on the floor beside a shoebox.

The lid was off.

The box was empty, but there were three cell phones on the carpet.

The pink casing on one of them and stickers and accessories on the other two made it clear that they were not the phones of a grown man.

CHAPTER FIFTY-TWO

Daniel crouched beside his friend. "This is not good."

"Yeah, why does a guy who doesn't have any kids have three girls' phones hidden in his closet?"

"In this case, I can only think of one reason."

"Me too. We need to tell your dad."

"Tell him what? That we broke into Mr. McKinney's house and found three phones in his bedroom? How is that gonna fly? It's not a crime to keep old phones in your house."

"Depends on whose they are."

Daniel realized the phones were on the floor. "Wait. Did you dump them out or did you touch them?"

Kyle bit his lip. "Dude, I wasn't thinking. I just . . ." His tone became intense. "They'll have my prints on 'em now, won't they?"

"Maybe, yeah, I don't know. Depends." To put it mildly, it was not a good thing that Kyle had touched those phones. "Did you try turning them on to see whose they are?"

"No."

Daniel tucked his hand beneath the corner of his shirt and used that so he wouldn't have to actually touch any of the phones.

He depressed the "on" button on each of them and waited.

Either the batteries were dead or they'd been removed, because none of the phones booted up.

"Makes sense," Kyle said. "I heard they can track phones, even if they're turned off."

Still avoiding touching them directly, Daniel laid the cell phones in the shoebox and processed everything.

Even though he and Kyle were in Mr. McKinney's house, if the phones had Kyle's prints on them, it could implicate him. Wiping the phones off might remove his prints, but it would also remove Mr. McKinney's if they were there—which they probably were.

A lawyer could argue that Kyle put them here, that he planted them.

"Should I point out the elephant in the room?" Kyle said.

"There are three phones."

"Which means three girls . . ."

"Yeah." Daniel eyed the closet. "Was there anything else in there that—"

But before he could finish his thought, he heard the crunch of gravel outside from the driveway, and the simultaneous rattle of the garage door.

Mr. McKinney had come home.

CHAPTER
FIFTY-THREE

"We can get back out through the cellar," Daniel said. "Let's go."

Kyle disappeared into the closet with the shoebox and when he reemerged they hustled down the hallway.

By the time they were halfway to the kitchen, the garage door was beginning to close.

No, no, no!

"Hurry," Daniel whispered urgently

They rushed across the kitchen to the cellar door. Kyle swung it open. As they stepped through, a car door slammed in the garage.

Silently, Daniel closed the basement door behind him and they started down the stairs, walking as softly as they could.

He heard the door leading from the garage to the kitchen bang open. "Hello?" Mr. McKinney called into the empty house.

How does he know someone is here?

Somebody saw you come in and called him!

Daniel counted the steps. *The sixth one from the bottom creaks!*

Kyle was in front and Daniel laid his hand on his friend's shoulder to stop him, but it was too late. He put pressure on the step and it made the same squeaking sound it'd made earlier when the two of them were going up the stairs.

Daniel's heart nearly stopped beating.

He and Kyle froze.

Footsteps began to cross the kitchen.

"Go." Daniel did his best to keep his voice low.

The boys scrambled down the rest of the stairs and shot across the basement. They raced up the steps that led outside.

"Is anybody down there?" Mr. McKinney said loudly.

Kyle pressed the cellar doors open, they exited, and Daniel was closing them behind him when he heard the kitchen door to the basement opening up.

Hoping that Mr. McKinney hadn't seen any light slip down the cellar steps, they bolted across the yard to the woods and dove behind a couple large oak trees to catch their breath and make sure the coast was clear before moving on through the forest.

Breathe, breathe, breathe.

Daniel felt the chug of adrenaline, just like he did during games. His heart churned, thrummed in his chest.

You need to see if he's coming.

No. Wait here. Don't move—

But he might come across the lawn. You have to look. You have to find out if he's following you.

Daniel finally decided he needed to check before moving any farther into the woods.

Slowly, he edged over to peer around the tree.

Mr. McKinney was standing near the cellar doors, staring directly toward him through the forest.

Daniel whipped back behind the tree.

No, no, no!

He saw you, he did, he saw you!

No, there are too many shadows here in the woods, he couldn't have.

No, he did!

He looked in Kyle's direction, then patted one hand against the air and put a finger to his lips with the other to signal for him to be still and not make a sound.

Daniel strained to listen for any movement coming his way and heard soft stirrings in the brush piles and leaves, but no sound of anyone running toward him across the lawn.

No one called out.

He sat there for what seemed like forever. Kyle waited too. Neither boy moved an inch.

Daniel didn't want to peek at the house again, but he knew that before escaping through the woods they needed to make sure Mr. McKinney wasn't still watching or on his way toward them. Taking a deep breath, he carefully tipped his gaze around the side of the tree.

This time the yard was empty.

Mr. McKinney had gone back into the house.

To call the police?

To get his shotgun?

"We need to get out of here," Daniel told his friend, but Kyle was already moving and didn't need any convincing.

They hurried through the woods, neither of them speaking, and emerged from the trees near their cars.

Looking back, Daniel confirmed that no one had followed them. No cars were on their way down the street. No police sirens cut through the afternoon.

"One of the neighbors must have seen us and called him," Daniel said.

"That or he finished up early at school. It's not far from here; maybe he got suspicious when I phoned the school to talk about rescheduling." Kyle thought about that. "I said I needed to do it for my son. What if Mr. McKinney only had girls scheduled for the rest of the day?"

"I don't think that would be enough."

"Whatever it was, he suspected something—he called out to see if anyone was in his house as soon as he entered."

Daniel decided to bring up what he'd discovered. "When we were in there I saw a bunch of high school yearbooks on the shelf in his office. They were from a couple of different schools in our conference."

He listed them off, the schools and the academic years of the yearbooks. "I say we go online, search to see if any other girls might have disappeared or drowned while Mr. McKinney was teaching at their schools."

"Nice."

"I know we don't have a lot to go on, but maybe I should tell my dad, or at least we could call in an anonymous tip. I mean, if Mr. McKinney does think someone was in his house just now he might get rid of the phones." Daniel could tell something was really bothering his friend. "What's wrong?"

"You can't call your dad."

"Why not?"

"You're not going to like this."

"Like what?" He began to imagine the worst—that Kyle had left his car keys in the house or something like that—but he never would have imagined what Kyle did next.

His friend reached into his jacket pockets, produced the three phones from Mr. McKinney's house, and laid them on the hood of his car.

CHAPTER FIFTY-FOUR

"You took the phones!" Daniel gasped.

"I wasn't thinking. They had my prints on 'em. I freaked out."

"Do you realize what you've done? You took evidence from a possible crime scene—not to mention now you have in your possession three phones that likely belonged to girls who might very well have been murdered."

"Yeah." His voice was soft and low. "Like I said, I freaked out."

Kyle was eyeing the neighborhood. He saw a sedan turn onto their street and quickly hid the phones in his car. "If we show 'em to Ronnie he'll be able to tell us if one is his sister's. Her charger will still be at their house, don't you think? We can plug her phone in, turn it on, see if there are any messages from people she might have been planning to meet at the lake."

"Kyle, you're not making any sense. What then? What? Do we sneak into Mr. McKinney's house again and put them back in his closet? Besides, if he thought someone was in his house, he's probably already checked to see if the phones are missing!"

"Don't worry, he would never call the cops. I mean, really? Tell them someone broke into his home and stole three cell phones that he took from dead girls?"

"But you've just implicated yourself."

"I did that when I touched the phones in the house."

Daniel had no idea what to say.

Kyle didn't seem to either.

"I have to get to Rizzo's," he said finally. "Don't say anything about this, okay?"

"Are you kidding? Who would I tell?"

"We'll talk after I'm off work and you're done with football practice."

Slightly dazed, Daniel watched Kyle drive away.

Unbelievable.

What were they going to do now?

His head wasn't in practice. There were too many other things on his mind. Everything seemed to be both somehow coming together and unraveling at the same time.

There were three cell phones in Mr. McKinney's home.

All from girls.

And Kyle had taken them from the house.

How were they going to get the sheriff's department to look into Mr. McKinney if Kyle had the phones?

Then another realization hit him: he hadn't replaced the padlock in the hasp when he and Kyle fled the house. If Mr. McKinney noticed that, he would know for sure that someone had been there.

After practice, Coach Jostens told the offensive team he was going to be gone tomorrow, but gave them drills to work on. "I'll be here right after school for a few minutes in case you have any questions before I take off. Don't worry, I'll be back on Friday for the game. I wouldn't miss that for the world."

When Daniel left the locker room, he called Kyle immediately and found that he was still at work. "I forgot I need to watch Michele tonight," Kyle told him. "I can't go over to Ronnie's to see if he can identify which phone was his sister's."

"Well, I know his mom wouldn't be too excited to see me, so I can't pick them up from you and take them over there by myself, even if I wanted to. Besides, if she found out we have Emily's phone, well, that could cause all sorts of misunderstandings."

"No kidding."

"I'll text Ronnie. Maybe we can meet up tomorrow between classes. I'll ask him to bring Emily's charger."

"He'll know we have her phone if you tell him to do that," Kyle noted.

"I'll just tell him we might have a lead. If we meet in the library they'll have copies of yearbooks from the years before we started attending here—who knows, maybe even from the other schools in our conference. There might be something in them."

"You're impressing me now, buddy. I can tell you've been thinking about this."

"My mind wasn't exactly on practice this afternoon. Also, you know how cell phones evolve and change styles every year or two? Well, you have the phones. Go online tonight, see if you can figure out, by the shape of the charging inputs, the design, whatever, what years they came out. We'll try to match the dates up with any instances of girls who might have disappeared or died in the towns Mr. McKinney used to teach in."

"Sounds like a plan."

After they hung up, Daniel headed home and went online, searching for class rosters from the years Mr. McKinney was at the other high schools, then he looked for articles about other girls who might have disappeared.

He found that last year, a girl from Roosevelt High had apparently killed herself with carbon monoxide poisoning by running her car in her garage with the doors closed, and one girl from Coulee High was found dead from a drug overdose two years ago.

Both had died on nights when Beldon High had away football games at the girls' schools.

Daniel's heart seemed to stop and somehow race forward at the same time.

Tell your dad. You have to tell your dad.

Really? And tell him what? You don't have any evidence they were murdered. There's no proof. It's all circumstantial.

No, it wasn't enough, not yet.

But tomorrow when he met up with Kyle and Ronnie, he would find out more.

And then he would go to his dad with everything and tell him about the other girls. And what Mr. McKinney had done to them.

CHAPTER
FIFTY-FIVE

Thursday.

Daniel woke up with a headache.

Severe headaches had preceded each of the other times Emily had appeared to him. So already that was a bad sign for the day.

His dad had the morning off and was sleeping in.

Daniel rose, got dressed, and rounded up some breakfast.

Before heading to school, he texted Ronnie asking him to bring the charger. They agreed to meet in the library between fifth and sixth hour.

Over the course of the morning, Daniel glimpsed Stacy twice at the far end of the hallway, but she avoided him. And based on what he'd told her the other night about losing touch with reality, he wasn't exactly surprised.

Ronnie and Kyle were waiting for him in a quiet corner of the library behind an expansive row of bookshelves.

Daniel didn't see the phones yet and assumed Kyle was waiting until he'd gotten there before showing them to Ronnie.

He had no idea how Ronnie would respond when he saw them.

Since they were in the library, he lowered his voice as he warned Ronnie not to get too upset right away.

"About what?"

"We found something and we're not sure exactly what it means."

"You wanted me to bring her phone charger. Is that what you found?" He sounded anxious, but also excited. "Did you find her phone?"

"We might have. I don't know." Daniel nodded for Kyle to show him the phones and, using a bandanna he'd brought with him so he wouldn't leave more prints, he gingerly drew them out of his backpack.

"That's hers." Ronnie pointed to the older-model Samsung Galaxy in the pink case. "My dad gave it to her when he upgraded."

"Plug the charger into the wall," Daniel said.

Ronnie found an outlet at one of the study desks nearby and plugged the phone in.

The three of them watched, hardly breathing, while it booted up.

The home screen became visible.

A photo of a golden retriever.

"Trevor," Ronnie whispered.

No password prompt.

For a moment none of the boys spoke. Finally, Kyle said, "Daniel, there's no way he would have this phone if Emily drowned by accident."

"I agree."

"Who?" Ronnie asked urgently. "Who had it?"

"We'll tell you later," Daniel replied. "We need—"

"Who? Tell me!"

"Shh. We'll—"

"Hang on." Suddenly Ronnie looked at them askance, his eyes wide. "Why are there three phones?"

"We're not sure," Daniel told him honestly. He didn't want to handle Emily's phone, so, just as Kyle had done, he used the bandanna beneath his finger when he tapped the screen to check the most recent texts.

In addition to the messages from Emily's mom on the night she disappeared asking where she was, the last text message, received Friday afternoon, read, "Meet me by Windy Pt 6:30. Kyle G."

Both Daniel and Ronnie stared disbelievingly at Kyle.

"You did it!" Ronnie gasped. Even though he was much smaller, he shoved Kyle hard against the wall.

"Easy." He held Ronnie back at arm's length. "It wasn't me. Check the number. Someone else sent it to lure her out there."

"You could have used another phone."

"Quiet." Daniel took hold of Ronnie's shoulders and pulled him away from Kyle. "Don't make the librarian come over here. Hang on now. Let's figure this out."

Ronnie jerked away from Daniel but, at least for the moment, held back from going after Kyle, though he glared at him and looked like he was ready to go at him again any moment.

It only took a second to verify that the number wasn't from

Kyle's phone. Daniel asked him, "Is there any way Emily would have known that the text wasn't from you? I mean, she didn't have your actual number, did she?"

"No. No way."

"Then somehow, whoever texted her knew she had a crush on you and—"

"She had a crush on you?" Ronnie snapped.

"It only means," Daniel said, "that someone was able to use that to get her out to Windy Point alone. It doesn't mean it was Kyle."

He scrolled through the texts and didn't see any others from that number. When he went to the incoming and outgoing calls, the number never came up.

"There's one way to figure out whose number that is." Kyle pulled out his cell. "Call it."

CHAPTER FIFTY-SIX

Kyle tapped in the number.

No one picked up.

No voicemail.

No surprise.

Whoever had sent the text could easily have used a pre-paid phone and destroyed it, or maybe he—or she—just wasn't answering it.

The three boys only had a couple minutes before the tardy bell would ring.

Ronnie had class on the other end of the building and had to leave, but told them to fill him in if they found out anything. He didn't look convinced that Kyle was innocent, but apparently trusted Daniel enough to let things be for the time being.

Daniel and Kyle had class on this wing, so they decided they could spare another minute or two.

Kyle replaced the three phones in his backpack. "When I was looking up info on 'em I found that they're all pretty new, only from the last couple years."

"That fits with when the two girls died at those other schools."

"So you found some girls who died?"

"Yeah. A girl in her car in her garage and an overdose. The first was a suicide. They called the second one accidental." Then he added, "Both of them died on nights when we had away football games at their schools."

"Mr. McKinney might very well have attended the games," Kyle replied. "And if he did kill girls in those other towns, who would suspect him?" He gestured toward a nearby bookshelf. "Come on. We need to see if there are any pictures of those games."

The two of them quickly flipped through the library's reference copies of Beldon High yearbooks from the years when the girls had died.

They found photos from each of the football games.

In the picture that the school photographer had taken of the Roosevelt High game, Daniel recognized one of the cheerleaders as also being in the photo of the math club that Mr. McKinney had led there, the photo he'd seen in his house.

She was in the background, walking right past Coach Jostens.

"That's the girl who overdosed," he said softly.

The tardy bell rang and they both scooted out of the library, agreeing to touch base tonight as soon as they could after Daniel's football practice.

For the remainder of the school day, Daniel wrestled with the headache, but it was making it harder and harder for him to concentrate.

He tried desperately to piece things together.

The football games.

Three dead girls.

Three phones in Mr. McKinney's closet.

He's friends with Coach Jostens, plus he's a teacher. Going to the games makes sense.

After school, Nicole met up with him while he was on his way to change for practice. She smiled warmly at him. "Thank you, Daniel."

"For what?"

She looked at him curiously. "You know."

"I'm sorry, I . . ."

"The necklace, silly."

"What are you talking about?"

She reached down and untucked the necklace she had on.

It was the one that Emily Jackson had been wearing in the photos at the funeral and on her grave, the necklace she'd pulled through her neck when she appeared to Daniel at the football game.

He could barely get the words out. "Where did you get that?"

"It was in my locker."

"It's not from me."

"Of course it is." Nicole unsnapped the clasp on the locket and flicked it open.

Inside was a picture of Daniel's face, cut out from the newspaper article about last week's game.

He stared at it.

"No . . . Nicole, that's . . ."

"Are you saying someone else put your picture in the locket and then gave it to me? Who would do that? It doesn't make any sense."

Mr. McKinney.

He slid it through the ventilation holes at the top of her locker.

But why Nicole?

The dance. He was there at the punch table. He could have seen you talking with her, maybe even saw you two leave together. Teachers hear things too. Maybe he heard she likes you.

He knows.

He gave her Emily's necklace.

He's setting you up for—

Mr. Reicher, the school principal, was striding down the hallway toward them.

"Something's up, Nicole," Daniel said. "I want you to go straight home."

"What is it?" The confusion on her face descended into fear. "Is it something to do with—"

Before she could finish, Principal Reicher arrived. "Daniel, may I speak with you, please?"

"Um, sure." He turned to Nicole. "I'll text you."

"Okay."

Daniel had no idea what this was about, but expected they would be going to the school office. However, they headed to the boys' locker room instead.

Inside, a bunch of guys were getting ready for football

and cross-country practice and stared uncertainly at their star quarterback entering with the school's principal.

Both Daniel's football coaches, Coach Warner and Coach Jostens, were waiting for him by his locker.

And so was his dad.

CHAPTER
FIFTY-SEVEN

"Can you open this for us, Dan?" his father said.

"What's going on?"

Mr. Reicher answered. "We received word that there's something in your locker that's not yours."

Received word—what's that supposed to mean? And why did they call in your dad?

"No." Daniel had a sinking, unsettling feeling as he remembered Nicole finding the necklace in hers. "I didn't take anything from anyone."

"Can you open your locker, please?" his dad repeated.

Daniel flipped through the combination and swung the door to the side.

His father donned latex crime scene gloves and removed Daniel's football equipment one item at a time, inspecting them as he did.

It didn't take long to find the item that shouldn't have been in his locker.

A lens.

The one from Emily's glasses.

His father held it up.

"I don't know how that got in there." Daniel's voice caught as he tried to explain himself.

But he thought he did know how it'd gotten in there.

Yes.

Mr. McKinney.

Daniel's eyes went to the ventilation holes in the locker.

Yes, just like with Nicole's locker. He slid it in there!

"What's that from?" Principal Reicher asked Daniel's father.

"We'll have to see."

Coach Warner looked at them quizzically. "What's going on?"

"Someone must have dropped it in there," Daniel exclaimed.

"I'm afraid Daniel is going to miss practice," his dad told the coaches.

"I'm telling you," Daniel said, "I didn't put that in there."

Coach Warner looked worried, which only seemed natural, given the circumstances. "Well, let us know if there's anything you need us to do."

Daniel didn't like the sound of that. It might very well mean they wouldn't let him play in tomorrow night's game.

His dad went through the rest of the things in his locker, but found nothing else unusual.

Without a word, he replaced the items and then gestured for Daniel to follow him. From across the room, Coach Jostens's eyes followed them all the way to the door.

"You told me you didn't find the lens," Daniel's dad said to him quietly.

"I was telling the truth. He stuck it in there. He's trying to set me up."

"Who's trying to set you up?"

"Mr. McKinney."

"What are you talking about?"

Daniel was aware that his father knew Mr. McKinney, but he felt like he didn't have any choice at this point other than telling the truth, even if it meant getting in trouble for sneaking into his house.

He told his dad about finding Emily's phone, but left out Kyle's name.

"And how do you know it was her phone?"

Mentioning Ronnie and the charger might not be good either. "Um . . ."

"What aren't you telling me here?"

He finally realized that he needed to be as up-front as possible. "Kyle has it. He's the one who found it in Mr. McKinney's bedroom—along with the phones of two other girls we think Mr. McKinney killed."

Daniel wasn't sure if he should tell his dad about the text that'd been sent to lure Emily out to Windy Point—the message that was supposedly from Kyle.

He decided to go ahead.

His father listened in silence. Daniel thought for sure he would rip into him for going into Mr. McKinney's house, but instead he asked about the cell phones. "And you're telling me Kyle has these phones?"

"Yes. He wasn't thinking and took them from the house."

No reaction. "Your books are in your hall locker?"

"Did you hear what I said?"

"Yes, I heard you. Let's have a look in your hall locker."

"For what?"

His didn't answer him. "Come on."

They didn't find anything unusual in Daniel's locker. His dad had him gather any books he needed for homework for tomorrow and Monday.

"What's going on, Dad?"

The students who were still in the halls watched—but pretended not to watch—as the sheriff, dressed in his law enforcement uniform, led his son in the direction of the school entrance.

As they walked, Daniel texted Nicole to stay at school instead of going home, to stay there with Kyle.

She didn't reply.

Daniel's dad waited until they were away from the other students, then said, "On Monday when we were at the lake you told me you'd gone out there for closure."

"Yeah. From the things I'd been seeing."

"You said Kyle was the one who found the cell phones in Mr. McKinney's house?"

"Yes."

"Were you in the bedroom before he was?"

"What?"

His dad stopped walking. Daniel stood beside him.

"Did you go in there first, Dan?"

"Yeah, but just for a minute. Mainly I was looking around Mr. McKinney's office."

His father was silent.

Daniel felt a stab of concern.

Why would he even ask you that?

"Why don't you ride with me?" his dad said, but it didn't sound like a question. He started for the doors. "We'll pick up your car later."

No, no, no.

He thinks you had something to do with this.

That's ridiculous.

You didn't do anything.

But he's right, you were in the bedroom first. You could have planted the phones.

No, you would remember.

You've been having these blurs. If you can go sleepwalking in the rain and don't remember it, you could have . . .

No.

He couldn't have.

You know details about her death that no one else seems to know. You knew about Trevor, about the glasses. You dreamt of killing her.

A terrible, terrible thought: Was that a dream or could it have been a memory?

A nightmare or a reality?

Grayland.

Caught between black and white.

Between good and evil.

That night when Ty and his buddies tried to attack Nicole, he said he saw you at the lake. What if he wasn't talking about Saturday morning, but about the night Emily died?

No.

The lens was in your locker.

You fainted at her funeral. You keep seeing her.

Stay on this. Seek the truth. Learn what happened.

Stay. Seek. Learn.

No!

The headache split through him, getting worse, taking over. Bright, needle-sharp spikes invading his mind.

A blur.

Everything was a blur.

The barrier is gone, just like you told Stacy.

Fantasy meeting reality, blending, intertwining, becoming one.

There was no football game the night Emily died.

You were free. You might have—

They made it to the doors. "Dad, I forgot something in my locker." He tried to sound casual. "I'll be right back. Okay?"

A slight pause. "Alright. I'll wait here."

As Daniel passed through the hall he was in a daze.

He had to talk to Kyle.

When he got to his locker he made sure his father wasn't following him, then snuck down a side hallway and out one of the school's rear exits, and phoned his friend.

"Daniel? Where are you? I got a text from Nicole. Why did you tell her to meet up with me?"

"Is she there?"

"No, I'm with Mia. I told her to meet us. We're still waiting for her."

Well, at least she's on her way.

"Have you ever thought you might be capable of doing something unspeakable?" Daniel asked him.

"What are you talking about?"

"I mean, you hear about it all the time. Someone snaps and goes on a shooting spree at his school, or some dad takes an axe to his family, or a mom drives off a pier with her babies in the backseat."

"Okay, you're scaring me a little bit here, bro."

"I'm just saying, did you ever wonder if you might come to the place in your life where you could do something like that?"

"No, I haven't. Some people are whacked out. They lose it."

Like I have.

This last week.

Blurs.

The headache didn't ease up, just bristled and regrouped and came at him in consuming waves, each one harsher than the one before.

"But how do you know you won't someday become one of them?"

A pause. "Why are you bringing this up anyway?"

"I'm wondering if I might have done something terrible."

"What?"

"I think I might have killed Emily Jackson."

CHAPTER
FIFTY-EIGHT

"Why would you even say something like that?"

"The other two girls died the nights of our away games. I would have been there, I could have . . . I can't remember things lately—like digging up Akira's grave. I could have been the one to put the flowers on those graves."

"No, that's not even—"

"How come I seem to know more about this than anyone else?"

"We talked about it before, your mind, you're piecing this together, you're—"

"I dreamed that I killed her."

"Well, for the better part of a week we've been suspecting that somebody murdered her. It's been on your mind."

"What about Trevor? Or the glasses? How did I just happen to find them? My prints were the only ones on them."

Kyle was slow in replying. "Where are you? Stay there. I'm coming over. We'll sort all this out."

"Behind the school. But I think my dad suspects me. He'll be looking for me, so don't pick me up here. You know the woods back here? Meet me on the other side of 'em, on River Drive."

It was a quiet road, not too much traffic. No one would see them.

As Daniel slipped away, he heard police sirens approaching the school.

Yeah, his dad was looking for him.

And he'd already called in backup.

CHAPTER
FIFTY-NINE

Daniel had just entered the woods when he heard his name being called, but it wasn't his dad who was yelling for him to stop.

"Daniel, wait!"

He turned and saw Stacy hurrying toward him.

"Stacy, not now."

"It's important. I need to tell you something."

His cell rang, his dad's ringtone. He didn't answer it. "I have to go. We can talk later."

But she didn't stop. She had a strange look on her face. Maybe it was fear. Maybe it was—

A thought struck him: back at the lake, Stacy was the one who'd pointed out where Emily's body was found. She'd used almost the same phrase Ronnie had when he was explaining his suspicions regarding Emily's death, about someone holding her under the water.

Only Kyle and you were there when Ronnie said that.

Daniel took a step backward.

What's real?

What's not?

Grayland.

A blur.

Stacy lives near the Jacksons' house, out by Lake Algonquin.

She's the one who suggested you find out who was at the lake when Emily died.

His phone vibrated. A text.

Stacy came closer.

"Hang on," he said. "Where were you on that night when Emily disappeared?"

The phone stopped vibrating.

"What?"

"Were you at the lake?"

"Listen to me, Daniel." She was only a few feet away from him. "This is very important."

A blur.

It's all a blur.

Stay. Seek. Learn.

He glanced at his phone and saw that the text was from Nicole: "Wolf Cave. 30 minutes."

What?

He looked back at Stacy.

She took another step and held out her hand. "Daniel, take it easy. You have to—"

He reached out to push her back, and his fingers closed on nothing but thin air.

At first he thought she'd somehow pulled her arm out of the way before he could touch her, but then he realized she had not.

No.

She.

Had not.

His fingers had passed through her arm as if it didn't exist. He reached for her again, tried to hold her wrist, came up with nothing.

He stumbled backward as she simply stood there, quietly watching him.

No. It can't be.

Thoughts raced through his mind, cycling around each other, vying for his attention, closing in and then fading away as if they were mist caught in a breeze.

She's not real.

She's—

Every time you talked with her you were alone—after school, at the lake, at your house, in your bedroom.

She wouldn't let you help her through the window at your house. She didn't want you to touch her. She knew where you live and that you were at the doctor's on Monday, even though you only told Kyle and Nicole.

She never answered her phone calls or texts.

Because she isn't there.

She isn't real.

His gaze dropped to his hands. They were shaking.

"Daniel," she said. "Look at me. It's time to stop him. It's not who you think it is."

His headache splintered apart in his mind.

He lifted his head and locked eyes with her.

Mia couldn't find anyone who knew her.

Nicole was confused when you said her name.

Stacy had no Facebook page.

Nothing came up for her when they Googled her name.

It was all an illusion. All a dream.

A blur.

The biggest one of all.

Stacy Clern only existed in his mind.

Or maybe she's a ghost.

Maybe—

"The away games," she said. "The other girls. That's the key. Who would have been at those football games? Think of the photos, the girls. Look it up. Stay on this, Daniel. Seek the truth. Learn what happened. Don't give up." As she spoke, she began to transform before his eyes.

Her skin became mottled, her hair changed from dark brown to blond, her clothes went from dry to soaking wet. Her flesh began to swell and become bluish. Clumps of lake-bottom weeds appeared in her hair, just like they had when he first saw Emily at the funeral.

Her face morphed from one girl to the other.

He was no longer looking at Stacy Clern.

But at Emily Jackson.

How do people wake up from a dream? They pinch themselves.

He tried it, pinching his forearm fiercely, just like he had when he first saw Emily move in her casket, fingernails digging into his skin, but the image didn't go away.

You're awake. This is really happening.

Stacy.

Emily.

Stay. Seek. Learn.

Stacy Clern.

Her name.

No, no, no, no, no!

It couldn't be.

But it was.

And then she began to disintegrate before his eyes, fading back into time and space as the memories of Stacy swarmed, merged, combined with his memories of Emily, and they all began to become an inseparable part of the moment.

The image faded away until only the outline of a girl remained.

And then even that was gone.

Another text came through.

Also from Nicole's phone.

As he read it, a terrible shiver shot through him: "Come alone. I have her."

No!

Stacy told you the key is the photos.

The photos.

Using his phone, he quickly surfed to the articles that reported the deaths of the other two girls and saw that each of the girls was wearing a necklace with a heart-shaped locket in the smiling press photos the newspaper had used to report their deaths.

He gave them each a necklace.

He gave one to Nicole.

She's next.

Wolf Cave.

Get there.

Go!

Now!

With the sheriff's department looking for him at the school, using his own car was out of the question.

He angled through the woods to the place where he'd agreed to meet Kyle.

CHAPTER SIXTY

Mia and Kyle were standing beside his Mustang waiting for Daniel when he burst out of the forest.

"Nicole's in trouble!" he shouted.

"I think we were followed," Kyle replied.

"What? Who?"

"A pickup."

Ty?

His friends?

As if on cue, a maroon SUV rounded the corner in front of them. The same one Daniel had seen at the lake when he was there with Stacy.

No, when you were there alone.

"We need to go." Reality seemed to be crumbling around him. "He's got Nicole, and Stacy's not real."

"What are you talking about?" Mia asked. "Who has Nicole? And what do you mean, Stacy's not real?"

The sound of an engine roaring behind them grabbed their attention and they turned to see a pickup swerve around the corner.

Daniel hadn't gotten a good look at the pickup that Ty's buddies had been driving Saturday night when they confronted him and Nicole, but he ventured a guess that this was the same one.

"Stacy Clern," Daniel told Mia. "Say her name slowly— Stay. Seek. Learn. That's what she told me. That's what I need to do: learn what happened."

He was about to tell Kyle where Nicole was, but then remembered that the text from her phone had told him to come alone.

"You said he has Nicole," Kyle exclaimed. "Who? Mr. McKinney?"

"Yes. I think. I'm . . ."

Both the SUV and the pickup were closing fast.

Kyle threw open the passenger door of his car. "Get in, Daniel. We'll go get her. We'll take care of everything. Trust me."

Daniel stared at him.

He wants you to trust him.

To—

All at once, everything Daniel thought was real began to shift, to fade, to swirl away in a sea of questions and doubt.

Kyle's the one who found the phones.

He snuck them out of the house—he could have snuck them in.

Daniel stood motionless.

"What is it?" Kyle asked. "What's wrong?"

The SUV skidded to a stop in front of them, and the pickup rolled in behind. They were blocked in both directions.

"Daniel," his friend said, "we have to get out of here."

314

He's the one who suggested you go out to the graveyard in the first place. He knew that killers visit the graves of their victims. He could've set the flowers out there beforehand.

Emily had a crush on him.

The text inviting her to the lake had his name on it.

He suggested Ty might've done it—to make you suspect someone else?

He could have gotten into the locker room, placed the lens in your locker. He could have put the necklace in Nicole's—

Stacy said it's not who you think it is.

"You?" Daniel said softly to his friend.

"What?"

"How did you know someone had found Emily's notebook in her locker?"

"I heard it around school, like I told you."

Daniel eyed the SUV warily. The windows were tinted and it was impossible to see how many people were inside.

"Let's go," Kyle said.

Ty and one of his buddies climbed out of the SUV. Two other guys exited the pickup.

"Byers and Goessel," Ty called. "I was hoping our paths would cross again this week. And, oh, look: the little emo girl too. I'm gonna enjoy this."

She flipped him off. "Enjoy this."

Thoughts flew through Daniel's mind.

The yearbook.

The girls.

It's not who you think it is.

Those other girls had necklaces.

The girls died on the nights of your away games.

The necklaces.

The photos in the yearbooks.

The ones in the papers.

Girls dying over the last two years.

No, Kyle hasn't been driving long enough.

It wasn't him. Not at all. It couldn't have been.

How could you have even suspected it was him?

How do you know what to—

Ty approached them.

Daniel thought of Nicole at Wolf Cave. The text had said thirty minutes. "I don't have time for this, Ty."

"It shouldn't take long."

Kyle threw Daniel his keys. "Go. I got this."

"Really?" Ty and his friends scoffed.

"Really," Mia replied, and positioned herself next to her boyfriend.

Daniel debated for a moment if he should leave.

Ty flicked out his switchblade.

"Is that the best you've got?" Mia whipped out a butterfly knife and flipped it around in her hand in a smooth, well-practiced motion.

Okay, that was unexpected.

Well, knowing Mia, maybe not so unexpected after all.

Ty's buddies backed away a couple steps, and the looks on their faces told Daniel that Mia and Kyle were probably going to be just fine.

"Go," Kyle urged Daniel. "Find her."

The killer has Nicole.

You have to stop him.

But as he turned toward the car, Ty came at him. He swiped the blade and Daniel leapt to the side, but it grazed his left arm, leaving a narrow red slash behind. Not deep; he'd be alright, but it was enough to get Daniel's attention. At school and out on the road near Nicole's house, he'd held back from punching Ty.

Now he broke his streak.

He swung hard, left-handed, to protect his throwing hand, connected against the side of Ty's jaw, and sent him spinning around, off balance, but it took him only a moment to recover. He came at Daniel again with the knife.

But Daniel balled up his fists and swung them simultaneously at Ty's hand, hitting it the way his dad had taught him to do to knock a knife away from someone. By hitting the nerve endings, the hand involuntarily opens. And that was what happened—the knife went spinning across the pavement.

While Ty was momentarily stunned, Daniel landed another punch, this time an uppercut that put Ty on the ground. Hard.

Go. Find Nicole.

"Get going!" Kyle retrieved the knife before Ty could get to it. "We'll be alright."

Daniel jumped into the car and fired up the engine.

To get around the SUV blocking the road he had to drive half on the shoulder and smack the vehicle's side panel to ram it out of the way, so he did. He didn't care.

Right now he needed to get to the cave.

Ty leapt up and hollered at him about the SUV, even chased him for a little ways.

Well, too bad.

Daniel phoned his dad and told him where Kyle and Mia were and that he needed to get over there.

"Are you with them?"

He didn't reply, just ended the call.

River Drive wasn't far from school, his dad could be there in a couple minutes, and Kyle and Mia could take care of themselves until then.

His dad called back. Daniel didn't answer.

Their house was on the way to Wolf Cave. If Nicole and her kidnapper were inside, Daniel realized he would need a flashlight to get to her. He swung by home, rushed inside, grabbed his headlamp and caving gear, then tore out of the driveway, aimed the car east, and sped toward Wolf Cave.

CHAPTER
SIXTY-ONE

There was no official parking area near the cave, just a gravel pull-off near the trailhead.

As Daniel neared it, he could see that a car he didn't recognize was already there.

It was a wild cave and you had to know what you were doing to make your way through it. No overhead lights, no paved walkways, nothing like that.

In addition to tight crawl spaces and loose boulders, there were pits and drop-offs to avoid—one shaft that plunged more than 120 feet. The kids called it Devil's Throat. An underground stream snaked through the west end of the cave. With the recent rains they'd had, it might have risen, might be swift.

It was not a gentle cave.

It was an angry cave.

He parked.

And looked in the window of the other car. Yes. Dog hair all over the black cloth seats. He'd seen this car at the funeral, had momentarily taken note of it, but only now remembered. Only now made the connection.

Trevor was in the car. That's what Emily had said.

This guy put him in here while he was with Emily. He might not have known she would bring her dog along with her out to the lake. He needed to get her alone.

Though the text from Nicole's phone had said to come alone, Daniel knew he would need his dad eventually. It would still take him a while to get here, so he texted him his location, then grabbed his pack of caving gear.

From the road it was a ten-minute walk to the cave.

Daniel did not walk.

As he sprinted through the woods he tried to thread everything together.

There were flowers on Emily's and Grace McKinney's graves.

But you don't know Mr. McKinney put them there.

Stacy said it isn't who you think it is.

But Stacy wasn't real, was only a figment of his imagination, an invention of his subconscious, so somewhere his mind held the answer. He needed to find that place, root it out, unriddle what he already knew.

The girls died on game nights. It has to be someone who was in those towns on those nights.

McKinney?

Maybe.

He neared the cave.

There was no game two weeks ago on the night Emily disappeared. So maybe . . .

He came to Wolf Cave's entrance and slowed to a stop.

The ground opened up in a tumbledown hole that descended quickly into thick darkness.

As he stood beside it trying to calm his breathing, he felt a breeze coming from the entrance, as if the earth were exhaling around him.

He knew it was from currents of air passing through the cave and meeting with the warmer air out here in the sun, but still, it gave the impression that the cave was some great living beast buried in the hillside, breathing on him.

Daniel put on his headlamp and started his descent.

CHAPTER SIXTY-TWO

The path down was muddy and strewn with moss-covered rocks, making the trek into the darkness even more slippery and treacherous than it appeared.

Despite carefully watching his footing, he slipped twice as he scrambled into the deepening shadows of the first room of the cave.

The sunlight bleeding down through the entrance was no longer warm, but was overpowered by the cave's cool interior.

Dank. Damp.

Smelling of lichen and mold.

From being in here before, he knew there were three main sections to the cave, but there were also numerous side tunnels that fingered off, some supposedly making their way all the way down to the underground river that fed into Lake Algonquin.

Who is it? Who has her?

Where would she be?

The photos in Mr. McKinney's hallway showed two different chambers, both of which Daniel had recognized.

The first was close, just to the left.

To get there he needed to pass through a relatively small room—only about the size of two minivans. A narrow passageway on the other side of it led to one of the cave's largest caverns, a sweeping, expansive room more than eighty feet long and fifty feet wide.

Daniel made his way through the small room into the larger one.

Massive stalagmites and stalactites rose from the cave's floor or hung thick and heavy from the ceiling. A few columns reached all the way to the roof of the cave from stalagmites and stalactites that had met in the middle sometime in the distant past.

Someone had been in here burning candles on one of the boulders, and melted wax had oozed down the sides of the rock and cooled, making it look like some kind of artificial formation itself.

"I'm here," Daniel called. No response save the echo of his own voice coming back to him. "I came alone!"

Alone . . . Alone . . . Alone . . . the cave replied.

"Where is she?" The words reverberated eerily through the cavern. "I know you're in here."

In here . . . In here . . . In here . . .

When the echoes faded away, the only sounds that remained were the rasp of his quickened breathing, the dribble of water seeping from the ceiling, and the rushing gurgle of the stream as it coursed through the cavern nearby and then disappeared into the unmapped portions of the cave.

Alright, it didn't look like they were here. Maybe the other room from the photos.

To get there, Daniel had to slide sideways through a series of tight squeezes that slanted deeper into the earth.

If her kidnapper had brought Nicole down here, it would not be good. This was the most dangerous part of the cave, the one that ended at Devil's Throat.

Daniel had rappelled into it twice with his dad. The last time they'd been down there they'd discovered the carcass of a raccoon at the bottom. It seemed unlikely for an animal to have found its way that far down the cave in the dark, and he'd wondered if someone had brought it in after it was dead and thrown it down.

The carcass was covered with spongy-looking white mold. It was a little hard to identify the type of animal because of the force of impact when it had landed on the boulder-covered bottom.

He adjusted his headlamp and worked his way through the passageway.

A line of thin stalactites about a foot long hung from the ceiling. No large formations in here.

The sound of the stream became fainter and fainter as he moved away from it through the cave.

He got on his hands and knees and edged forward through a small crawl hole. From here it wasn't far to the chamber that held Devil's Throat. Just another fifty feet or so.

Daniel sorted through what he knew, trying to make sense of everything that'd happened since he arrived at the church for Emily's funeral.

The girls in the photos were wearing necklaces, all wearing the necklaces with the heart-shaped lockets.

Maybe you saw their photos in the news after they died, and the pictures, just like the reference to Trevor, lodged in your mind and only jarred loose when you heard about Emily's death.

Maybe . . .

They say our brains record everything, and Daniel's had always been able to notice things, to calculate things, that no one else seemed to be able to do—

That's why Emily held up the necklace for you at the game. Because you already knew it was the key to this.

She did it at a football game.

Then there was the photo of his offensive coordinator near that girl who'd died.

He thought of the photos of the football games.

Who would have been there from your school?

The team. The coaches.

Roosevelt High.

Coulee High.

The press photos of the girls—

Who could have gotten access to your things in the locker room?

Who could have seen you and Kyle enter Mr. McKinney's house while all the teachers were in their parent meetings at school?

The teachers were there. Yes, but not—

Oh.

Yes.

Daniel knew who it was.

He was at the prom. He could have seen you leave with Nicole.

He's around students all the time. He could hear which kids like each other. He could have heard about Emily liking Kyle.

He can enter and leave schools without anyone being suspicious.

Of course.

And he had to be at the games. It was his job.

Daniel shone his light forward.

He was almost to the cavern that held Devil's Throat.

Football.

Yes, the yearbooks, the football games, the photos all pointed to one person.

"I'm here," Daniel shouted as he reached the edge of the crawl hole. "I know who you are!"

"Oh, really?" the man shouted.

Really? . . . Really? . . . Really? . . . came the echoed reply. It was distorted by the acoustics of the cave, making it impossible to tell who was speaking.

But that didn't matter to Daniel.

He already knew who was waiting for him in that cavern.

Yes, his offensive coordinator, Coach Jostens, had been there at those games.

But it wasn't him.

It was the man who'd photographed him beside that Roosevelt High girl who'd died.

"Yes, I do," he yelled, "and you better not hurt her, Mr. Ackerman!"

CHAPTER
SIXTY-THREE

"Come out where I can see you," the photographer called.

Daniel entered the chamber, stood up, and directed his light toward the far end of the cavern.

Quickly, in the breadth of a moment, he took everything in.

The room swept before him: twenty feet wide, but seventy feet long. It contained no gentle, sloping formations, only jagged boulders and rough fall-down.

Devil's Throat lay at the far end and slit through the floor of the cave like an uneven gaping wound. It spanned the cavern and yawned open four yards wide.

A natural outcropping stretched across the other side, ten feet higher than the floor Daniel was standing on. It was just wide enough for five people to stand on, shoulder-to-shoulder. A few large boulders lay on top of it.

Running along the right side of Devil's Throat was a narrow rock shelf just large enough to walk on that allowed cavers to traverse around the yawning pit toward the higher ledge. Someone had tied a thick rope off one of the boulders on it so people could access that level of the cave if they dared.

The rope had knots every foot or so to help climbers keep from slipping down and falling into the shaft. It was precarious and dangerous. Daniel had been up there twice.

At the far edge of the saber of light cast from his head-lamp, Daniel saw Nicole and Ackerman standing on that rock platform on the other side of Devil's Throat. The photographer was behind her, holding her fast.

Daniel called out, "Nicole! Are you okay?"

"Yeah! Get out of here, Daniel. He wants you to—"

Ackerman interrupted her: "Daniel, come here."

"Leave, he wants—" Nicole began.

He grabbed her hair with one hand and yanked. "Quiet now."

"Ow!"

"Stop it!" Daniel yelled.

Ackerman wore a headlamp, Nicole did not. It would have been a good way to make sure she didn't run off while he was bringing her down here. Without a light she would've been lost in complete and total darkness if she'd tried to get away.

Daniel crossed the room toward them, trying to think of a way to save her.

Come on, man, think! How can you do this? You need to get her away from him!

"You called my name before you came in here," Ackerman said. "How did you know it was me?"

"The press photos that ran in the newspaper articles about the dead girls: in the pictures, the girls were all wearing the same-style necklace. That couldn't be a coincidence. You're the one who took the photos. You're the only one who'd know they would have them on. You chose to submit those photos to the papers. You found a way to give them the necklaces, and whoever killed those girls had to have been at our away games. You went to take pictures for the newspaper."

Daniel arrived at the edge of Devil's Throat.

"That's not enough," Ackerman said.

"There was a picture in Mr. McKinney's hallway of the two of you in here. The key is the cell phones—someone put them in his closet. He's your friend, you cave with him. You planted the phones—maybe you were in there because you know him, maybe you snuck in through the unlocked cellar—I don't know. Your home studio is right there in the neighborhood. Is that it? Is that how you saw us enter Mr. McKinney's house?"

"Very good."

"Then what? Did you stop by his place that night and see that the phones were gone?"

"Nicely done. Yes. That's when I knew it was time to end this."

"Daniel, go—" Nicole hollered.

"Quiet!" Ackerman cut her off again. He moved her closer to the edge of the outcropping.

"Don't!" Daniel yelled.

You need to stall until your dad can get here. Keep him talking.

"You chose girls from the schools Mr. McKinney taught at on purpose, targeted ones he had in class back when he was a teacher there," Daniel said. "You've been planning this, setting him up for years. Why?"

"To make sure there were arrows that pointed somewhere other than at me."

Why is he telling you this? That can't be good. He's not going to let you walk out of here alive.

"But why did you plant the cell phones now, this week?"

"I heard your dad was looking into Emily's death a little more closely. That was reason enough."

Daniel dropped his pack of equipment. "Were there more than those three girls?"

"Just those. But there will be. Once you start"—he took a deep, satisfied breath—"it's very hard to stop. Now—"

"But why?" Daniel's voice was strained as he thought of the appalling crimes Ackerman had committed. "Why did you kill them?"

"The thrill. The challenge. The adrenaline—you must know what that's like from your games. It can be addicting, can't it? Now, let's get this over with. Do you see that rock shelf on your right?"

Daniel glanced toward it.

Waist-high. Not very large.

Nicole's cell phone sat among a cluster of rocks. The smallest was softball-sized, the rest were as big as bowling balls.

"What about Mrs. McKinney, did you kill her too?" Daniel said.

"That was actually an accident. That's why I chose drowning for Emily. To wrap it all up in a sweet little bow. Enough talking. Now, toss your phone down the shaft."

There were a few questions Daniel still had, but Ackerman seemed to have thought things through pretty well, and right now Daniel realized he needed to focus completely on rescuing Nicole and not worry about tying all the remaining threads together.

"Throw it down," Ackerman repeated.

Daniel tossed his phone into Devil's Throat.

It clattered against the walls, then, after what seemed like an impossibly long time, it shattered to pieces with a sharp *crack!* on the bottom of the shaft.

"Now, take Nicole's phone. You're going to type in your confession and suicide note."

"What?"

"You lured Emily out to the lake, where you drowned her. Guilt-stricken, you fainted at her funeral. Nicole found out about it and you had to kill her too. You brought her here to do it. And then, overcome with remorse, you felt compelled to take your own life."

"No. No one will believe it."

But Daniel had the sense that they just might, considering his dad already suspected him: he'd told him about the blurs—then there was digging up Akira's corpse, the interest he'd shown in Emily's death, the lens in his locker, his prints being the only ones on the glasses.

If Ackerman had deleted the last couple texts from Nicole's phone, with Daniel's destroyed—unless the phone company kept records of them—there wouldn't be any proof that anyone had texted Daniel to get him to come out here to Wolf Cave, or any proof that Daniel hadn't picked up Nicole after he left Kyle. . . .

"What about your car?" Daniel said. "You being out here?"

"I came here to stop you, but, tragically, I was too late to save either of you."

No, it'll never—

"I trust you, Daniel," Nicole called.

"I'll—" Daniel started

"Take the phone, Daniel," Ackerman told him. "I'll tell you what to type."

He's going to kill her anyway!

You need a bargaining chip. Something to—

"I trust you!" she shouted again.

Her eyes were on the wall beside him, where the phone lay beside those rocks.

Does she mean the phone or—

He glanced up at her and saw her slyly tuck her leg between two boulders to lock herself in place.

No. She didn't mean the phone.

She means the rock.

"Pick up the phone, Daniel," Ackerman ordered.

"Okay." He held up his hands palms forward to try to reassure him. "I'll do it, just don't hurt her."

Only Ackerman's shoulders and head were visible as he held Nicole in front of him.

He's nine yards away. You could hit her.

No, you can do it. You're that accurate with a football at twice this distance, you can hit him with a rock from here.

When he looked back at Nicole, she made an okay sign with her fingers.

Do it.

Reaching toward the phone, Daniel chose the softball-sized rock instead and spun toward Ackerman. Instantly, subconsciously, he calculated velocity, trajectory, muscle flexion, the weight of the rock, the distance—all in a private, hidden corner of his mind, just like he did on the field, just like he did when he solved problems in math.

He fired the rock at Ackerman's head.

Instinctively, the man ducked, and when he did, he loosened his grip on Nicole, who pulled away and leapt deftly to the side.

The rock smashed against the cave wall and bounced off, clunked across the platform, and dropped into Devil's Throat.

If the other rocks had been small enough, Daniel might have tried again, but they were all too big to throw.

He didn't have a choice. He needed to get Nicole safely off that platform as fast as possible, and there was only one way to do that.

Knock Ackerman off it first—

—the rock hit the bottom—

Devil's Throat loomed before him, a jagged twelve-foot-wide gash on the floor of the world.

The rope dangled on the other side. If he actually made it across, it would be possible to grab it, but the momentum from the jump would mean he would slam hard against the wall.

Traversing over there will take too long. Ackerman will throw her off before you can get to them!

But if you do this, you cannot miss that rope.

No choice.

Go!

He backed up to get a running start, sprinted toward the fissure that plummeted twelve stories into the earth, aimed for the rope hanging on the other side, and launched himself into space.

CHAPTER
SIXTY-FOUR

Time seemed to slow to a crawl as he flew over Devil's Throat, just like it had at the game when Emily appeared to him on the field. He saw Nicole scrambling as far as she could away from Ackerman, the murderous look on the man's face, the rope coming closer, and then—

Hands open, he grabbed for it. He missed with his left hand, but managed to snag it with his right. He rotated his body to take the force of impact against his side, but his knee was what hit the rock wall first.

For a brief moment adrenaline smothered the pain, then it rolled up his leg.

Even though he was clenching the rope as tightly as he could, the force of impact jarred him harshly, and his hand slid down to the next knot, ripping skin off his palm as it did.

Fire blazed through his hand, down his arm, but he didn't let go. Instead, he gripped the rope with both hands and, ignoring the pain of his shredded palm, climbed to the ledge, pressed his toes against a small foothold, and clambered over the edge onto the platform.

He rose to his feet and faced Ackerman.

The man's demeanor had changed and he had transformed into something dark and demonic, as if all the evil inside of him had risen to the surface, overwhelming any good that used to be there. He hardly looked like the same person. Narrowed eyes. Tight fists. Bared teeth. Fierce. Primal.

You're the bigger threat.

He'll kill you, then he'll throw her off too.

No.

He won't.

Daniel tried to keep his injured leg from giving way under his weight, tried to disguise how much it hurt. "Don't worry, Nicole. It's okay."

Ackerman said coolly, "They won't be able to sort out the bones of the two of you on the bottom."

He lunged toward Daniel, who managed to spin to the side, just as he would've if he were evading a tackle on the football field, but his leg buckled and he collapsed. Before he could stand again, Ackerman kicked him fiercely in the ribs.

Pain chugged through him, but Daniel kept from crying out.

You might have a broken rib.

Yeah, well, deal with that later.

Ackerman kicked at him again, but Daniel was able to roll to the side, get hold of a boulder, and work his way to his feet.

The photographer swung a roundhouse punch and Daniel threw an arm up to block it. The force of the blow sent him reeling against the rock face. He tried to land a punch of his own, but Ackerman ducked out of the way faster than Daniel guessed he would and he almost lost his balance, almost went down again.

Behind Ackerman, Nicole went for the rope. She yanked it up, tugged it toward another boulder, and pulled it tight between them, forming a line about knee height behind Ackerman.

"Do it!" she yelled.

Ackerman came at Daniel, punched him violently in the face, driving him back against the side of the cave again.

"Now!" Nicole called.

"Say good-bye, Daniel," Ackerman hissed.

Daniel leaned against the wall for leverage, swung his left leg up, and kicked Ackerman hard in the chest, driving him toward the rope.

"Good-bye."

The photographer stumbled backward, hit the back of his legs against the rope that Nicole was holding taut, and toppled toward the shaft.

He seemed to hover for a moment at the edge of the sheer drop-off as he flailed his arms to try to regain his balance, then he tipped back and disappeared. The beam of light from his headlamp swirled crazily up through the shaft as he fell. A long, thin scream trailed behind him as he hurtled toward the bottom.

And then the scream stopped as a thick crunch echoed up through the fissure, the light blinked out, and Devil's Throat devoured the man who had killed three people.

But Daniel's attention wasn't on the scream.

Or the thud.

It was on Nicole, who'd slipped to the side from the force of Ackerman's legs smacking against the rope she'd been holding.

"Daniel!" she cried as her legs dipped over the edge and the rest of her began to follow.

No!

He dove toward her, trying to keep his momentum from taking him over the ledge.

Just as her arm was disappearing, he snagged her wrist with his right hand. Her weight dragged him forward until he was lying on his stomach, bent over the lip of the outcropping, holding her with only that one hand.

"I've got you! It's okay!"

Get her up fast. You can't hold on like this, you need to—

Someone called out from the other end of the room. At first Daniel couldn't tell who it was, but when he momentarily tilted his headlamp up, he saw that it was his dad, flashlight in hand, emerging from the crawl hole.

He shouted for them to hold on and started to rush toward them, but Daniel didn't think he had time to wait for his dad to get across the traverse before helping Nicole up to the ledge.

He grabbed her other wrist with his free hand, then worked to hoist her toward the ridge of the outcropping so she could hold on while he repositioned himself to help her up.

"You can do this," he told her.

"Don't let me fall," she gasped.

"I won't."

He lifted her right arm, bringing her hand to the edge. She clung to it while he got a better grip on her and then leaned back, heaving her the rest of the way up.

She swung her legs over the edge, rolled onto the outcropping, and collapsed into his arms.

For a long moment neither of them spoke. They were both breathing heavily, riding on the rush of adrenaline and the lingering fear coursing through them.

"That was a good idea," he said at last, "with the rope."

"That was a good throw," she replied, "with the rock."

"I might have hit you."

"Yeah, that would have really ruined my day."

It took a little bit for them to catch their breath, then he pulled back from her slightly. "Listen, I need to explain something about Stacy." Whether or not this was a good time, he didn't know, but he felt like he needed to do this.

"No, it's . . ." Nicole sounded suddenly distant. "It's okay, I . . ."

"Listen, there was never anything there between us."

"What do you mean?"

"Everything I thought I felt toward her was . . . well, I can honestly say it was an illusion."

She looked at him curiously. "Are you sure?"

"Yeah. She's not someone I plan on ever seeing again. When I look at you it's as if she never even existed."

A faint smile. "Really?"

"Really."

And then, as Daniel's dad once again told them to stay

where they were and made his way around the traverse that led along the rim of Devil's Throat, Daniel held Nicole tight.

He felt her heart beating against him.

Not like a ghost.

Not like a blur.

Just like a girl he should have drawn close to him a long time ago.

CHAPTER
SIXTY-FIVE

Daniel thought they might cancel school, but they didn't.

"So, Mr. Byers," Miss Flynn said as class officially began, "I know you don't really like speaking in front of the class, but we all want to hear what happened in that cave—well, at least those of us who haven't already been told—or texted—all the details yet."

Last night after leaving Wolf Cave, he and Nicole had filled Kyle and Mia in about everything.

"Kyle's a lot better storyteller than I am," Daniel said. "Maybe he could . . . ?"

"I got it, Teach," Kyle told Miss Flynn. "No problem."

He stepped to the front of the room and spun the tale, leaving out the investigative details Daniel's dad had informed them the previous night needed to remain confidential. He also bypassed mentioning their suspicions that the killer was Mr. McKinney.

Or Daniel.

Or himself.

Or the girl who didn't exist.

Also, Daniel and his friends had agreed to keep the blurs to themselves, so Kyle skipped over those too.

Actually, that really cut down on what he could say, but somehow he managed to encapsulate the rest of the facts in a way that contained the essential truth of what had happened, even if he wasn't exactly, entirely, one hundred percent forthcoming.

When he was done, the class peppered him, Daniel, and Nicole with questions. Some they offered answers to, some they couldn't, some they chose not to.

Brad Talbot said to Kyle, "So your Mustang got smashed up? That sucks. That thing is sweet."

"It's not nearly as bad as Ty's SUV."

"And you fought him?"

"Well, mostly Daniel took care of that, but one of his friends smiled at Mia in a way I didn't like and I was really tempted to smack it off his face."

"So, what happened?"

"I gave in to temptation."

"Sweet."

Ty and his three buddies had taken off before Daniel's dad arrived on River Drive and hadn't shown up for school today. However, Daniel had disarmed Ty in front of his friends, undoubtedly embarrassing him, and he had a feeling that it was not the last time he'd be hearing from Ty Bell.

When the class was done asking questions, Miss Flynn

said, "There's one last poem I would like to share with you before the bell rings."

She read:

> And here is the truth from which all others grow;
>> here is the spring from which all others flow:
>> soon I will be dead.
> *Soon, as measured by stardust and time.*
> *Soon as measured by comets and dreams.*
> Soon. Soon.
> Soon, I will be dead.
> And here is the question that determines everything—
>> what will I do until then?

The meaning of that poem wasn't too hard at all to unpack.

Soon I will be dead.

What will I do until then?

And the answer was evident too, and resonated through Daniel's mind: *Live each moment, each precious moment that you have. Live each one as if it were your last. And your first.*

Miss Flynn gave them a short writing assignment for Monday, class ended, and as the students were gathering up their things, she asked to speak with Daniel for a moment.

She waited until the room cleared out. "I wanted to take a second to talk to you about your blog entries from last week."

Oh, that's right—she hadn't said anything earlier about either of them. Daniel didn't even know if she'd given him a completion grade.

"Okay," he said somewhat uneasily.

"You wrote about vultures picking away at your dreams. First there was that, and now everything this week with Mr. Ackerman, and what happened in the cave. I wondered . . . well, how you're doing."

"I'm okay."

"You sure?"

No, but as long as the blurs stop, I might be.

"We'll see."

She hesitated, evidently at a loss for how to respond to that. "Okay."

After handing back his assignment with the completion grade on top, she said, "Daniel, remember to cling to the one thing that the vultures can never devour unless you let them."

"What's that?"

"This moment."

He found Kyle waiting for him in the hall.

They hadn't had a chance to connect that morning before class, and now Kyle asked him, "So what did Coach say about tonight's game?"

Daniel held up his bandaged, rope-burned right hand. In addition, even though he'd wrapped his banged-up knee in an ACE bandage, he couldn't keep from limping. At least the previous night's X-rays showed he hadn't ended up with any cracked ribs, and the cut from Ty's knife wasn't severe. "It's just a flesh wound," Kyle had told him last night in his best Monty Python accent.

Now Daniel said, "Coach said it's a no-go. I guess I agree. I'm not sure how well I'd be able to throw."

"Next week?"

"I'll be back then for sure, if I have anything to say about it."

They started down the hallway. "And your mom?"

"She's coming up tomorrow. After she heard about everything that's happened she told me she was coming no matter what I thought."

"What did you say to that?"

"I told her it'd be good to see her." He paused. "We'll see how that goes."

"And this is her first time visiting? I mean, since she left?"

"Yes."

They walked a little way, then Kyle said softly, "Your dad knows all about the blurs now."

"Yeah, and he's worried, I can tell. But when I explained everything about how they were helping me figure things out, he told me he needed to think about that. I'm not sure where that's gonna lead. At least he doesn't suspect me of anything anymore. By the way, sorry about yesterday, when I thought you might've been a serial killer."

"It's all good. You suspected yourself too. And Stacy, who never even existed—which I have to say is a little bit psycho. Anyway, at least I'm in good company. I think."

"How's Mia today?"

"As she would say, 'Smokin'.'"

"What was up with that butterfly knife she pulled out?"

"She's a girl who's full of surprises."

"Your kind of girl."

"My kind of girl."

Daniel got a text from Nicole, and when Kyle left for class, he decided to chance another tardy slip and meet up with her near the snack machines Emily had written about on the sheet of paper that'd fallen out of her notebook when he picked it up at her house.

He greeted Nicole, but caught himself peering past her at the vending machines, thinking of Emily's words about watching the popular kids talk and wishing she were part of their group and never quite finding the right way to fit in.

The words must have been lodged in his mind, in that cryptic corner that didn't let anything slip by, the one that seemed to be opening up lately more and more—maybe too much. He heard the words about her yearning to belong as clearly as if she were reading them herself, "I watch them and I despise them and I envy them and I hate myself for wanting to be like them."

"Daniel?" Nicole was waving her hand in front of his face.

"Huh?" It took him a moment to collect himself. "Yeah?"

"Are you okay? You just zoned out on me."

"Sorry, I was just remembering. . . ."

"Remembering what?"

"Something I read that Emily wrote."

"What's that?"

"About how much she wanted to belong."

Nicole processed that. "We all do, I guess."

No one should slip through the cracks.

It's so easy to close up circles so kids like Emily can't come in. It's a lot harder to open them up.

But it was worth it to at least try. It was one thing he could do, one thing he decided he was going to do.

He asked Nicole, "What were you saying when I blanked out?"

"There's still one thing I don't understand."

"What's that?"

"The marks on your arm. They formed just because of your thoughts? Because you were convinced Emily had touched you?"

"I don't know. Maybe we'll figure that out next week. I have an appointment with a shrink on Wednesday. I hope he'll finally be able to tell what's wrong with me."

"Or what's right."

"What do you mean?"

"I mean you've got this . . . I don't know, ability, gift—even though it doesn't seem like a gift—whatever it is, it helped you solve all this. Maybe it's not something you need diagnosed and treated, but something you need to figure out a way to use again."

"Yeah, I'm not so sure about that. I think I'm done seeing blurs—at least, I hope I am."

He didn't think that bringing up what he'd told Stacy that night in his room—that the barrier between reality and fantasy was gone for him—would reassure Nicole too much, so he kept that to himself.

The tardy bell rang.

"This'll be my first tardy slip this year." Nicole sighed.

"I'm a bad influence on you."

"I think I can live with that."

He thought about everything that'd happened over the past two weeks. In a way it reminded him of the themes of the stories and poems Miss Flynn preferred, the ones that were about death—or about life, depending on how you looked at the endings.

Soon, as measured by stardust and time. Soon as measured by comets and dreams.

Soon. Soon.

Soon, I will be dead.

And here is the question that determines everything—what will I do until then?

Yeah, that was the key. To realize it's not about dreams and death at all.

It's about dreams.

And life.

He took Nicole's hand and as they headed to class, he started to calculate how many minutes he'd been alive, but stopped himself, and simply embraced the one he had instead.

TO BE CONTINUED IN

FURY

SPRING 2015

Special thanks to
Eden, Pam, Trinity, J.P., Randy, Liesl,
Todd, Tiffany, Amy and Larry.

STEVEN JAMES

is the bestselling, award-winning author of nine thrillers. This is his first suspense novel for teens. When he's not writing or traveling, you'll find him trail running, playing disc golf, or drinking really strong java at a coffee shop near his home at the base of the Blue Ridge Mountains in eastern Tennessee.